BOOK 13

THE
PUZZLE
OF PARHAM
HOUSE

A 1920s MYSTERY

BENEDICT BROWN

COPYRIGHT

For my father, Kevin,
I hope you would have liked this book an awful lot.

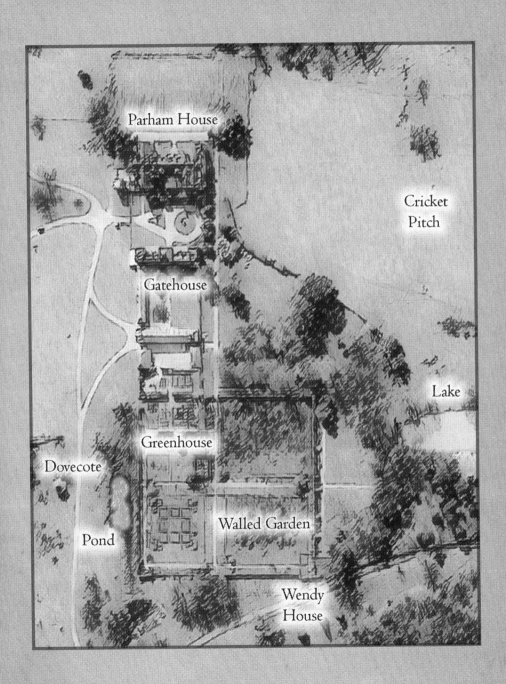

READER'S NOTE

I wouldn't have been able to write this book without the kind permission of the current owners of Parham House and Gardens in Sussex. For that reason, I'd like to make it clear from the beginning that this is a work of fiction and, while I've included many wonderful details about the real house, the events in this book are largely made up.

The Pearson family were the owners from the 1920s onwards, and though I greatly enjoyed reading up on their time in Parham, I am no authority on their lives. It goes without saying that Lord Edgington's fictional daughter was not a friend of the Pearsons, and there were no murders in the house in 1928.

And with all that established, I hope this book stands as a tribute to the incredible estate and the remarkable people who have lived there. At the back of the book, you will find a character list and a glossary of unusual terms, along with information about my reasons for writing, the fascinating things I discovered through my research, and the true history of Parham House.

Happy reading!

PROLOGUE

A scream. That's what woke me, though I didn't know it at the time. It was the second and third that brought me back to consciousness. They were desperate sounds that echoed about the old building and up to the first floor. In that disorientated, in-between state, I didn't know where I was or which way the door should be, but I knew that I had to get out of bed.

I didn't think about waking my cleverer, more experienced, master-detective grandfather. I just felt my way along the wall to leave the pitch-black room. By the time I reached the corridor, my eyes must have adjusted, as I could make out blurry shapes. It was something like an artist's shadowy impression of the world we know – an English country house reinterpreted by Francisco Goya. I stumbled through it, trying to get my thoughts in order so that I could locate the staircase down to the ground floor. My hands were more use than my eyes, but I eventually found what I needed and continued on my way.

I don't know why I decided to go to the Great Hall, but that's where I found the body. I suppose that it was simply because it was the heart of the house and the room I knew best, rather than any sixth sense that told me it should be my destination. Well, that and the fact it was the only room with a candle burning in it.

He was lying face down in the moonlight, his back to the door through which I'd entered. I didn't know who he was – had never seen him before in my life, in fact – but I knew he wasn't dressed like a footman, guest, or inmate of the house. I hesitated for a moment, afraid that he was the thief we had come there to find. Dressed all in black, he wore a thick woollen jumper and looked just the type to rummage through a house in the darkness. He hadn't moved an inch in the minute I'd been watching him, though, and so I summoned the courage to step inside.

As I ventured deeper into that remarkable old chamber, it was as if the countless Elizabethan portraits on the wall were following my progress. Queen Elizabeth herself looked down from her frame, and I felt as though she were willing me onwards. I stretched my hand out as I got closer to the motionless figure, and I was about to bend down to touch whoever was lying there when a sudden spasm passed through his body. I instinctively jumped backwards as the man screamed out once more.

"It was a dragon with a great crooked claw," he declared in a throaty voice as his eyes latched onto me. "That monster took my breath away. It's a wonder he didn't eat me alive."

I could see no wound on him, no knife protruding from his body or blood dripping from his head as I might have expected, but he clearly wasn't well. His eyes burned wild and blue in the half-light, and I could make out a labyrinth of deeply etched lines on his face. He was older than I'd first imagined, around sixty years of age at the very least, with long grey hair like my grandfather's. He tried to stand up, but the effort was too much, so I placed a firm hand on his shoulder to support him.

"What happened?" I asked, my voice unusually high and urgent. "What can I do?"

He held his hand to his chest, and it was clear that he couldn't breathe as normal. His fear was tangible and, somehow, I knew that it was already too late. Even when the sound of people moving around the house reached my ears and my Grandfather arrived at my side, there was an inevitability about the whole thing.

"I don't want to go like this," the wretched fellow said as another bolt of agony coursed through him, and he tore at his heart. "I don't want to die."

CHAPTER ONE

It was a sunny morning in March when the crime occurred, I read for approximately the fourth time without being able to concentrate.

Bang!

It was a sunny morning in March when the crime occurred, I tried once more, but it happened again.

Bang!

This time, the sound was followed by a burst of laughter, and I took a deep breath so as not to get angry.

"Grandfather, do you mind?" I asked, which made the dear old fellow and his factotum turn sheepish.

"Oh, I am sorry, Christopher." He rubbed the end of his shiny leather brogue against the back of one trouser leg as he replied. "We certainly didn't mean to disturb you."

"My apologies, Master Prentiss," Todd added, in a similarly guilty tone, and I picked up the pile of papers once more.

It was a sunny morning in March when the crime occurred. Wallington was a sleepy town to the south of London. Little of note ever occurred there, which made P.C. Robbyns's discovery all the more extraordinary. He was going about his usual round at approximately seven o'clock that Saturday when he noticed something out of the—

Bang!

"Grandfather, I thought you were going to stop."

He held his pistol towards the library ceiling and looked confused. "We have stopped. We didn't laugh at all that time."

"I was talking about the gunfire. I'm studying the Anderson file. I'm never going to solve this old case of yours without a little peace and quiet."

The obdurate detective could not see the problem. "This is a very large house, my boy. There are plenty of spaces within it where you won't be bothered by gunfire."

I considered reminding him that I had been in the library before they had set up the large target and cleaned their weapons, but I knew it would do me no good. Todd had already reloaded, and was clearly eager to take his next shot, so I gathered up my belongings and –

in an exaggeratedly flustered fashion, so that they knew just how unreasonable they were being – stomped from the room.

There was one last bang which was timed perfectly with the closing door as it slammed behind me.

"That was an exceptional shot, Todd," I heard my forebear comment, and they both indulged in another great laugh.

Out in the bright corridor, our golden retriever Delilah was sitting in the shade of a walnut armoire. It was hard to say whether she was scared, depressed or just lonely, but she was enjoying Grandfather's shooting practice just as little as I was. She followed me along the endless checker-board corridor as I searched for a better place to read. The paintings on the wall and porcelain plates on every dresser shook as more ammunition was discharged.

I'd always liked the petit salon at Cranley Hall as it was one of the least ostentatious of the many sitting rooms, lounges and parlours there. It had a homeliness that was rare in the sprawling property, and so I nipped inside. I sat down on one of the well-sprung velvet sofas, atop a thick Chinese carpet, and opened Grandfather's case file. I was determined to solve it, just as the great Lord Edgington had many years earlier. Delilah sat with her flank against me to keep us both warm, and I stroked her absentmindedly as I returned to that sunny town on a Saturday in 1879.

"P.C. Robbyns," I began out loud before finding my place and continuing in my head, ...*noticed something out of the ordinary a little way off. At first, he took it to be a pile of rags or perhaps some sacks of grain that had fallen from a passing carriage. The road was nothing more than a pockmarked muddy ditch in that part of the town, and it would not have been the first time that a merchant had lost a sample or two of his wares. However, upon approaching the mysterious object, Robbyns could see that his initial impression was greatly at odds with the reality of the scene.*

Just as in everyday life, I sometimes wished that Grandfather could be a little more succinct in his written accounts. I was reading a police report, not a Victorian novel.

The fabric that the constable had spotted was not the characteristic beige of sackcloth, nor did it have the mismatched patterns of a bundle of rags. It was of a high quality, with straight black lines running down it. While half of it was covered with mud and branches, he should at least have realised what the elongated shape suggested. Before him was a—

"Albert!" a voice called to interrupt my thoughts. "We will be fine in here." My father swept into the room, followed by my brother. The pair were dressed in identical grey suits. Even their navy blue ties matched, and they seemed to have adopted the same upright, bouncy walk as they stalked over to the table in the middle of the room and pulled out two chairs.

"Jolly good," my once soppy, now oddly business-like brother declared as he emptied a glossy leather briefcase of its contents.

Father mirrored this action, and I had to wonder whether they had choreographed their entrance for some reason. I kept expecting them to make fun of me for being so gullible as to believe that anyone really acted in such a manner.

Instead, Albert rose from his seat and held up the first file. "With regard to the Smithurst account, I sought advice from our colleague Gilbert Baines at Hargreaves Bank. I believe that the best option is to continue with the series of investments that we had previously envisioned."

"I am inclined to agree," my father... agreed.

Albert's voice only grew louder, and he struck the file loudly with the back of his hand. "I cannot stress enough just how important consistency is in our line of work. The smallest backward step could be viewed as weakness by our clients."

I had never seen our blessed pater look so proud. I was surprised he didn't jump up from his seat to celebrate the son who had finally lived up to his expectations. "That is it in a nutshell, dear boy. How often have I said that consistency is the watchword of this business? The very watchword! In just six months, you've grasped the essence of what we do."

Albert showed no emotion, but nodded sagely, as if he was an old hand who was only too used to such praise. I hadn't a clue what they were talking about (or exactly what my father did, for that matter) but I knew that I couldn't concentrate with the pair of them blathering on about the fascinating world of finance.

"I'm terribly sorry to interrupt—" I began.

"Then please don't, Chrissy." My brother didn't look at me but simply picked up the next file. "Father and I have important work that must be completed this morning."

"I was in here before you!" I stated a little too keenly and immediately regretted sounding like a brat.

The two of them stopped what they were doing to fix their eyes on me.

"Come along now, Chrissy." Father touched the hair at the top of his head ever so gingerly, as though checking to see that he hadn't gone bald. "There's plenty of space for everyone. And you're only reading."

"Only reading!?" I practically exploded, as I'd rarely heard a more offensive expression. "There is no such thing as *only* reading. There's *only* banking and *only* work, but only reading is a contradiction in terms."

"We've already settled here for our meeting, Christopher. You'll have to go elsewhere." Ever since Albert had decided to devote his every waking moment to his work in the City, it had sapped him of his previously mawkish character. I can't say this was an entirely bad thing, though I missed his more pliable nature.

"Or…" I began, hoping that a stellar argument would occur to me. "Or… you could…"

The implacable businessmen stared back, unimpressed. I knew I would have no luck, so I seized the Anderson file once more and flounced from the room, mumbling to myself. "The heartless machine known as business spares not a thought for the little man. I am but an ant before the might of…" I would have continued like this for some time, but I was already out in the hall, and they could no longer hear.

At least Delilah padded after me, looking just as forlorn as when I'd found her.

"Where can one possibly go in this oversized castle where one will not be disturbed?" I asked and, as I'd started in this mode, I felt compelled to continue. "One has an idea!"

Looking down the corridor in either direction (to make sure that no one would realise what we were doing and follow us) I shot along to the silver room and opened the door. It was the perfect place to hide, as the only person who ever went in there was our head footman, Halfpenny. Inside, there were two large cabinets filled with silver dinner services, various implements for polishing and a single chair. There was only room for one person to sit (and a dog to perch), so even if someone had intended to use the space to practice operatic singing, celebrate a Greek wedding or something equally loud and disturbing, they would have been hard pressed to do so.

"Where did we get to, girl?" I asked my patient companion before finding my place on the second page. "Of course, P.C. Robbyns had just discovered something unexpected at the side of the road and Grandfather had waffled for some time about a selection of things that it would not turn out to be."

I fell quiet and began to read.

Before him was a corpse in a pin-striped suit. At his side, there was a small, stuffed duck which might belong to a young child. Robbyns could not see the man's face at first but, upon removing the foliage from atop the cadaver, he discovered the cause of death. A short-handled hatchet was buried in the victim's back. Having undertaken a brief search for significant clues, Robbyns knocked on the door of the nearest cottage, where a childless, elderly couple lived, and asked them to keep watch over the scene of the crime until he could report to his superior officers and return.

As a detective at Scotland Yard, I was informed of the murder forthwith, and my chief inspector dispatched me to Wallington to investigate. My first thought when I arrived was that the soft duck was a strange contrast to the violent spectacle before me, and—

"Master Christopher," our head footman said from the doorway, and I wondered how I could have failed to predict this outcome. "I didn't realise… Or rather, I mean to say… What are you doing in the silver room?" Halfpenny stood there looking awkward as I sought an explanation and failed to find one.

"I suppose you have come to clean the silver."

He did not disagree. In fact, he continued smiling in a hesitant manner which suggested that a beloved pet had recently died, but it wasn't his place to share the bad news. Luckily, Delilah was right beside me, so I could rule out that sad prospect.

Accepting defeat, I sighed and put my papers back into their file for the third time. I was about to give up altogether and head to the kitchen in search of a pork pie when I bumped into my mother. I mean that quite literally. I positively crashed into her as I was coming out of the silver room. The file dropped from my hand and the papers went everywhere.

"Do look where you're going, Christopher," she told me in a voice that was quite different from her usual warm, empathetic tone.

She stared down at the mess of papers on the black and white tiles, but I don't think she really saw them. The way she held herself – as if she wanted to leave but couldn't bring herself to move – told me that something was very wrong.

"Are you perfectly all right?" I asked and, when she didn't reply, I spoke again. "Mother, what's the matter?"

I'd rarely seen her look quite so hesitant before. She held her fingers to her mouth and shook her head, but her gaze was still directed towards the floor as if it had become attached.

"I'm sure there's no reason for anyone to worry." She was trying to convince herself that this was true. "It's just, I would never have expected…"

I noticed at this point that she was clutching a letter in her other hand. It was written in the neatest writing I'd seen in some time. I could only think it had been penned by a calligraphy teacher, or perhaps a medieval monk. I glanced at the name of the sender, but it meant nothing to me.

"Who's Alicia Pearson?" I asked as Delilah nuzzled my mother's leg through her long skirt.

Finally relaxing a little, Mother smiled and seemed to come back to herself. "She is someone I respect a great deal." She breathed out long and thoughtfully before continuing. "I'm sorry if I've alarmed you, Christopher, but I would simply never have imagined her needing our help."

CHAPTER TWO

If Alicia Pearson never asked for help, then she had that in common with my mother. Grandfather was eccentric, my brother Albert either wildly emotional or, as it would now appear, quite the opposite, and our father was one of those typical Englanders that public schools work so hard to produce – complete with a stiff upper lip and a remarkable inability to discuss anything more sentimental than cricket scores and patterns in the stock market.

It was my mother Violet who bridged the seemingly unbridgeable gulfs between us. She was the one on whom we could rely to make her father a little less… what's the expression? Oh, yes: barmy in the crumpet! She always looked after my brother when a young lady broke his heart, or he was distraught over a missing cufflink. And she was the only person I knew who could make my father seem like a normal human being. Without her, what hope was there for any of us?

The smoking room smelt like a chimney, and the other comfortable sitting rooms were occupied, so I escorted her to the grand salon then rang for refreshments from the kitchen.

I sat down in a chair opposite hers, still unable to fathom what had so upset her. "Has Alicia written to you on a matter of business? Is it Grandfather she needs?"

"Precisely. It seems that there have been a series of strange occurrences at her estate, and we must…"

I had the definite impression that she was struggling to put her story into words and so, rather than hurry her along, I simply sat back and waited for her to gather her thoughts. I'd seen my grandfather use this approach with witnesses on a number of occasions, and I was rather proud of myself for doing the right thing.

"I should probably start from the beginning. You see, Alicia Pearson and I sit on the boards of several worthy charities together. She is an exceptional woman who devotes much time and energy to a number of important causes. I've known her now for almost twenty years, and I suppose that we might call one another friends, but she is such a competent and capable person, I've always felt like a child around her. I run about in her wake, forever trying to keep up with all her plans and ideas."

She looked up at the ceiling at this moment and her eyes caught the light that was coming through the windows beside us.

"Her husband is equally brilliant. Clive is the chairman of S. Pearson & Son and has overseen engineering projects from tunnels and dams to harbours and railways all over the world. Alicia used to travel with him to Mexico and Panama and all sorts of places, but since they had children, she has stayed here in Britain. They bought an Elizabethan estate called Parham Park and have been renovating the house there."

I was still struggling to see how any of this might interest the great Lord Edgington of Scotland Yard, but before I could ask, she sensed my uncertainty and tried to explain.

"Perhaps I'm not being clear enough. What I'm trying to say is that Alicia is made of different material from the likes of you and me, Chrissy. And so, when I received this letter, I knew that something must be very wrong. It's all the more alarming because she doesn't say exactly what has happened. You see—"

The story came to a sudden stop, and I still didn't know how to respond. The letter had upset her, and she evidently thought highly of its sender, but it was not like my mother to be so anxious. Most of all, she was a practical person, and I thought her first concern would be to find a solution to her friend's dilemma.

"Chrissy, do you understand what I'm trying to say?" She shook her head then, as though to answer her own question, and I tried to set her mind at ease.

"Don't worry, Mother." I put my hand on hers. "If I read the letter, we can decide what to do from there."

She gave an appreciative nod and handed over the thick, cream paper. I unfolded it and began to read.

My dearest Violet,

It has been far too long since we last met, and I can only offer my most heartfelt apologies. Life here at Parham has been somewhat trying lately. With my husband Clive away in South America for so long, I must admit that I am all at sea. I have my three girls for company, and their bright minds and boundless hunger for life and living are a superb distraction from my problems, but I still struggle sometimes.

If you happened to visit the house before we bought it, you would not recognise it today. We have done all we can to return Parham to the state it was in when first built three hundred and fifty years ago. As a result, the estate is forever abuzz with workers and historical experts. We have created a wonderful life, in a wonderful place, but I can't help feeling that we will never finish the task in which we are engaged.

Although I am normally resilient, events of the last fortnight weigh upon me more than I can say. The long and the short of it is that certain items from the house have gone missing, and I would greatly appreciate your and your father's assistance. It is not a question of their value, or a desire to see the culprit punished, but I need someone to help me understand what is happening and why.

Even if you are unable to come, it is a great relief to write this letter, and I sincerely appreciate your time.

Yours with gratitude,

Alicia Pearson

"It really is quite odd," I said as soon as I'd finished reading. "If it is merely a question of theft, why hasn't she contacted the local police?"

With this challenge presented, Mother instantly lost the fog that had seemed to surround her. "That's just it! All I can say is that for Alicia to have written such a letter shows that something has deeply upset her. I don't know if this makes a great deal of sense, but—"

"It does," I interrupted. "I know exactly what you're feeling, because there is someone in my life who is really very similar to your friend Alicia."

"Oh, yes?" She sat up higher in her chair.

"Or perhaps even two." I smiled as Delilah rolled over in a patch of sunlight on the shiny wooden floorboards. "You see, if grandfather wrote such a letter, it would be most distressing. I don't believe he's ever asked me for help. He is generally grateful for my assistance on our cases, of course, but that's different."

"And the other person?" she asked, her voice rising self-consciously.

"It's you, Mother." I felt the slightest twinge in my throat at that moment, but I ignored it to tell her how special she was. "There is no one I know who is quite so capable and caring as you are. And so, if you need us to accompany you to see your friend, you only have to ask."

"Where are we off to now?" Grandfather asked from the doorway. "It's been far too long since we've had anything exciting to do." He scratched his chin with the muzzle of his (hopefully unloaded) pistol as he said this, and I could only conclude that he was telling the truth.

CHAPTER THREE

Before anyone accuses me of telling fibs, I'm not suggesting that we simply jumped into the car and drove off in search of adventure. There were formalities to observe and preparations to make. Mother called the Honourable Alicia Pearson at Parham House and told her that we would be only too happy to assist her in any way we could.

"There's nothing to say that whatever we find there will measure up to one of your cases," she warned her father when she'd hung up the telephone.

"All I'm expecting is a trip to a historically significant property which, unless I'm very much mistaken, is older than Cranley Hall." It would be wrong to say that my grandfather was a terrible liar, as he had tricked and trapped any number of criminals during his career on the Metropolitan Police force. However, this made the fact that he was abysmal at keeping secrets in the family all the stranger. Rather than maintaining a neutral expression to convince his daughter that his response was genuine, he winked across at me theatrically.

"I mean it," Mother continued. "You mustn't accompany me to Parham on the off-chance that you'll stumble across a body or unearth a gang of international spies. I imagine it is a simple household matter that will be resolved with a few short enquiries."

He held his hand to the breast pocket of his long grey morning coat. "If some nefarious criminal has unsettled the poor lady, I will do my best to solve the case."

With each word he said, Mother looked a little sterner, and so I decided to intervene.

"Really, Grandfather, there is no sense in getting your hopes up. The most likely scenario is that one of the staff at Parham has been helping himself to a few antiques. I very much doubt that we will uncover a plot worthy of your talents." I waited until Mother had turned away before returning his wink.

With our invitation swiftly confirmed, the staff were told of our plans, our cases were packed, and we ate a seven-course meal for lunch. There's no time to go into what we ate. The affair at Parham would take two whole days to resolve, with six main meals consumed in that time, and so I will have plenty of opportunities to describe the luscious offerings of a good stately home. For that reason, I won't provide any details of the mulligatawny soup or kedgeree that Cook made, nor the forest fruit pudding and blackcurrant sorbet that we had for afters. What I will say is that every mouthful was delicious, though I didn't like the way the fish heads peered out at me from the curry dish.

With our bellies full, we were free to set off to wherever it was we were going – I hadn't actually thought to ask how far Parham Park was. We warned Father and Albert that we might be away for some time, though the pair of them were only concerned with their business problems and wouldn't have missed us anyway.

I thought Grandfather was fairly reasonable for once in that he only took three cars and four members of staff with us. In addition to our Cook, our head footman and Grandfather's right-hand man, our gigantic and formerly terrifying maid Dorie came along, which was nice as she'd missed out on our last few adventures. I sat with my grandfather in his favoured Aston Martin, and I could hear her singing 'Nellie Dean' in the car behind us whenever we pulled up at a junction or had to stop for a flock of sheep. To begin with, it was quite amusing and, every time she said the name of the song, I would sing it back to her.

> **"I can hear the robins singing, Nellie Dean."**
> **"Nellie Dean!"**
> **"Sweetest recollections ringing, Nellie Dean."**
> **"Nellie Dean!"**
> **"And they seem to sing of you,**
> **With your tender eyes of blue,**
> **For I know they miss you too, Nellie Dean."**
> **"Nellie Dean!"**

Of course, by the time she'd sung it five or so times, it had become less entertaining.

"Do stop encouraging her, Christopher," Grandfather politely requested as we skirted Rudgwick, driving south towards the village of The Haven.

"It's all a bit of fun," I replied. "And it's a nice distraction for Mother. I was quite worried about her when she received that letter this morning."

"No, the song was a bit of fun the first time. It is now quite irritating." He could always be relied upon to focus on the least important thing I'd said.

I looked over my shoulder at my mother, who was sitting in the passenger seat of the Daimler limousine, just behind our car. She certainly didn't look as though our maid's singing had alleviated her woes. She was quite removed from the scene, and once more kept her eyes on the exterior world without appearing to notice what was before her. It was rather a shame as, for much of the journey, we were bordered by the first blooms of the season. Exotic eastern Magnolias with bright pink blossoms brightened up the villages we passed, along with cherry and plum trees that had burst into life to mark the imminent arrival of spring.

Because I am just as petty as my grandfather, I would not let the discussion die. "Of course, you could simply drive faster if you don't like the song. I've rarely seen you crawl along at such a pace."

He did not reply, but glanced at his side mirror to prove that he was just as concerned about his daughter as I was. It might seem odd to worry about someone just because she was worrying about someone, but as I've tried to explain, my mother's steady presence in the family was one of those unshakable constants that we never questioned. Just as my father was a closed book, Mother was the rock upon which we built our lives.

Remembering that I still hadn't made it through the first page of the Anderson file, I eventually snapped out of my contemplation and returned to work. Delilah was keeping Todd company in the far roomier Silver Ghost, and so I asked myself how far I had read. To which I replied, *the fifth paragraph!* Only in my head, of course. I didn't want my grandfather to roll his eyes at me.

...the soft duck was a strange contrast to the violent spectacle before me, and I instantly considered the possibility that the dead man had been travelling with a child. This idea was reinforced when I turned the body to discover that the face looking back at me was a familiar one. Martin Anderson was as corrupt a fellow as any I'd encountered. I'd never known him to be violent, but he was the exception to the rule that there was honour among thieves. He would have picked the pocket of any man alive, then wasted that money on

whichever three-legged beast with the longest odds was running that day at Epsom.

Again, I must apologise for my grandfather's loquacious tendencies. I'd rarely come across such a lengthy sentence as that one, and I was certain that a competent editor could have shorn the paragraph of a good deal of unnecessary detail.

Anderson's most redeeming feature was the love he showed his family. He was not a responsible man, but he was an attentive father to his little boy, Daniel, and had been truly heartbroken when his wife died of consumption. The fact is that I felt something approaching affection for the man and, scoundrel though he may have been, I was sorry to learn of his fate.

I could only think that he had cheated the wrong person and paid the price. Such vengeance was common in the circles in which Anderson moved and the case might not have held my attention had it not been for the stuffed duck he held. In the nearby bushes, we found a bag that resembled a military map case, worn as a sling across the body. Its contents had been scattered there, and I found pins, a length of terry towelling and bottles of lotion. If the duck hadn't already implied as much, I could only conclude that Anderson's little boy had been with him when he died.

"We are not just dealing with a murder," I told Constable Robbyns once I'd completed my inspection of the scene, "I believe we have a case of a missing child on our hands."

I sent him off to the nearest—

"Here we are! Parham Park," Grandfather announced with some glee to interrupt my reading.

I didn't know what to say. "We've only been driving for half an hour."

"That is correct." For a famously perceptive sleuth, it was amazing how often he failed to interpret my meaning.

"But the cars were packed as if we were embarking on an international voyage."

"Oh, no, Christopher," he corrected me as he pulled off the leafy road to take a bumpy path onto the estate. "As you will learn when we

24

set off on our international voyage, the provisions we have with us are only enough for a few days."

I didn't like to argue with him – mainly because I knew I'd lose – but I couldn't comprehend his thinking. For one thing, I already knew that Parham House dated back to the Elizabethan era and that the Pearsons had devoted their time and resources to restoring it. Surely such a property would have everything we could require.

We followed the long, twisting path through woods and a steep-banked valley. On either side, stags with dark brown coats looked down upon us as if they'd been posted there to make certain that only the right kind of people obtained access. Were this true, they were apparently not selective enough. Not only did we glide past without any complaints, when we drove around the curve in the road and caught sight of the house in the distance, I could see that there were any number of people milling about in front of it.

The house itself was brilliantly old and perfectly grand, with pointed gables and chimneys in twos and threes all over. While my ancestral home at Cranley Hall may have been larger and just a touch more luxurious by most people's standards, Parham House immediately spoke to me of its secrets. That view from up on the hillside told me that there were any number of stories waiting to be uncovered, and I couldn't wait to get started.

Of course, my mother would have been able to tell you all about the malmstone in which the house had been built, which was distinctive of the architecture of the South Downs. She would have probably noticed the contrasting sandstone and ashlar quoins, too, but I'm not nearly so knowledgeable as she is. All I can tell you is that it was an exquisite house, surrounded by several matching outbuildings, and, oh yes, one facade was covered in scaffolding.

"This brings back memories!" Grandfather hooted as we rolled down the path towards an attractive church that was set away from the main complex of buildings.

For a moment, I thought he meant that he'd been to Parham before, but then I remembered that it really wasn't so long ago that his own house had been redecorated in time for his seventy-fifth birthday celebrations. Perhaps understandably, seeing as both my aunt and uncle had been killed in quick succession, I wasn't given to thinking of that period too often.

I would have said that it was a welcoming property, but the work that was taking place was a little too distracting for that. It felt as if we were visiting an unfinished masterpiece and, although I'd only just arrived, I already wished to return when the work was done.

The path curled around, and we drove through an arch in an old stone wall. This led us to a large gatehouse topped with a clocktower before we brought the cars to a stop in a courtyard beside the main building. Mother had regained her composure by now and got down from the Daimler in search of her friend. Our arrival must have been noted from within the house as a heavy wooden door swung open, and an elegantly attired woman of around thirty-five came out to us. She was followed by three girls in height order, with the oldest being a good head shorter than me.

"Welcome, all of you," the woman called, and my mother increased her pace.

"Alicia, my dear. We're so glad to be here."

My grandfather and I hurried around a circular pool and fountain to catch up with her.

"I can't believe that you came so quickly," the chatelaine of Parham House declared in a tone which was really not so far off disbelief.

There was an awkward moment during which neither of them knew how to greet the other before my mother abandoned any sense of stuffy old propriety and embraced our hostess.

It seemed that neither of them would address the reason we'd come there, and so Mother found something else to say. "I can't believe we've been living a short drive from one another for so long without coming to visit."

My grandfather and I were standing next to them by this point, while Todd and Halfpenny drove the others away to wherever it was our servants would call home during our stay.

"Ahem," Lord Edgington said when no one had paid him any attention. That's right, he didn't clear his throat, he said the word *ahem* very clearly and loudly so that the women had to turn to look at him.

"Oh, Father, my apologies." Mother stood aside to introduce our wise and always humble leader. "This is my friend Alicia Pearson. You may remember her from a brief visit she paid us some years ago."

"Of course I do." The old fop bowed ever so graciously. "And I knew your father, the first Lord Brabourne, when I was a good bit younger."

"I can't tell you how happy I am that you're here, Lord Edgington," Alicia told him, but she glanced at her daughters at the same time, and I had the sense that she would not reveal anything significant in their presence.

There was something very youthful about her. She had pale, clear skin, and an elegantly pointed nose. Perhaps it was the note of hesitancy in her voice that lent her a certain vulnerability, or perhaps it was because it so closely matched the tone in the letter she'd sent. As for her clothes, she was extremely well presented, as if great thought had gone into the positioning of the collar of her plain pink blouse and the creases in her silken floral skirt.

"Allow me to introduce my daughters, Veronica, Lavinia and Dione," she continued, pointing to the three small girls who had hair in lengths corresponding to their apparent ages.

The girls copied their mother's curtsy, taking the skirts of their white cotton dresses between pinched fingers as they did so. They tried not to smile too broadly, but they were clearly excited by our visit.

"I'm Veronica, I'm twelve," the eldest told me in a tone that suggested she believed this the most natural way to start a polite conversation. "Mother says you've come to play with us."

"I said nothing of the sort," Alicia chastised her daughter in a serious tone, which was slightly undermined by the affectionate way she regarded Veronica. "Christopher is an adult. He has not come here to spend time in your Wendy House."

"But you will play with us, won't you?" the second girl asked in a pleading tone, whereas her younger sister looked intimidated by the encounter and hid behind the others. The older girls stared at me intently, and I must confess that I failed to understand their real meaning.

"I'm sure my grandson would love to join in a game or three," Grandfather kindly volunteered on my behalf. "He may be a few years older than you, but he is very young at heart."

In response, the three children each produced a sigh of contentment, or perhaps it was relief, as they glanced back and forth at one another conspiratorially. The whole lot of us fell to silence then, though the topic that no one dare broach was almost deafening. When this continued for a few moments longer than was comfortable, Alicia's eyes narrowed in discomfort, and she seemed to shrug without moving her shoulders.

"I must show you the house before it's time for tea." Without another word, she turned to take us inside.

CHAPTER FOUR

Although our hostess would not yet explain her reason for asking us there, we were treated to a really very fascinating tour of the property. I'd visited many country houses by this time in my life, but I'd rarely come across one whose very essence had been in a state of flux for so long.

"There were various stages of transformation enacted upon Parham over the centuries," Alicia revealed as she took us up a staircase at the back of the house towards the state rooms. Every wall was covered with portraits stretching back through the centuries, and there was a particularly striking painting of a woman in a ruff, with snow white skin. "That is the first mistress of Parham when it was built in the sixteenth century," she said without looking at me, as if she knew that my eyes would be drawn to that very portrait. "She was Queen Elizabeth's goddaughter."

The woman in the picture had immense, puffy sleeves in the fashion of her day. Her hair was styled close to her head and decorated with a jewel, much as her own godmother was often depicted.

"It's a marvellous portrait," Grandfather responded ever so politely, though I could tell what he really wanted to ask was, *Is anyone here, by chance, plotting a murder?*

"I sometimes feel as if this house offers us a path back through time to the days of Elizabeth herself." In this one sentence, Alicia showed how fortunate she felt to live in such a place. Whatever her distress might be, it seemed that the building itself was not the cause.

She led us on through a dark corridor typical of the Tudor houses I've visited. The girls bustled along behind their mother like three ducklings. They were perfectly well behaved and seemed at ease in adult company – though they were no doubt impatient to return to their games as Alicia described the work that she and her husband had overseen.

"As I said in my letter, we are trying to return this house to the way it was when first built. Our architect has worked tirelessly to study the plans and documents that relate to the original building." Her eyes sparkled in the light that came through a leaded window at the end of the corridor and she stopped beside a firmly closed door. "It's rather amazing when we peel back one layer of paint or knock away a false wall to discover something ancient and astonishing. We started four years ago, and we've already made great progress."

She pushed the door open, and a flood of bright light poured out to us. It only took a moment for my eyes to adjust but, when they had, I had to squint once more at the wonders on display. It was not just the selection of portraits on every wall that I found impressive, but the space in which they were displayed. I had been to the National Gallery in London, and in this respect, at least, it could not compare with the Great Hall of Parham House.

There was an elaborate plaster ceiling above our heads with inverted peaks that reached down to us like stalactites in a cave. One wall was decorated with an ornately carved oaken screen. There were two arches cut into it that gave onto other rooms and inlaid pilasters on either side of them. The floor was made up of square stone tiles laid on the diagonal, and there was a banqueting table in the centre of the room that made me wish we'd come there for a grand feast, rather than whatever the problem was that required Grandfather's help.

"Many of the items here and throughout the building are from the sixteenth century, when Parham was built," Alicia continued as though we were paying visitors or historians on a formal visit. "Clive and I have had to hunt down many pieces that had been here in centuries past. From the paintings on the walls to the Jacobean chairs and benches, we have done our very best to put the house back together as it once would have been."

She wasn't the only one who was pleased with the progress they'd made. Grandfather nodded his approval, and the middle girl whispered to her older sister, who passed on the message with an excited look.

"Mother, don't go on about all those fusty antiques without showing them the unicorn's horn."

Even Dione, the shy youngest child who could not have been more than eight years old, stepped forward to see. For her part, our hostess rolled her eyes and shook her head as if to say, *If you insist.*

I have come to understand, now that I am nineteen, that there is not some perceptible line one crosses between childhood and what comes next. However, while I have grown up a great deal over the last few years, there was nothing to stop me crossing my fingers that unicorns would turn out to be real – perhaps hiding away in a jungle somewhere that no one had thought to explore just yet. And so I waited almost as eagerly as the three children to see what marvel Alicia would produce. To my amazement, it did not disappoint.

"It's a genuine unicorn's horn," I muttered as she held up the immense and twisted object that was housed in a long red case. Though far longer than such things tended to be in picture books, there was no doubt that it had grown organically, and I was well and truly convinced that it belonged to a magical horse.

"It's not from a real unicorn," Alicia said to dash my hopes. The girls must have already known the truth but still looked at the immense thing with reverence. "It's the tusk of a narwhal. Sailors sold them as unicorn horns, and any number of sensible people bought them because, deep down, we all want to believe in fairy tales."

It was as if she'd read my mind. Another person who tended to do just that now cast a reproachful look in my direction as if to say, *Really, Christopher, when will you grow up?*

I stared back at my grandfather with a look that surely implied, *I have no desire to grow up if being older means being boring. If it's all the same to you, I'd rather enjoy the freedoms of adulthood and the creative instincts of youth simultaneously.*

In reply, his expression seemed to say, *I haven't a clue what you mean, boy. That was far too complex a thought to express in just one look.*

As no one had said anything since I'd so foolishly thought all this, Lord Edgington stepped forward to bring us to more relevant matters than the existence or otherwise of mythical creatures.

"I must say that I am truly in awe of all you have done here. To turn back time as you and your husband have is quite the feat."

"You're most kind. Not everywhere has been so easy to fix as this magnificent old room, of course. Aside from uncovering a few windows that had been bricked up over the centuries, we've done really very little here."

This was another moment when it felt as though she might finally tell us why she needed our help, but she pushed any such thoughts aside and continued with the tour. Just as she'd promised, there were some rooms there that had been greatly overhauled and others that didn't look as though they'd had so much as a splash of paint in a hundred years. Even more interesting, though, were the rooms that hadn't been finished, where workmen were toiling away to raise floors and lower ceilings or rip away wood panels and fireplaces in search of what had been there long before.

I could see that there was an element of play in the work of Parham's new owners. They were not just serious conservationists – striving to restore a once great house to its former glory – but children with a toy box, putting together the pieces of a truly magnificent new doll's house. I have to say that, in their position, I would have done very much the same thing.

"It's amazing," Mother told her friend when we'd completed a full circle on the ground floor.

"We feel it's our duty," Alicia replied, and she gazed out of the immense windows in the hall which looked over the hilly lawns and up to the deer park through which we'd entered. "Children," she said, coming back to herself, and I was uncertain at first whether this included me, "you'll have to go up to the nursery now. Nanny will get you ready for your lessons with Mrs Blythe."

In a second, the girls lost all the glee about them, and three frowns appeared.

"Do we really have to, Mother?" Veronica demanded with fists tightly clenched. "Blythe is such a terrible chatterbox. All she does is make us walk around in circles on the horses for hours on end as she whitters on about her own terribly dull affairs."

The middle girl, Lavinia, took up the cudgel. "She smells like sherry and horsehair, and she's always pinching my cheeks. Can't we stay with Chrissy instead and play Snakes and Ladders?"

"Or tennis!" Veronica added, warming to the idea. "My service has come along an awfully long way this year. We could give him a game."

"To the nursery!" was their mother's only response, and they knew there was no sense in arguing.

The oldest girl gave me another look that spoke volumes, though I couldn't quite read those volumes at the time, and then the three of them trailed off in a line with their heads down, like school children on their way to morning service. It was only when they got to the door that little Dione turned back to us and issued a rare comment.

"Mother, I don't like horses. Goodbye."

Alicia tried to keep the stern expression on her face, but it didn't last long and, once we were fairly certain that the girls couldn't hear, the four of us burst out laughing.

"My goodness," my mother said as she raised one hand to her mouth. "I remember when Chrissy and Albert were their age. I have often wondered whether girls are easier to handle than boys."

"I wouldn't be so sure." Grandfather's laughter only grew louder. "You and your siblings were all equally wicked."

Though the jolly mood lingered for a moment, the feeling that something very important had gone unsaid made our mirth seem out of place. It was Alicia who finally acknowledged what the rest of us were too polite to address.

"I must talk to you of course, but not here." Her expression had already turned to one of mild panic. "We'll go somewhere more private."

Even as she said this, a man entered the room in a long black robe that was somewhere between an officer's coat and a vampire's cloak. He had dark features, and his hair was arranged with pomade in a peak that swelled in the centre, as though it had been sculpted from a piece of black stone. I couldn't imagine who he was, but I felt that I wanted to know, especially when two smart young ladies hurried to catch him, squabbling between themselves as they went.

Alicia led us to a salon that was decorated in a comparatively modern style. I would have guessed it was late Georgian, though the educational part of our hostess's presentation was over, and the time for questions had passed. It rather reminded me of pictures I'd seen of French salons from the time of the French Revolution, and although the cream furniture was particularly elegant, it was hard and uncomfortable.

Alicia took a chair at a small table and invited us to do the same. A well-stocked bookshelf behind her framed my view, as she picked up a bell to ring for tea, then changed her mind and set it back down again.

"I'm so sorry," she said, and even before the first glimmer of moisture came to her eyes, I knew she was about to cry. "You must think I'm quite the loon, but that's the very problem. You see, I believe that someone is trying to drive me insane."

CHAPTER FIVE

I looked at my grandfather in the belief that he would be the one to reassure the poor lady, but it fell to his daughter to speak.

"When I read your letter this morning, I was alarmed that the tone of fear I detected could have come from the pen of the imperturbable person I know. Whatever has happened, Alicia, we are here to help."

The distressed woman before us readied herself to reply, then pulled her words back, just as she had done with the bell moments earlier. She tried a second time, though, and her response finally came.

"At first, I thought that it was caused by the stress of the work here and my husband being away for so long. Clive often has to travel to far-flung destinations for his work, but he's never been gone for so many months at a time before."

"I can only imagine how that must make you feel," Grandfather finally said to break his silence.

Alicia paused for a moment, as though she needed to put her thoughts back in order. "Before the girls were born, I would go with him. But for the last few years, he's hardly been home, which would have been fine in itself, but with everything that…"

While a younger version of me would have jumped in with a silly question, I waited impatiently to find out what was troubling her.

"What I'm trying to say is that it was easy to believe that the stress of the life that we have chosen for ourselves was simply too much for me. You see, I kept losing things." Her voice was so earnest at this moment, her expression wrought with unrest, and I felt something of her pain as I listened. "In a number of rooms across the house, things were turned around and upside down. And then certain items went missing altogether. There was an Italian vase in my sitting room. It wasn't particularly valuable, but I loved it, and it just disappeared one day."

"Could someone have stolen it?" Grandfather asked in a sympathetic murmur, though I knew he would have preferred to jump up and say, *When will we get to the actual crimes?*

Alicia straightened her silk skirt over her knees so that the fabric pulled taut for a moment. "I did consider the possibility. I even told our nightwatchman, Mr Stanton, to be extra vigilant, but there are so many more obvious valuables to take, it seemed an unlikely choice. And then, before I could think too much about it, the vase reappeared."

"You found it in your sitting room?" I asked, as I hadn't said anything for a while, and sometimes my voice goes a touch squeaky if I don't use it.

"No, that's another strange part of the story. It was in pieces in a pile at the far end of the walled garden. One of the children found it."

I immediately considered a solution but didn't want to accuse anyone directly, and so I tried to make myself look bad. "Mother, do you remember when the whole set of crystal goblets that you'd been given as a wedding present by the Spencer-Churchills was broken?"

As soon as I said this, I knew it was a terrible idea, and the grimace on my mother's face only confirmed it. "Yes, Christopher. I certainly do remember them."

"Ahh. Well, I think I'm old enough to own up to my part in their downfall. I was playing hide and seek with Albert when I was eight and, I must admit, I emptied out the glass cupboard and smashed them to pieces with the door when I tried to climb inside."

Thank goodness Alicia interrupted before Mother could translate her shock into words. "That's very sweet of you to put yourself in my daughters' places, Christopher, but I'm confident that they aren't to blame. They were away at their paternal grandmother's when the vase went missing."

That had been exactly what I was thinking, and my confession had done nothing but land me in trouble. I couldn't look at my mother, and so I asked another question as my grandfather chuckled at my predicament.

"Was there anything else that concerned you?" I believe I had to cough to get the words out.

"Just my grip on reality." She released a laugh, which soon turned into a sigh, and another silent tear descended her fine-boned cheek. "A few other insignificant items have gone missing, but it's the uncertainty of the whole thing that I find so frightening. It felt for a long time as though the floor beneath my feet had turned to sinking sand, but then whoever was responsible made a mistake."

Grandfather leaned forward to hear more, and a half-smile

illuminated Alicia's features. "Chrissy, would you please take a closer look at the four etchings beside the fireplace?"

I rose from my backless chair, glad to have escaped its poky clutches. I've genuinely sat on more comfortable hedgehogs before – not on purpose, I hasten to add, and in my defence, I thought that the spiky little fellow was some sort of cushion – what he was doing sitting on the bench in our garden, I will never know.

Anyway, back to my trip to the fireplace. It was a white plaster affair with pretty scrolling on the chimney breast and a golden mirror above the mantle. The etchings themselves were of an attractive young lady in four different poses. Her pale skin and wispy hair rather reminded me of Alicia's, but I didn't think that was why she'd sent me to look at them.

"They're the seasons," I finally concluded. "In one of them the subject has bladed shoes fitted to her feet, so I can assume she's on a frozen lake. In another, the plant life around her is abundant to symbolise the spring."

"That's correct." Alicia seemed to regain her composure when she was talking to me. Perhaps it was her natural instincts as a parent that enabled her to harness her emotion when necessary. "And do you notice anything significant about the way that they are arranged on the wall?"

I glanced over at the pair that were hanging on the far side of the chimney. "They're in the wrong order! Spring, autumn, summer, winter. No one would hang them in such a way. It's quite illogical."

A flush of confidence coursed through her. "That's just it. I know exactly how they were before. Unlike the other instances when I believed that I had misremembered features that had seemingly changed or become muddled, I know beyond any doubt that the four seasons were arranged in chronological order, starting with spring. And that tells me that someone really has been interfering with things in the house."

"So what we must decide," my grandfather began, and I realised that he was going to say something thoroughly Christopherish, "is why anyone would do such a thing."

It was usually my job to make points that were so obvious they barely needed uttering, but he'd decided to do it for me. He hadn't been himself for days, and this was yet more evidence – just in case his target practice in the library that morning hadn't proved it.

"It's quite a puzzle," Mother added, and at least she'd thought of a potential solution. "Unless whoever has been in here was searching for valuable items and took them down from the wall to examine them, then put them back without thinking."

"Yes, that makes perfect sense," her friend replied before standing up to point out a problem with the idea. "Except for one thing."

She hurried from the room, and we rose to go after her. Grandfather was unusually obedient, and I realised at this point that we'd left Delilah asleep in the car. We bustled along in our human train through ante rooms, grand chambers and up a curling flight of stairs before Alicia found the next piece of evidence she wished to show us. The duck egg green room where we finally came to a stop was full of the usual fascinating antiques, but our hostess hadn't taken us there to show off more of Parham's treasures.

"I should have known from the beginning that it wasn't just my bad memory. You see, all of the paintings and many of the artefacts in this room relate to a distant relative of mine. Sir Joseph Banks was a naturalist who became president of the Royal Society."

"Unless I'm very much mistaken, he travelled on the Endeavour with Captain Cook and helped found Kew Gardens," Grandfather added, though I doubted this would have any bearing on the case.

"Yes, but that's not why I thought to mention him." Alicia raised her chin with something approaching pride. "This room was the first in which I noticed that things had been moved around. The two largest paintings swapped places when I was out with the girls one day. And various smaller items disappeared into a wardrobe."

She motioned towards a series of wooden globes on the mantlepiece and two larger ones standing beside a chest of drawers.

It was my mother who would respond to her. "I don't understand, Alicia. What does any of this prove?"

We all walked over to look at the two paintings. One was of a rather commanding figure in long white robes with a turban on his head, and the other was a typical nineteenth century lady.

"I came here before I wrote the letter and it finally made sense to me."

Mother moved closer to encourage her. "Go on."

"I realised that all this must be a distraction from something. In the rooms where things were moved, nothing was missing." Her voice became more strained all of a sudden. "But I stayed up half the night trying to work out what whoever did this really wanted. I went through long lists of the possessions in the house and the items that aren't even on display yet, and it wasn't until I'd half given up, and collapsed on a chair in the Great Hall at three in the morning, that I noticed."

She rather reminded me of her daughters as she skipped from the room and back downstairs to the immense chamber where we'd started. "Everything in the Great Hall is in its original place. No paintings have moved, no items swapped. However, not everything is as it should be." She pointed to the immense mullioned windows and the rough stone window sills that were oddly unadorned. "There were two marble lions here. They were made in the nineteenth century and have been in Parham ever since. I don't know much more about them than that, but they would surely fetch a good price."

"So that's what this was?" I asked with a note of surprise. "The thief played an elaborate trick to make you think you couldn't trust your own memory in order to distract from the fact that he wanted to steal a pair of valuable lions?"

"The lion is something of a symbol of Parham House. You'll find them in tapestries and portraits all over the house, and the gate in the walled garden is guarded by a pair of them." A certain nervousness was noticeable once again in her manner. I could only conclude that she was eager to hear our thoughts but frightened what my imposing grandfather might say.

He looked about the room for a moment and his eyes danced from painting to painting and chair to chair. They finally came to rest on a large portrait of a queen in all her bejewelled and bepearled finery. He concentrated on it for a moment and, rather than explain what he was really thinking, he turned to Alicia with a wide smile. "It seems that you have hit on the solution, my dear. Perhaps you will not need our assistance after all."

CHAPTER SIX

Surely the biggest negative to following my grandfather into the life of a detective was that people were forever promising refreshments and then failing to deliver them. In normal society, one's day is built around those most British of institutions – breakfast, elevenses, lunch, tea, supper and dinner. But as soon as a case of murder, theft or blackmail is added to the equation, all regularity goes out of the window. Such corruption has many sins for which to answer, but this fundamental breakdown is surely the most irksome.

A rather gouty butler by the name of Mr Cridland came to show us to our rooms, and all talk of tea was forgotten. As tended to be the case with the grand houses we invariably visited whenever underhanded deeds were afoot, the great Lord Edgington was afforded a spectacular chamber with a grand four-poster bed, fine decoration, and a thick Persian rug to keep his tootsies warm. I, meanwhile, had the cupboard next door. For some reason, people always assume that I prize being at the old genius's side night and day over my own comfort.

"You didn't tell the truth downstairs, did you?" I put to him after Mother had left to see her own no doubt sparkling quarters. "You don't believe for one second what Alicia Pearson suggested."

He was standing at the window looking over the grounds of the immense estate. "I would not say that exactly." I thought he was set on being secretive, but if there is one thing that had improved in the last couple of years, it was the fact he adopted his lofty air of reticence less frequently than before. He had cut down from ten or so times a day to a mere three or four. "Alicia has certainly considered a range of potential explanations for the strange goings on here. I would even go so far as to say that she has approached the matter with the detached and rational mind of a fledgling detective."

"However..." I said for him, as he might never have got there otherwise.

"However, she contradicted herself."

I walked over to the window to stand alongside him. "Yes, I thought that was what you'd concluded. I saw you examining a portrait of a woman who looked remarkably similar to Queen Elizabeth."

"You noticed the very thing that caught my attention?" He spoke with such astonishment that he sounded just like I had when he'd first performed this trick on me. "You mean to say that you knew what I was thinking?"

His confidence in me was somehow more terrifying than the alternative, and my vocal cords turned into a gelatinous substance that would not do as it was told. "Come along, now. There's no need to exaggerate. I had a wild stab in the dark, and I'm probably wrong."

"That's enough false modesty, Christopher. What did you conclude?"

His penetrative stare cut through me, and I hurried to respond. "That it is just as Alicia said. There are far more valuable items in this house than a pair of marble lions of which she knew little of the provenance. If the portrait of Elizabeth is contemporary to the queen herself, it would be worth a small fortune."

"Oh." He sounded disappointed. "Is that what you think?"

Suddenly uncertain, I gave a lethargic moan in reply. It sounded like a dying horse.

"Because if it is, I must shake you by the hand." He did just this, and I wasn't sure what to make of it. "That is exceptional work, my boy. I'm proud of you. The fact is that, while Alicia was correct in her conclusion that someone has clearly attempted to hide his motives through the strange acts that she described, I see no reason why the criminal should do all that only to steal a couple of ornaments that no one had noticed were missing."

"So what *is* happening?"

"You tell me." He bothered his moustaches with the tips of his fingers. "What have you noticed about the people here since we arrived?"

I thought back over the last half hour and considered the various footmen and maids we'd seen before casting the net further to include the workmen at the front of the building and spilling out of various rooms that we'd passed.

"There's certainly a lot of them about. From the size of the house and what I've noticed so far, I would imagine that there must be twenty regular employees and just as many again who are dealing with the renovation work."

"And, of those people, who would you imagine are the most likely to know about fine antiques – if theft turns out to be the trickster's goal?"

Grandfather had a way of making perfectly simple questions difficult to answer.

"I would say…" I didn't actually pull at my collar or wheeze as I considered the possibilities, but I came very close. "We must consider the staff who know the house well and…"

"And?" Though his tone was light, this one word was enough to pile more pressure on me.

Talking to my grandfather must be similar to the feeling of competing against a master sportsman. I imagine I would be just as nervous facing down René Lacoste across a tennis court. Of course, I've never been particularly good at sports, but when it comes to sniffing out criminals, I am at least a competent amateur, so I took a deep breath and replied.

"And there are presumably experts around who know all about the best pieces to take. One of them may have spotted something precious and decided on a stratagem to vanish it away without anyone suspecting."

He clapped his hands together and shot off across the room with the energy of a man a quarter of his age. Having said that, I was almost exactly one quarter of his age, and I was desperate for an afternoon nap.

"You're right on every count. Not only do I believe that, if the situation here is as it first appears, a man with an eye for antiques is the likely culprit. We've already seen such a figure downstairs."

He didn't stick around to explain what he meant but disappeared through the door so that I had to bolt after him, calling as I went. "Who did we see? And where?"

Even though the only crimes that had been committed were a lot of moving things about and the possible theft of some large feline paperweights, he was too excited to wait for me and sped down the corridor towards the staircase. He at least had the good grace to whisper over his shoulder as I scampered.

"If I'm not mistaken, as we left the Great Hall soon after arriving, I caught sight of a man by the name of Elton Lockhart. He's an expert on ancient civilisations, a man fond of adventures in foreign lands and, by most accounts, an out-and-out rogue. If he's here, you can be certain that he's found something worthy of his time."

He led me all the way back to the centre of the house, which was deserted, then retraced our steps to the exit. To be honest, if he was hoping to find one particular person, I thought it unlikely that we'd be so lucky as to—

"Ah, Alicia," he said as we reached the outer door just as she entered with a bunch of freshly cut flowers in her arms.

"I'm sorry to leave you," she said with her usual warmth, "I thought you might like some time to settle in before we sit down to tea."

Oh, yes, that's what they all say, a small voice in my head replied. *Tea is always something that is on its way, and yet it rarely arrives.*

Oh, do be quiet, I told myself, and I did just that.

"That's very kind of you, but we're already settled." There was a real urgency about him, and I still did not know why. "I have a question for you, and it could be very important."

As we were talking, our dog Delilah pushed past Alicia looking disgruntled. She normally reserved her disapproval for her master, but this time she grizzled a little in my direction, too.

"Yes?" Alicia replied, but the dear hound's intervention had made him lose his train of thought.

"I have an important question," he tried once more before Alicia's daughters appeared, dressed in their riding clothes.

"Well that was worse than ever," Veronica complained, as she stepped around her mother.

Lavinia was the next to arrive. She stuck her head gingerly into the bright entrance hall but didn't say a word as she made way for her younger sister to step forward. Dione was covered from head to toe in mud.

"Oh, darling, what happened to you?"

The tiny child's face said, *I would think that was rather obvious,* whereas all she would say was, "I don't like horses, Mother," and her blue eyes shimmered with discontent.

It was at this moment that their nanny thundered down the stairs to us, looking just as perturbed by the little one's appearance as we were amused.

"Now, now, children. What mess have you got yourself into?"

44

She was a tall, formidable woman with a northern accent, and it was immediately apparent that the girls were more afraid of their nanny than their mother.

"It wasn't anyone's fault but our teacher," Veronica, who was evidently the bravest of the three, spoke up on her little sister's behalf. "She was blathering about nothing as poor Dione slipped off her pony and somehow managed to fall face first into the mud."

"Mud?" the nanny replied, as if she'd never heard of such a thing before. "Well-brought-up little girls like you went nowhere near the stuff when I was your age, and I won't have you playing in it now." She walked over in order to shoo them deeper into the house. "Miss Dione, we'll have to get you straight into the bath. I believe a good scrubbing is in order."

Dione planted her feet on the ground and looked quite unwilling to move, so the nanny picked her up by the shoulders and carried her along.

Veronica had other concerns than her little sister's ablutions and issued a request. "Mother, couldn't Chrissy come with us while Dione's getting clean? We never have anyone to play with here." She pulled on Alicia's arm and so Lavinia copied the gesture on the other side.

"Couldn't he please, Mummy?"

The two girls looked up expectantly, and my feelings on the matter were clearly not important.

"Oh, very well," she eventually gave in. "But if you hear the bell for tea, you're to be down in a flash."

"Yes, Mother. Of course, Mother," they sang in unison and hurried after the tempestuous nanny and their flying sister.

Grandfather looked alarmed by the proceedings. I do not believe he was used to allowing situations to escape his control, but it was not just Dione who was up in the air that day. Our investigation was nebulous. His own behaviour was strange, even by his standards, and I was now apparently off to the nursery for games with two infant girls.

CHAPTER SEVEN

I followed the chattering group up first one set of stairs, and then along a hallway to another. We eventually made it to the top floor of the house, and I was interested to discover that the long gallery up there was a building site.

It was incredible to see. In place of a floor were the bare timbers of the original beams. A board had been laid across them, upon which carpenters were racing back and forth as though there wasn't the slightest danger of them falling to the floor below. The other remarkable thing about it was the sheer size of the room. It appeared to span the length of the building, but whatever decoration had been there before the Pearsons arrived had been stripped back to reveal the bare bones of the house.

"It's this way if you're coming, young man." The nanny stepped through the first door on the right, and I pursued her into an entirely different world.

The nursery at Parham was serene and inviting and seemed a thousand miles away from the bustle and busyness of the renovations that were going on nearby. It was more like an apartment than a single space. It had its own telephone and a lift that transported food up from the kitchen. A budgie hopped about in its cage by the window, and Veronica and Lavinia had already disappeared into their respective rooms. The nanny wasn't the only member of staff there. Dressed in black with pretty bunches in her hair, a nurserymaid, who couldn't have been more than sixteen, was busy rearranging the girls' dolls and soft animals.

Like much of the house, the room was blessed with great inundations of light and, had I been ten to fifteen years younger, I would have liked nothing more than a ride on the rocking horse that sat waiting expectantly in the middle of the room. This serenity was somewhat disturbed by Nanny marching to the lift in the corner and slinging some dirty plates into it before scribbling out a note and sending the whole lot down with a bang. This apparently wasn't enough for her and so she put her mouth against the pipes underneath and, in a gravelly yell, exclaimed, "Just in case you can't read, Cook,

I said that lunch today was little better than average, and you should learn to use cinnamon more sparingly."

While this was taking place, Veronica emerged from her bedroom dressed in a red and white gingham dress and came to stand next to me. "Nanny and Cook have been at war for some time now. It almost came to blows when Cook stormed up here looking as though she wanted to murder poor Nanny, who, to be fair to Cook, had just described her Irish stew as 'swill unfit for a dead pig'."

With her rebuke delivered, the Amazonian nanny brushed off her hands and went to attend to other business.

"I need to talk to you," the eldest Pearson girl said in a conspiratorial whisper. "I tried to get your attention earlier, but you didn't understand." She said this as if it was a major failing in on my part.

"I can only apologise," I told the twelve(ish)-year-old. "What did you wish to—"

The nurserymaid came closer at this moment and Veronica interrupted me with a "Shhhh!" She waited until the maid had retreated to what I took to be a bathroom, and then she spoke a little faster, "Dione says that Nanny says that you're a detective."

"That's right." I tried to sound confident, as the idea that I was anything more than a hanger-on to my grandfather's magnificent coat tails was still difficult for me to state out loud. "I've solved any number of heinous crimes. Everything from murders to..." I may have faltered then as I realised just how narrow a field of experience I had. "...other murders."

"Good, then we're going to need your help." She was deadly serious, and I got the impression that she was listening to the sounds of the house in case someone should disturb us.

Much like her mother, Veronica seemed reluctant to discuss what she'd brought me there to say, and so I took over. "You must know a lot of what goes on around here. I'm sure there's any amount of intrigue in a place like Parham."

She looked up at me rather coyly, and I wondered whether the word *intrigue* was in the everyday vocabulary of such a young girl.

"Are you referring to Graham Perugino?" she asked to surprise me, and I instantly wanted to know all about that curiously named person.

"I might be," I said in the hope I could coax the story out of her,

48

but it was just then that Lavinia came to interrupt.

"Have you told him yet?" she asked her sister, but before she could answer, their nanny reappeared and sat down in a rocking chair to darn some thick woollen socks. The two girls exchanged disheartened looks and Veronica thought of something to pass the time until we were alone again.

"Come along, you two. We've got just enough time for a game of rude poetry before Dione escapes from the bathroom. She's terrible at it. She can't spell for one thing and her rhymes never make any sense."

"What's rude poetry?" I asked, instantly distracted.

Instead of answering, the rather strong child with shoulder-length, chestnut brown hair pushed me over to a small table, which I imagine was normally used for tea parties. I was directed to a chair that was approximately seven sizes too small for me, and pens and papers were soon produced.

"Each person is allowed to write two lines about another player," Veronica explained in a grown-up voice. I could tell that, as the oldest, she was the one in charge of such tasks. "We then pass the poem on, and the next person adds two more lines. They can be as insulting as you jolly well like. And then, when the poem gets back to its subject, he…"

"Or she!" her sister added.

"…must write two final lines to defend himself."

"Or herself!" Lavinia was eager to offer what I took to be a past example as she sat down beside me at the table. "So we could say:

Veronica is very dull; she really is a bore.

Which is the very reason no one likes her anymore.

She's as friendly as a polar bear, with extra sharp nails,

And her singing voice is dreadful, she positively wails.

And then Veronica would add…

Despite all that, she's a good gal.

Who always looks out for her pals."

"I see." I was not sure how I felt about indulging in such cruelty, especially against two innocent competitors. The imposing nanny had her disapproving eye on me the whole time, and I definitely didn't want to incite her wrath.

"Don't be afraid, Christopher," Veronica replied with a hint of wickedness in her voice and a raised eyebrow. "We won't be too hard on you."

Three pages were torn from a notebook, and I had to write about Lavinia for my first lines.

"Do you like life here at Parham?" I asked when I couldn't decide where to begin my poem.

"It's better than being in the city." The elder sister wrinkled her nose as she answered. "The staff are nicer here. Our old nanny in Grosvenor Square used to treat us just horribly. One day, Mother saw her seize Lavinia by the ponytail, so she dismissed her on the spot."

"I don't see much difference," Lavinia moaned in a low voice. "Life in general is a thoroughly daunting experience. All in all, I wish that it was shorter, warmer, and more comfortable."

Her sister turned to me to explain in a whisper. "Lavinia is scared of everything. She once fainted at Nanny's reading of Dr Doolittle because the idea of talking animals was too much for her to bear."

At this, the younger of the two screwed her eyes up and covered her ears. "It's the thought of pigs, rabbits and chickens delivering their final words before we eat them that so upsets me. Can you even imagine?"

I smiled at this and decided upon the first line of my poem. They were sweet children and at least as odd as Albert and I had been at their age (and presumably still are today). However, none of this would tell us who had been tormenting their mother.

"Does Graham Perugino scare you?" I not so subtly asked to change the topic.

Veronica glanced over at their nanny, but, as she didn't appear to have noticed my softly issued question, she nodded for her sister to answer.

"He didn't use to." Lavinia sighed and held her pencil to her lip. "I used to think he was lovely."

"We all thought he was lovely," Veronica added in a tone that suggested she was a great deal more worldly than her sister. "He is by far the most handsome footman that Parham has seen in its I don't quite remember how many centuries of history." She put her pencil down and said in a confidential whisper, "You know that he's half Italian."

"Change!" Lavinia suddenly screeched and, when I didn't

understand what she meant, she added a detail. "Fold the paper over and pass it to the next person."

I wasn't particularly happy with my rhyme, but it would have to do, and so I followed her instructions. My next task was to compose a couplet of insults about Veronica. They needed to be offensive but not cruel, which is far more difficult than you might think, especially as I was trying to figure out how to return to the topic of the mysterious half-Italian footman who may or may not have done something intriguing.

"How did you feel when you found out about Graham?" I used his first name as I'd quite forgotten his last.

"We were shocked, of course," Lavinia replied, before her sister warned her that it was not her turn to talk with a simple but effective glare.

"We were shocked until Mother told us that he had only stolen from us because he couldn't afford the quality of life to which he aspires."

I was quietly impressed that I'd managed to uncover this much, and I can't describe how happy I became when she added another key piece of information.

"That's why Father decided not to give him the sack."

If anyone had provided tea, I would have spat it out at this moment. "You mean a man stole from you and he's still working here?" It was hard to control my voice, but I managed not to shout.

"Oh, yes," she replied quite earnestly, her pale eyes suddenly growing larger. "Graham works below stairs. I don't know exactly what he does, but he always seems to have a cloth in his hand for polishing things."

The nanny looked at me, and so I pretended to be thinking over my poem. I scribbled down a line then crossed it out when I realised that I couldn't think of anything to rhyme with *disparage* except for *carriage* and *marriage*, which wouldn't do at all.

"I'm sorry," I said when she looked away, "but I don't understand why your parents would agree to have a thief in the house. That seems quite reckless."

"You really aren't listening, are you? It was Daddy." Lavinia replied in her usual drawn-out way of speaking. "Our chauffeur, Mr Petre, told the housekeeper, Mrs Evans, that he'd seen Graham in the silver room after hours. When an inventory was taken, a tray and two bowls were found to be missing." She was no longer whispering, so apparently this wasn't the sensitive topic that they wished to keep from the staff.

Veronica filled in the next part of the story. "Mrs Evans told Mother and Mother told Father, who surprised everyone by saying that if Graham Perugino felt the need to steal from us, we clearly weren't paying him enough. So instead of firing him, Daddy doubled his salary."

"My goodness," I replied quite involuntarily. "That may be the nicest thing I've ever heard."

"We have very kind parents." Veronica sighed, as if it was terribly difficult to live up to their example.

"Change!" Lavinia called, and I understood this time what she wanted.

I folded over my paper and handed it to Veronica, who passed hers to her sister and Lavinia's came to me. Oddly, I found it even more difficult to say anything good about myself than it had been to make up silly things for the two girls. This time, though, I didn't have to stoke the conversation, as Veronica did it for me.

"Poor Graham cried with gratitude when Father told him."

Lavinia was quick to provide an addendum. "And nothing has gone missing below stairs since."

It seemed unlikely that a man would steal again if he'd been given a second chance as Graham whatever-his-lovely-Italian-surname-was had. It would truly disappoint my grandfather if the known thief in the household turned out to be the mastermind behind poor Alicia's torment. He didn't approve of such prosaic solutions to our cases, and I didn't like the thought of having to tell him what I'd discovered.

"Finished," Lavinia announced with pride.

"Finished," her sister echoed.

"It will have to do," I concluded and put a line under my work to show that my stab at literary greatness was complete.

"Read yours first," Veronica demanded and so I cleared my throat and did just that.

"Christopher is pale and round, his trousers trail along the ground.

He's certainly no work of art, and I doubt that he is very smart."

"I wrote that!" Veronica beamed, and I continued to read.

"The truth is, he is awfully glum, and, like a baby, sucks his thumb.

His legs are bowed, his nose is pimpled." I had to stop for a moment to check this wasn't true. *"And people say he's very simple."*

Lavinia burst out laughing and I hurried to read my retort.

"But at least he's not a total fool.

He actually did quite well in his last year at school."

Silence filled the room, and the girls both looked a little sorry for me.

"Is that really the only nice thing you can say about yourself, Chrissy?" Lavinia's whole face had sunken. "How very sad."

I'd never been pitied by two children before – to my knowledge, at least. It was an odd feeling.

"You can think what you like," I said with a laugh, "but I'm really very proud of making it out of school on the first try. My geography teacher, Mr Anders, once told me that there was less chance of me obtaining my secondary education certificate than there was of the people of the Territory of Western Samoa invading the Cornish coast. I told him in reply that I didn't know where the Territory of Western Samoa was, which he said more than proved his point." Aware that this had made them frown even more, I changed tack. "What did you say about yourselves, anyway?"

Veronica did not hesitate to answer. "I wrote:

'Actually, none of that is true, and with her eyes of brilliant blue.

Veronica is quite exquisite – the nicest girl you'll ever visit."

"That is a bold and confident claim," I had to admit.

Lavinia decided to drive the point home. "I finished mine by simply stating:

But if anyone should disagree, that she's the best in history,

She'll make sure that you don't forget that Lavinia is the greatest yet."

I was rather glad when the third sister appeared from the bathroom, clean and changed and ready to play. Instead of joining in with our game, though, she stood on her own in the middle of the room.

Nanny finished her stitch and nodded approvingly. "Very good, Miss Dione," she said, getting to her feet to pat her on the head. "I'll clean the bathroom while you all play."

The big, bustling woman disappeared into the room which smelt of Pears soap. Finally free, the three girls nudged one another as they tried to choose who would get to reveal their secret.

To my surprise, it was little Dione with the bobbed hair and the chubby cheeks who was awarded the privilege. "You have to help us."

This phrasing was not to her big sister's liking, and so Veronica immediately took over. "What Dione means is that we've been waiting for you to arrive. Something strange has been going on here. Mother might not think we realise anything, but we've been investigating, and we think we can help."

CHAPTER EIGHT

If that afternoon told me anything, it was that, despite any evidence you might have noticed to the contrary, I was no longer so childish as I once had been. Seeing their games in the nursery reminded me that I wasn't playing anymore. Even Albert had moved on from his youthful follies, and things had clearly changed for us.

And so my first thought when three children told me that they were hot on the heels of a criminal in their own home was that they were ever so sweet and perhaps a little misguided.

"You've been investigating?" I doubt I hid my incredulity very well.

"That's right," the bravest of the three replied, throwing her head back with a confidence I only fleetingly possessed. "We've been compiling evidence which we have recorded in a notebook, the location of which no one outside of this room—"

"Except for Daphne," Lavinia told her big sister.

"I was just coming to that," Veronica replied. "We have hidden our secret findings in a place that no one except for the three of us and our cousin Daphne could possibly know."

They were all so serious that, rather than dismiss the idea, I paused and considered the possibility that they actually knew something. My grandfather was getting close to eighty, and yet he was considered one of Britain's great detectives. It wasn't such a stretch of the imagination that three well-educated young daughters of a cultured and prestigious family could have learnt something worth knowing.

I moved my chair back from the table and turned it to face them. "Very well. What do you wish to tell me?"

Veronica eyed the door, then nodded, and her two sisters rushed to fulfil tasks that had evidently been assigned in advance. Lavinia went to stand beside the budgie cage and felt behind the curtain in search of the book. Dione, meanwhile, walked to the bathroom door and put her weight against it. This was all ceremonial, as they didn't need the book to tell me what they knew. Instead, Lavinia handed it to Veronica, who held the slim volume and occasionally tapped it to offer support to what she had to say.

"We know exactly what has been happening to Mother and, despite what you might think, we had nothing to do with it. We haven't been moving paintings around. We did not destroy the vase from her sitting room, and we haven't taken the lion statues or anything else that went missing."

I had to wonder whether they'd caught any of the conversation we'd had with Alicia in the Georgian salon, but I didn't mention it directly. "So who do you think is doing all that?"

"It's obvious, isn't it?" Lavinia asked in her slow drawl.

I waited for one of them to explain as, if it was so obvious, I evidently didn't need to repeat my question.

Unsurprisingly, it was Veronica who would reveal the truth. "All this started after the experts arrived."

"The men who are here to examine Parham's historical artefacts?"

"No, the men *and women* who have come to pick over our treasures. I don't trust them." She suddenly sounded older. In fact, there was something quite commanding in her manner. Her eyes were ever so sharp, and she spoke with decision.

"I don't like them at all," little Dione added with her usual bluntness.

I got up from my tiny chair, perhaps subconsciously wishing to show that I was the senior and, at least in theory, most mature person there. I wasn't used to this, and I can't say I enjoyed the sensation.

"Have you found any evidence that could link them to the strange events of the last few weeks?"

The two girls looked at Lavinia, who would evidently be the one to reply. "I've heard them walking around at night. Sometimes they talk until late, and the language they use can be quite vulgar." I had no doubt that, for a child of ten or so, rude words were a sure sign of criminality. As I was now nineteen, I knew that this was not automatically the case.

"And you heard all this through the pipes, I assume?" I asked in a perhaps superior tone.

Veronica crossed her arms over the squares on her dress. "Well, yes. They're so old that they carry sound all over the place. It's like a system of speaking tubes. Daddy says he will replace them, as we often hear the kitchen staff talking when we're in the Great

56

Hall having dinner, and then we have to pretend that we don't know what Cook thinks of Willie, the odd man, or how Mother's grumpy lady's maid Miss Metcalf is secretly in love with Graham. It's terribly embarrassing."

I was distracted by her colourful description of the goings on below stairs and had to remind myself that there was a crime to investigate.

"Very well, but you can't say for certain that the historical experts are involved in any of the things that have scared your mother."

The three girls were dismayed. No matter what it said in their notebook, they presumably knew that they hadn't obtained any real proof. This did not stop Veronica from disagreeing with me. "But he's a rogue!" She was suddenly quite upset and gripped the book more tightly.

"Who is? Elton Lockhart?"

"Well… yes." Veronica became less sure of herself with every response she gave. I knew just how she felt because I had experienced the same thing a thousand times when I was learning from my grandfather. I must say, it made me quite the rotter to imply that my perspective on the situation was any more valid than hers, and so I softened my tone accordingly.

"He may well be, but that doesn't explain why he would decide to move things about in an old house. After all, he has direct access to your most valuable possessions. Why would he go to all that trouble?"

"We don't know," Lavinia said to help her sister. "But we don't trust him. At the very least, he's a bounder. And he's playing a game with the sisters that follow him around everywhere. He can't be trusted."

I suddenly understood my grandfather's side of things a little better, but I took a deep breath so as not to snap as he surely would have. "You were right when you said that I'm a detective. Lord Edgington is the expert, but I've helped him on a number of cases over the last few years, and we've managed to solve each of them. In that time, I've known every kind of individual. I've met savages who seem like saints, and ruffians who turned out to be thoroughly nice chaps. Just because two women are in love with the same man, and many people think that he is a rogue, it does not prove that he has some devious scheme to rob, upset or defraud your family."

Dione would be the person to summarise their feelings on the matter. "But I don't like him," she said rather sadly.

I wished that I could have told them that I had already amassed any amount of evidence on the cad in our midst and that I would soon have him ejected from the house. Sadly, life is not as simple as children like to believe, and I had to tell the truth.

"I quite understand why that would be the case, and I will bear in mind everything that you have told me." I sounded as diplomatic as my mother. "Until we find some clear and irrefutable evidence, however, there is no reason to suspect Elton Lockhart more than anyone else here."

For some reason, their dour little faces perked up, and they came together in the centre of the room.

"Wonderful," Veronica began, having hidden the book once more. "Then we'll set about accumulating evidence and let you know what we find."

"I beg your pardon?"

"You said, 'we'. *We'll* work together to solve the case. I have no doubt that *we* can solve it before any more deviousness occurs. And it isn't just Lockhart who could be involved. There's the very dull man who sends us all to sleep."

"And the rather handsome one who always wears a silly hat," Lavinia added.

"Oh, yes!" Veronica clapped her hands together. "His name is Dr Carbonell, and he dresses like a jungle explorer for some reason."

"Then there's the young one," Dione reminded them. "I like him. He painted me a picture of a donkey."

"Hold on just one moment." I raised my hands to stop them, but they didn't notice. They were too busy chattering amongst themselves about the potential suspects. "That wasn't quite what I meant. I was only trying to—"

"I think I heard the bell for tea." Veronica moved to leave before she'd finished her sentence and, with their nanny appearing from the bathroom again, they marched downstairs in their neat line.

I looked about the deserted nursery and tried to comprehend what had just happened.

CHAPTER NINE

Tea! O, that most wondrous of inter-meal diversions (joint first with elevenses). We Britons have invented a pantheon of great things. The telephone (as Alexander Graham Bell was Scottish)! The electric toaster (thirty-five years ago, back in 1893)! The… toothbrush! But are any of them comparable to the simple concept of eating sandwiches and cakes *between* other meals? I will let you be the judge of that.

After this brief soliloquy, you can be in no doubt as to my feelings when I descended the stairs. I followed the sound of the girls' chatter, which carried through the house even without the help of old metal pipes. I travelled down the winding staircase and soon found myself stepping outside at the front of the building, where a large round table had been set up and Todd was serving drinks. I should have taken this as a first negative sign, but I am not as good a detective as my grandfather claims and thought nothing of it.

"Hello there, Chrissy," he said as our footman Halfpenny arrived with a laden trolley.

The south façade of Parham House was, without question, the most attractive, even with scaffolding covering one part of it. There was an impressively large wisteria growing up the visible parts of the property, seven gables of varying sizes, and banks upon banks of windows. It was a harmonious spot to while away the afternoon, and I took my place at the table in front of it.

"Have you had a nice time with Alicia's daughters?" Mother asked, and Veronica answered for me.

"We truly did," the eldest girl said with a knowing smile. "We played a game of rude poetry, and I told Christopher he must learn to be more confident."

I had just identified the food on the trolley as being a selection of our cook Henrietta's more experimental creations and was overcome with disappointment.

"He really must," Lavinia added, which I thought was rather rich coming from a girl who'd fainted at the thought of talking animals.

Alicia changed the topic to spare my blushes. "Your grandfather has kindly lent us your cook for the afternoon. I remember your mother telling me of Henrietta's unique cuisine when we first met." This surprised me, as I had no idea Henrietta had been working at Cranley for so long. Even more incredible was that, having heard reports of her work, Alicia requested that she make afternoon tea.

On the table now in front of me were several trays bearing, for want of a better word, food. There was everything from smoked pilchard surprise to macerated swede, but not a ham or cucumber sandwich in sight. I sighed and helped myself to the least offensive-looking option. For some reason, the others all seemed happy with the choices before us. I thought that the girls would at least have shared my conviction that the best kind of sandwich must always contain cucumber.

Once more trapped within the rigid confines of a polite discussion, it was impossible to get any further with the investigation. I was hoping that I might extrapolate something significant from Alicia's light conversation, but apart from a few nervous glances she gave in the direction of the house, there was nothing obviously amiss.

As we ate, a chattering group rounded the house. The manual labourers had finished work for the duration of our stay, but these noisy scholarly types remained and were deep in discussion as they crossed the lawn. In addition to that dashing figure, Elton Lockhart, and the two young women who were undoubtedly twin sisters, there were three men we hadn't yet seen.

The first was dressed like a jungle explorer, as the girls had already described. He was talking over his grey-faced companion, who did not seem to have noticed and continued prattling regardless. A young, skinny fellow with bright red hair trailed after them, whistling to himself as he went. It was a rather happy cacophony, and I was glad when Grandfather asked for our hostess's permission to call over to them.

"Ladies, gentlemen," he shouted rather loudly to get their attention. "Won't you join us for a moment?"

Lockhart glanced about as though to ensure that my grandfather was talking to him, then nodded and waved his comrades over to us. Up close, I could see that he was just as handsome as such celebrated rogues tend to be. There was something that put me in mind of the mercurial Lord Byron, rolled together with the famously affable Charles II. It was an appealing combination, to say the least.

"Good afternoon, all," he said, not standing on ceremony, even as he offered a florid bow. His colleagues and acolytes mumbled their greetings, but it was clear that he would be the one to direct the conversation.

"Good afternoon, Mr Lockhart," Alicia responded with a genial look. "This is my friend Violet Prentiss and her father and son. They will be staying with us for a short time." I noticed that the words "Lord Edgington" were not spoken, and I wondered whether she wished to keep my grandfather's identity a secret. He was well enough known for that not to be possible, but I saw nothing to suggest that any of them had recognised him.

"How nice for you, madam." Lockhart had an impressively full and dramatic voice. It was as if he'd practiced his lines in advance.

I watched the two blonde sisters who flanked him – this arrangement only adding to the impression of the dark, brooding fellow's rakishness. It was immediately evident that neither one of them was happy that he would lavish his attention on anyone but them.

"Elton Lockhart, I assume," my grandfather interjected. "I've heard much about you."

Lockhart laughed to himself quietly before responding. "All of it bad, I'm sure."

"I wouldn't say that, but I won't deny you're an intriguing character." Grandfather froze with his teacup and saucer raised above the table. "If your employer does not mind, perhaps you could all join us for dinner this evening. I would love to hear the tales of your adventures abroad. My grandson and I are planning a grand tour of Europe that we intend to commence very soon."

Rather than replying, he turned to Alicia for her thoughts on the matter. She looked nervous once more, and I wondered whether she knew of her daughters' belief that the unpleasantness at Parham House had been caused by one of the experts before us. She nodded, and, approximately two hours later, we'd changed for dinner and were due downstairs in the dining room.

"All I wish to know is your general impression of our time here," I complained as Grandfather tied his cravat in the mirror in one corner of his room.

He was in a particularly unhelpful mood. "My general impression is that I'm having a lovely time. Aren't you?"

"What has got into you? You're acting like a perfect lunatic."

He sighed and turned to me. "Nothing has 'got into' me, as you so inelegantly put it. I'm simply not taking this matter too seriously for once. No one has been murdered, thank the Lord, and until that changes, I will thrill in this rare chance to investigate something which is barely even a crime."

"Terrifying a woman who is the caretaker of one of the oldest country houses in Great Britain: do you really not consider that a crime?"

He put one hand on my shoulder, as I was overreacting – by his standards, at least. "My boy, I'm not trying to play down the possibility that something more nefarious is at play. And as you can tell from the deft way in which I engineered this evening's soiree, I am hard at work. However, I will go about it with a smile on my face."

As he danced lightly about the room, I tried to return to the topic I actually wished to discuss. "Fine. You are an elderly man, and you deserve to enjoy your simple pleasures." I had 'engineered' this sentence to pique him, but he continued his jolly movement. "However, you can still tell me what you think of my findings. First of all, there is the half-Italian footman who has a history of stealing from his employers, and then the girls told me that nothing unusual happened here until the team of experts we met on the lawn arrived."

He was not surprised by my news. "That's right. Alicia informed me that they came here to study a large batch of antiques that were bought from Chatterton Hall in Yorkshire. A number of treasures that were originally in Parham were sent there by the previous occupants."

"So you know more about them than I do," I replied. "What a surprise."

He finally stopped his shuffling and walked to the door. "Yes, Christopher. Despite the long, painful absence I suffered while you were in the nursery this afternoon, I was capable of interviewing Alicia without your assistance."

"Very good, Grandfather. Does that mean you hold to the same idea as her daughters? Do you think that Lockhart and his colleagues are the reason we're here today?"

He raised one finger to respond, and I knew he was playing with me. "I would answer those questions, my dear boy. You know I would.

But we mustn't be late for dinner."

I had hoped that he would be more willing to reveal his thinking now that I had solved a case or two. Such optimism would only lead to disappointment.

I followed him from the bedroom and down to the ground floor. When we got there, I found the three girls, all in their finest pale blue silk dresses, standing at the bottom of the stairs, pulling a great rope that looked as though it belonged in a bell tower. This description wasn't nearly as creative as I first thought, as I soon realised that they were ringing the dinner bell. The ashen butler, Mr Cridland, was standing nearby looking rather paternal. I know how it is in such houses. Until I was approximately nine years old, I was sure that our old butler, Jessop, was my real father. He certainly paid me more attention than Daddy ever did.

Even the normally listless Lavinia was pulling on the bell with all her might, and I could hear doors opening and closing on the higher floors as people got the hint that their presence was required in the dining room. I paused before entering, as something important had come to the fore in my mind. Even before I stepped inside, I knew that I was about to meet the suspects to a crime that, for the most part, hadn't happened yet.

CHAPTER TEN

To my disappointment, the only person there was jungle Joseph – that wasn't actually his name, but with his plain beige attire, it might as well have been. He had a black moustache to rival my grandfather's white one, and he seemed to be very much engrossed in the suit of armour in the corner of the room. He had at least taken his helmet off for once but still held it at his side.

"My apologies," he said when he noticed that he was not alone. "My name's Dr Raymond Carbonell. War relics."

"I beg your pardon," I found myself replying, though what I should have said was absolutely nothing at all; a good detective would have nodded his head and looked impressed.

Grandfather took a few steps closer and held his hand out. "I believe what Dr Carbonell meant was that he is an expert on military equipment. That would be armour, swords, firearms and the like."

I nodded my head and looked impressed.

"My father was a collector of civil war memorabilia," the rather engaging doctor continued, and I took my turn to shake his hand. "He would have me out first thing every Saturday morning from spring right through to autumn. We spent our time in fields where he believed important battles had taken place, and we would dig holes until we found scraps of armour or lead shot. I thought it was terribly boring back then but, for some reason, when the time came to choose what I wished to study at university, the only thing on my mind was history and warfare. After the Great War was over, I threw myself into my work and have been at it ever since."

He smiled to himself and stared into space, as if his old man was right there with us in the room. I must say that I instantly liked him. There was something open and appealing about the way he spoke and, though not as flamboyant or enigmatic as his colleague Lockhart, he had chiselled features and a crop of messy dark hair perched on his head that made me think he was the type to lead a platoon into battle.

Of course, the fact I liked him made me worry that he would turn out to be the troublemaker we had gone there to find. I did a quick calculation in my head to work out how many such amiable characters we'd met had turned out to be rotters. I counted at least three but couldn't decide whether this made it more or less likely that Dr Carbonell was a scoundrel. I opted to think the worst of him, just in case.

"It must be a fascinating field," Grandfather replied before noticing his unintended pun, "metaphorically speaking!"

The two enjoyed a brief titter, and I cursed our new acquaintance for his potential scheming. Before I could nod and look impressed again, we were joined by more guests.

The young red-haired fellow arrived next with the singularly drab man I'd spotted during tea. It was not just his suit that was grey; his fleshy, pockmarked skin had a sickly quality, which was nothing compared to the dull yet simultaneously arrogant tone in which he spoke.

"Good evening, gentlemen." He had thick glasses which magnified the area around his eyes so that he looked like a rather patronising owl. I instantly wanted to return to my room for a lie down. "I was just saying to my colleague, Mr Mark Isaac here, that it is not every day I am invited to dine in such exquisite surroundings with such exquisite company." Another person would have injected some energy and animation into this comment but not this man. Oh, no, not Mr... Actually, I hadn't learnt his name yet. "My name is Eric Uhland. That's Uhland: U-H-L-A-N-D, and I am a specialist in portraiture. I'm sure that Dr Carbonell will already have told you about me. I am highly respected, and my work on a number of significant paintings over the years surely precedes me."

He closed his eyes, as if waiting for someone to confirm just how good he was at his job. He didn't talk like a normal person, and I had to wonder whether he actually believed his own claims of excellence. I could see that my grandfather wasn't impressed, but he was saved from saying anything rude – or having to lie – when the curly-headed man kindly cut into the conversation.

"And I'm Mark Isaac, as Mr Uhland just mentioned." He had an interesting accent that I didn't recognise. If I had to guess, I'd say that he was from somewhere up north like Sheffield, Leeds or Watford. "Unlike my companions, I'm not an expert on anything. I'm just a student, and I've been assigned to help Mr Uhland with the work he is undertaking."

He was yet another cheerful, honest-seeming fellow I would have to add to my list of likely villains. Thank goodness Uhland was a terrible, pompous bore, as I could be fairly certain that he would never do anything so noteworthy as to plot a devious criminal enterprise. Unless, of course, he had assumed his persona in order to throw everyone off the scent. Being a detective can lead to such paranoid thinking, and it has become genuinely difficult to trust the world before me.

"Vyvyan, all I'm saying is that you could be a mite more subtle," a woman's voice declared, and the two blonde sisters who we'd seen with Elton Lockhart made their noisy entrance.

"And all I'm saying, Frances, is that you are a sore loser," the second replied in a bitter tone.

"You're being ridiculous." The first twin would have continued this argument if she hadn't noticed the group of people who had turned to watch her. "Oh, my apologies, gentlemen. I didn't realise I was interrupting."

"There is nothing to worry about, my dear. We were just getting acquainted." My grandfather was instantly charming. I'd be happy if I could be charming with five minutes' notice, but he could turn it on and off like an electric light. I suppose that I was good at pretending to be marginally stupider than I really am, but I can only get away with that because of my age. In a few years' time, no one will find me sweet anymore, and then what will I do?

"I'm Vyvyan Horniman... with two Ys. And this is my sister Frances," the first explained, and it took me a moment to work out where the two Ys would fit into her name. In my defence, I was busy trying to spot the differences between them. They were both terribly beautiful, with skin the colour of fluffy clouds, hair as yellow as the sun and, perhaps inevitably after those comparisons, sky-blue eyes. I finally spotted a beauty mark on Frances's right cheek that would help me in telling them apart – as long as they were looking at me face on and the room was bright enough.

The staff from Cranley Hall were nowhere to be seen, but Mr Cridland was there to provide refreshments. I would have asked Todd for a champagne flip but had a feeling that Parham's ancient retainer would not offer such a wide range of drinks as our factotum did. At least this told me that Henrietta would not be in charge of dinner, and I could look forward to something that featured neither jam-smothered beetroot nor horseradish Eccles cakes.

From the look on Grandfather's face as my mother, our hostess and her daughters arrived, it was not just the meal that he was anticipating. Everyone sat down at the long, oval table, and he wore much the same expression as when we'd arrived at the house that afternoon; I was quite sure he was looking forward to this dinner as a chance to assess the potential guilt of those present.

There seemed to be the expectation that the oldest and, let's be honest, best dressed member of the party would be the one to lead the conversation. However, before Lord Edgington could begin, the final member of the group arrived to topple him from his perch. Trust that peacock Lockhart to make the biggest entrance. A lazy detective would have pinned the blame on him as the most notorious suspect and then headed off home. Sadly, my grandfather insisted on doing things correctly or not at all.

"I'm terribly sorry to be late," he told Alicia as he sat at the opposite end of the table from my family and me.

There were a few good-spirited groans from his colleagues, but Carbonell looked put out by his behaviour.

"I don't suppose it can be helped." There was something rather frightening about Grandfather just then. Though his delivery was neutral, the fact he had replied in place of Alicia was evidently noted around the table. Even the children looked surprised, but two footmen in dark brown liveries with contrasting cream cuffs arrived with the first course, and the tension was soon forgotten.

"This reminds me of a dinner I had on a ship on the Irrawaddy River in Burma," Lockhart began, and we were soon all engrossed in his tale.

As a dish of turbot and sea kale in a butter sauce was served, I watched the faces of those around me. They were an unusual bunch, from the shy and reserved apprentice, Mark Isaac, to the exuberant confidence of Elton Lockhart. But it wasn't just their moods I attempted to observe; I was curious as to how they interacted and, in particular, how they viewed their unelected leader.

Dr Carbonell could not hide a look of displeasure when Lockhart spoke. They evidently were not the best of friends, whereas the two Horniman sisters practically swooned as they listened to their companion's many anecdotes. Eric Uhland was paying careful attention to everything his more exciting colleague said, and even the three girls' eyes flicked back and forth as they followed the jolly conversation.

Once the first course had been served, and the staff retreated to the kitchen, my grandfather cleared his throat, and the real excitement began. "What a remarkable world you all must occupy. Of course, even experts like yourselves can rarely be certain of the provenance of an item. Many of the artefacts in the British Museum have passed through the hands of smugglers and fences. Is there any way of knowing whether important items have been forged or stolen?"

He watched with some satisfaction as the seed of the idea he'd planted immediately sprouted. No one had mentioned criminality until now. The talk had been of incredible finds and distant voyages, with each anecdote painting the teller in a flattering light. But with my grandfather's change of tack, it was almost as if he had dripped poison into their wineglasses and dared them all to drink.

It was the student and his mentor who most noticeably flinched. Uhland's eyes seemed to shrink down in themselves as if he wanted to go into hiding and, a few seats around from mine, Mark Isaac swallowed noisily. Neither said anything as the gallant military expert, Dr Carbonell, responded to my grandfather's unexpected comment.

"It's odd that you would equate the work of scholars and antiquarians with such behaviour. It is true that unscrupulous treasure hunters exist in the world, and even that Western nations have a history of ransacking the countries we occupied, but that doesn't mean that every person in our profession can be tarred with the same brush, Mr...?"

Lord Edgington was clearly intent on keeping his identity a secret for some time longer and, rather than giving the man his name, he delivered a measured response. "I am not seeking to accuse anyone of a crime," he said quite civilly before undermining this very notion, "but that doesn't mean you should be considered saints."

One of the twins laughed at this. I couldn't see her right cheek, but I believe it was Frances who said, "Well, I've certainly met a few rogues," and then winked at the man directly across from her.

Lockhart's silence was noticeable. He examined the table in front of him and gently touched a silver knife as though valuing it for auction. I thought he would ignore the discussion entirely, but then he looked straight down the table at Grandfather.

"If your comments are in any way directed at me, sir, all I can say is that you shouldn't believe everything you hear."

"That's right," Carbonell added. "Only one third of the stories about Elton are true and some of those are positive."

"Watch your tongue, Raymond." Lockhart's cheerfully mischievous grin disappeared, and a devilish aspect took its place. "Whatever you might think of me, I'm no criminal."

They held one another's gaze for a few tense moments before Carbonell turned away and, in little more than a whisper, said, "Certain people I know might disagree."

"Ladies and gentlemen," Alicia said when the hush that had consumed the room would not go away, "I believe we have started the evening on the wrong foot. I'm sure that all Lord Edgington wished to imply, was that—"

I didn't hear much more than this because of the reaction to her (perhaps unintentional) revelation.

"Edgington?" Lockhart exclaimed as someone dropped their cutlery and the second Horniman sister clapped in excitement.

"The detective?" Vyvyan with two Ys sang. "Oh, what fun. It feels as if we've assembled here to participate in a detective play. I'll be the first to die, of course. The prettiest young ladies tend to have the shortest roles in this sort of thing."

Frances looked disapprovingly at her twin, and I could see that she took umbrage at the idea that Vyvyan was the most beautiful woman there.

"What's all this about?" Eric Uhland asked and, even in this moment of heightened emotions, his voice was as flat as an anvil. "Have we been brought here under false pretences? I do not like to be duped."

"Few people do," I said when no one spoke. "But this is not a trap. My grandfather thought it would be a good idea to get to know you better, and so here we all are."

I looked across at him, unsure whether he wished to reveal the reason for our visit or not. He'd spent the last minute or two finishing his plate, as if the discussion was all very humdrum. Having done so, he wiped the corners of his mouth with his napkin, took a sip of (thankfully unpoisoned) wine and addressed the room.

"As we told you this afternoon, my daughter and Mrs Alicia Pearson have been friends for many years. We are here as guests of the family. Perhaps I should not have suggested that your profession is linked to criminality any more than if you were bankers, politicians or fortune tellers in a carnival." He said this with such sincerity that it took me a moment to realise that he was speaking ironically.

"Or policemen." Frances was far less jolly than her sister, and I wondered about their background. How had two well-bred young ladies come to dedicate their lives to searching out dusty artefacts and digging in the mud?

"Indeed," Grandfather replied with an impish smile of his own. "There are bad eggs in every profession…"

"But even more so when great works of art and rediscovered treasure are involved," Lockhart put to him. "Is that what you're not saying?"

Much like my grandfather, he knew how to use his words sparingly. It made a nice change for the great detective to meet another person with whom to spar. Instead of continuing the back-and-forth discussion, Frances asked a question.

"There's evidently something happening here," she murmured as the footmen arrived to collect the dirty plates. "What is it that you haven't told us?"

Grandfather sat back from the table for the staff to do their work. "Since your party arrived at Parham House, a series of unusual events has occurred. Items have been rearranged or gone missing altogether. Our hostess Alicia has been frightened by the behaviour of someone in this room, and I believe that everything that has happened up to now is just a prelude to that which is still to come." I would have loved to ask how he could be so certain, but he continued straight on with his speech. "So I am here to say that it must stop. If one of you is plotting something, I can assure you that it will come to nothing. Whatever it is you hope to achieve, as long as I am here, you will not succeed."

Of everyone around that table, it was the three Pearson girls who were most enjoying themselves. Like children on their first visit to the theatre, they sat with their mouths open as they got to see the famous sleuth at his dramatic best. Their heads twitched at every new comment from the supporting cast, and I noticed Veronica gasp, Lavinia close her eyes out of fear and Dione clasp her fists in quiet agitation when, at this point in the proceedings, Lockhart stood up from the table.

"I'll have you know that I am no thief." He first spoke to my grandfather, before turning to beg Alicia to believe him. "You must know that I would never wish you any harm, Mrs Pearson, and I am grateful for the chance to examine some truly exceptional artefacts that would not have been available to me anywhere else in the world. To jeopardise that would be foolish in the extreme."

"That is a high-minded sentiment," my grandfather replied with some ambiguity.

From the look of things, several members of our party doubted the sincerity of Elton Lockhart's speech. I evidently wasn't the only one to notice as, his head held high and with a ripple of the eyebrows, he pushed back his chair and swiftly left the room.

"He is just as dashing as everyone says." Grandfather spoke in such a dry and serious tone that it was hard to imagine he was about to make a joke. "He dashed off before he'd eaten the main course."

CHAPTER ELEVEN

As main courses go, the battalia pie was an exceptionally tasty one. Game pie has always been a favourite of mine, but when it is filled with venison, French boar, partridge, and the most delicious gravy, then topped off with spices, lemon and sealed in the crenellated pastry coffin, it is quite heavenly. I doubt there'll be time later, so I'll tell you now that we finished the meal with Cornish saffron cake, which was the perfect balance between light and luscious, flavoursome and subtle. And now I will stop talking about food until at least the next meal.

Even more captivating than the contents of my plate was the reaction to Lockhart's departure from those who remained. My mother considered the scene with quiet detachment, and I had no doubt she was weighing up what she had seen with the critical mind she had inherited from her father. The assorted experts could no longer look at one another. The twins sat together, staring down at the newly delivered dish as though it were an optical illusion. Whatever discomfort Uhland and his curly-haired assistant had suffered before, they now looked relieved, and Carbonell studied my grandfather as if bemused by the whole thing.

The person who really caught my attention, though, was our hostess. She had sat calmly through the argument my grandfather had instigated and was apparently resigned to his trouble making. She had invited us there to solve her problem, and so it shouldn't have surprised me, and yet I would not have expected her to be so accepting of his unconventional methods.

What she couldn't tolerate, however, was an awkward silence. Once we had finished the pie, she begged her daughters to stand up and perform for our entertainment.

"I don't like performing, Mother," Dione told her, whereas Lavinia looked as though she would rather fall asleep on the table, and Veronica refused point blank to leave her seat.

After a great deal more cajoling and promises of extra dessert, the three lined up in their matching outfits to recite a poem.

"Past eight o'clock and it's bedtime for Dolly,
Past eight o'clock and it's bedtime for me,

Dolly must lie on her sweet little pillow,
Dolly and I we must always agree!"

Veronica stared pleadingly at me, presumably hoping I could save her from embarrassment as the second verse began, and the three changed position in a shuffling step.

"Goodnight Mama! Goodnight Papa!
Goodnight to all the rest.
Goodnight Mama, Goodnight Papa,
I must love Dolly best!"

The audience cheered and smiled, and the two Horniman sisters rushed forward to pat the darling little children on their heads, which at least cheered up the two youngest sisters, though Veronica gritted her teeth throughout. For all the girls' discomfort, their mother had achieved her goal. Conversation flowed for the remainder of the meal, and the uncomfortable atmosphere appeared to have been forgotten. In reality, I noticed countless sly glances in my grandfather's direction from the five remaining experts. We may have feigned joviality, but the truth was that every last person knew that something wasn't right at Parham House that night.

"The poem was quite accurate, girls," Alicia told them once that exquisite saffron cake had been golloped. "It is past eight o'clock and bedtime for all three of you."

They could not ignore this but took their time saying good night to each of us before leaving the room. I was not the only one who was astounded to see Dione climb up into Lord Edgington's lap and give him a kiss on the cheek. If she had known that his warm, Father Christmas-like appearance belied a stickler's interior, I very much doubt she would have gone anywhere near him. For his part, Grandfather was amused by the normally reserved girl's show of affection and patted her on the back appreciatively.

There was talk of digestifs and cigars, but no one was in the mood, and each of the experts made their excuses and went up to bed. Mother and Alicia retired to the Saloon, which left my grandfather and me alone at the table.

"What a riveting experience that was, Christopher," he told me, and I believed that he'd discovered something worth discovering – or

74

perhaps he just wanted me to think that was the case.

"Come along," I told him with a yawn. "I'm not going to stay up all night, so if you want to show off the impressive observation you've made, then this is the moment."

He shook his head and looked stern. "No, no. It's nothing like that. It's just the day in general. Twelve hours ago, we were home in Cranley with no knowledge of the goings-on here, and now we've put the fear of God into a group of queer fish, one of whom clearly has an ulterior motive for accepting this work."

"But how can you be so sure?" I asked as I sipped the fresh lemonade that Todd had evidently had a hand in preparing. "You said to their faces that you thought one of them was up to no good. The way I see it, very little has happened. And now that you've warned them, it's even less likely that we will have a serious crime to solve."

He remained silent for some time, then reacted as though my words had only just reached him. "You may be right. We do not have a *serious* crime to solve, but we still have a puzzle to unravel." He placed both fists on the table and there was something animalistic about the way he rose to standing. "As for the future, I do not expect the person who has started down this path to turn back now, but only time will tell."

I wanted to put forward some theories of my own and ask him more questions, but his behaviour left me quite bemused. I followed him upstairs, reflecting once more that the biggest mystery in my life would always be my grandfather – a man who seemed to contradict himself on an hourly basis and yet rarely turned out to be entirely wrong; a man who understood everyone and everything but tended to leave those around him scratching their heads.

I saw him up to his room, then went to my cupboard to get into bed. At least there was enough space inside to open and close the door, so it was an improvement on a case we'd investigated a year earlier. And when I'd changed into my pyjamas, I lay there turning over questions in my head.

That really is a detective's job in one sentence. Of course, there's always an element of investigation involved, but the element that attracts people like my grandfather to our line of work is the mental agility it requires. So I tried to give my brain a good stretch before I drifted off to sleep.

I stacked up hypotheses like boxes in a warehouse. I remembered my grandfather's reactions to Alicia's tale and the various suspects we had met. The three Pearson girls were there in my head, too, and I added their half-Italian footman to the list of potential culprits for a crime that was still incomplete. Thoughts and images melded together and, for a moment, I thought that I'd solved the case before we'd really begun. This certainty didn't last, and I became acutely aware of the fact that reality was slipping away from me. There was moonlight coming in through the window, and I truly believed I could hold on to it, but a few seconds later, the room had turned black, and I was fast asleep.

A scream. That's what woke me, though I didn't know it at the time.

CHAPTER TWELVE

I don't know how long I'd been asleep, but the moon had abandoned me, and the room was as black as can be. I found my way downstairs somehow, and all the way to the Great Hall, only to meet a dying man who thought he'd been attacked by a monster.

"I don't want to go like this," the wretched fellow said as another bolt of agony coursed through him, and he clawed at his heart. "I don't want to die."

I had heard sounds from around the house and knew I wasn't the only one who had heard the screams. Quick to action, Grandfather was already there next to me, and he turned the invalid onto his side to examine him.

"What else did he tell you?" he asked as the man's breathing became even shorter. It was as if the act of inhaling required too much energy – as if a weight was pressing down on him and he didn't have the strength to push it off.

"He was talking about dragons. He said that something landed on his face."

He nodded and took his patient's pulse, then loosened his collar to give him more air. I don't believe my grandfather showed any great emotion; he was concentrating too hard to give anything away, but at the moment that the victim cried out for the last time, Lord Edgington sighed a deep sigh and sat back on the floor.

"You have to do something," I shouted, my voice still not my own.

"He's dead, Christopher. What would you have me do?"

I looked from the body to the man who should have saved him. "I don't know. It's your job to work miracles, not mine. Save him, Grandfather. Move his arms about, blow air into his lungs, tickle him until he starts laughing if that will do the trick, just do something."

"He hasn't been in an accident. I believe he's inhaled something and so, while I might be able to restore his breathing momentarily, I would not be able to reverse the effects of whatever is inside him."

"But he was alive…" I said, looking down at my own hands and wishing that they knew what to do. I made a mental note that I should learn one day, but that would do nothing for the man who had drawn his last breath just moments before – the man whose name we didn't even know until…

"Stanton!" Alicia screamed from the doorway. She ran over to us, her wispy cotton dressing gown dragging behind her across the tiled floor.

"You knew him?" I asked, because stupid questions are a speciality of mine, particularly at tense moments.

The house was alive with noise by now. I could hear servants running about in the corridors beyond the hall and several gathered in the doorway to see what was happening. It took Alicia some time to respond. At first, she just stood over the body, frozen in place until she could find her tongue.

"It's our nightwatchman, Michael Stanton. He's been working for us ever since we moved to Parham."

Grandfather turned to Mr Cridland, who looked unhealthy at the best of times and was positively ghostlike after being woken at such an uncongenial hour. "Telephone the police and then take all the staff you can find to inspect the house for anything that might have been taken. If anyone saw anything suspicious, send them to me."

The butler hobbled off to do as he'd been told, and Grandfather knelt once more to examine the corpse. "It could be chloroform or perhaps ether," he stated in a harsh whisper, and I believe he was debating the point with himself rather than informing me of his findings. He put his hand to Mr Stanton's face, and I couldn't say at first what he wished to examine, but then he pulled the skin taught around the nightwatchman's lips and I could see the colour more clearly in the light of the electric chandelier that someone had just illuminated.

"There are early signs of cyanosis. If someone had put a rag soaked in chloroform over his mouth, that would explain the hallucination and his shortness of breath. I didn't see him for long before he died, but he appeared to be suffering from respiratory depression."

"I thought chloroform was supposed to knock people out, not kill them."

He looked up at me with a wry smile. "That's just it. It's *supposed* to knock people out, but it doesn't. In carefully controlled and continuously administered doses, it can work as an anaesthetic, which is why it was used for some time to ease the pain of childbirth. Forcing

78

someone to inhale it, however, is just as likely to lead to hallucinations and heart failure. I can't say for certain that was the cause of this man's death, but it certainly fits with my knowledge of the drug."

The onlookers had dispersed by this point, no doubt with orders from the butler to make up an inventory of the major valuables from each room. In their place, a young girl stood in the dim corridor, peering through the open door. The look on Veronica's face was a mix of curiosity and fear, and I knew just how she was feeling. She didn't stand there for long, but I could read her emotion just as I would an enormous sign on the side of a bus. A moment later, a woman I took to be the housekeeper gathered her up in her arms and ushered her away.

"What were Mr Stanton's duties?" Grandfather asked our hostess, who still appeared shocked by that terrible alarm call.

"He…" She looked down at her employee once more and had to turn away entirely before she could answer. "He patrolled the house at night. He would check in at key points around the building on a schedule. We'd been lucky that there weren't any thefts before. As you will surely know, old houses like this one have become a target for burglars, and it's necessary to have someone on duty at all times."

Grandfather didn't reveal any more thoughts on the matter but moved closer to Alicia to offer his sympathy. "I am so sorry. I feel that I should have prevented this from happening. I really haven't taken things seriously enough, and I can only apologise."

This seemed to go against what he'd told me in the dining room the night before, but I didn't wish to contradict him in front of her. I'd do that a little later when we were alone.

"You mustn't blame yourself." Her words sounded as if they had come from somewhere very far away. "Even at my most pessimistic, I had not considered murder to be a likely outcome. I assumed that someone here was plotting to rob us. I never imagined…"

She didn't finish her sentence, but it was not necessary to do so. It was clear how she felt. She wished to leave the scene of the crime, and perhaps even the house entirely and forget all that she had seen. To this end, she drifted across the room without another word and, though I didn't follow her to find out, I could only imagine that she went up to the nursery to check on her children.

I believe this was not only the first time that someone had died in my arms, but the first of our cases in which an innocent servant had been caught up in a killer's plan. I'd investigated the deaths of dukes and barons, and Michael Stanton was just as important as any of them. As I stood over his body, I made a promise to myself that I would find the blackguard who had ended his life.

"I've been a blasted fool." Grandfather didn't use the word blasted, or fool for that matter, but I don't think it's polite to repeat his words here. "I thought this was a little game we could enjoy. I thought that we would take our time working out which of the sneaky, self-interested historians we met yesterday was using his time here at Parham to siphon off priceless artefacts. I didn't seriously believe that anyone would get hurt." He had left me before he finished speaking, but I lingered behind. "I'll be waiting for the police at the front of the house, Chrissy," the great and greatly upset detective told me as he trundled away. "Go to bed."

Although I hadn't known Michael Stanton in life, or even seen him in the house the day before, I didn't feel that he should be left alone. I felt that the least I could do was wait until the coroner came, which is just what I did, though I admit I yawned a lot and nearly fell asleep on a number of occasions.

When I finally returned to my room, I was on the point of collapsing. I lay back down and tried to sleep, but, as the grandfather clock in the hallway tolled four, my brain decided to wake up again. For the next hour, it was alive with thoughts and theories. There was a small desk beside my bed that doubled as a nightstand, and so I finally took a pen and a few sheets of paper and wrote down my ideas.

The first thing that struck me was that none of the experts with whom we'd shared dinner had come down to see what was happening. They were notable for their absence, and I had to wonder where in the house they were staying. It was also clear that this would not be a normal investigation during which we'd trawl through the victim's past to find a connection to one of the suspects. Stanton was not a famous actor or a politician. I was fairly certain he'd held no title beyond Mr, and there was as much chance of his being a millionaire in disguise as my being a mathematical genius.

Grandfather clearly believed that Stanton's death was connected to the series of events that had so upset Alicia Pearson. It seemed safe to assume that the killer had been prowling the house in search of whatever it was he wished to take when the nightwatchman appeared. It was all rather sad, as it was unlikely that the culprit had meant to kill him. Two lives would be ruined because of human greed. Unless it turned out that Stanton had once been a passionate archaeologist in his spare time, or that he had a degree in fine art, it was hard to imagine that he shared any knowledge of his killer, and so we would have to approach our suspects in a different manner. Come the morning, my grandfather would surely lecture me on the technique we would employ and, most likely, tell me off for not considering it myself.

When my eyelids finally grew heavy again, and I returned to my bed, I heard the most dreadful sounds coming from outside my window. At first, I thought it was the burglar, climbing the drainpipe to break into the house. It was a sort of grunting noise, interspersed with heavy breathing, and instead of running from the room in search of one of the police officers who were scouring the house, I stayed perfectly still and awaited my fate. I'd like to put it down to exhaustion, but it was more likely cowardice. I was a deer in a car's headlights, awaiting my extinction. To my great relief, no one smashed the window, no one came inside and, as I lay there in abject terror, the owl in the tree outside gave a more recognisable hoot, and I could breathe again.

With relief rushing through me like rain along a gutter, I was soon dead to the world... metaphorically speaking, of course.

CHAPTER THIRTEEN

Sometimes all one really needs is a good night's sleep to make sense of even the most taxing problem. Sometimes a few winks are just what the doctor ordered.

When I went to bed, I hadn't the faintest idea what was happening at Parham. This was not a killing for the sake of an inheritance, hidden diamonds, a decades' old rivalry or any of the other common-or-garden motives we'd investigated before. And yet, I woke up feeling as though I could take on the world, learn Swahili and solve the case before breakfast was over. Which reminded me that I had to eat breakfast before I could get anything else done.

I went downstairs to look for food – and clues to the murder if any happened to be at hand. There was no sign of my grandfather, but there were plenty of servants milling about, and I could only think that they'd taken it upon themselves to patrol the halls in case the unidentified killer should pop up and confess to the crime.

I found my mother in the Great Parlour, which was in the western wing of the house. The view across the grounds was exquisite and the sight of the morning buffet almost as stirring.

"Isn't it terrible, Chrissy?" she said from her comfortable chair in the large bay window. She did not get up but stared across at me hopelessly. "Did you wake up last night when Mr Stanton was killed?"

I wanted to take a plate and fill it, but that would have been insensitive and so I went to comfort my mother instead. "I'm afraid to say I was there when he died. Grandfather thinks that the blighter who's responsible covered Stanton's mouth with a cloth soaked in chloroform."

"Did he suffer hallucinations?" Mother was as good a detective as her father and apparently knew just as much about noxious substances as well.

"He believed he'd been attacked by a dragon. And now that I think about it, there is a hint of logic in what he told me. He claimed that the fabled monster took his breath away, which fits with a rag laced with some volatile chemical being held there."

Mother shuddered. "Does Father have any hope of catching the killer?" Somewhat disconcertingly, she didn't wait for an answer, but moved onto a doubt of her own. "It makes me wonder what's behind it. Why would anyone go to such trouble just to steal something?"

"I've been asking myself the very same question," I replied, unable to hide quite how much that exemplary woman had impressed me. "It's easy to dismiss the idea that a nightwatchman would have any connection to the geniuses who've come to the house to assess the valuables here, but what if there's more to Michael Stanton than there first appears? What if he had a remarkable past that we must work to uncover?"

"If that is the case, then that is what we'll do. We can only solve what is before us." She spoke just like her father, and her pithy aphorism reminded me of a quotation from Charles Dickens that was on the tip of my tongue but would not spring from it.

As we were speaking, other people arrived to help themselves to crumpets, pastries and toast. The Horniman twins were first and, though they didn't actually say anything to one another, they still fought over who would take the top plate from the pile, who got the biggest Chelsea bun, and who got to sit beside the unlit fireplace. I was more curious about their story each time I saw them, but I was not inclined to interview any suspects without my grandfather there to look disapproving. Of course, that didn't prevent one of them from talking to me.

"It's a rum business," despairingly dull Eric Uhland declared. "A rum, rum, really just abysmally rum business. Imagine going about your job like that and being cut down in your—"

"Thank you, Mr Uhland," I had to interrupt because, if he wasn't already boring enough, he was also now breathtakingly gloomy. "I don't suppose you heard anything last night that might explain who the killer was or where he went?"

"Me?" A smile formed on that sickly grey face. "I sleep like a baby who's been dosed up with whisky. I certainly didn't hear anything. My room is in the gatehouse, anyway, so it's no wonder I slept a full nine hours."

I had the definite impression that he was about to inform me of the minutes and seconds he had slept, but I was too quick and cut him off.

"I appreciate your time," I told him, without meaning to make a pun, and then launched myself from my seat to fetch a plate of food. I felt sorry to leave mother with that monstrous bore, but it gave me the chance to observe his student.

I'd barely had the time to take notice of Mark Isaac the night before, but he was an odd sort. His clothes all looked too tight for him, and his glasses seemed to have been glued back together after an accident of some kind. He was both messy and neat at the same time in that his movements, as he loaded baked goods onto his plate and buttered the relevant components, were exact and considered, but his overall impression, with the curly red hair that sprang from his head in all directions, was quite the opposite.

Even more noticeable than his clothes and appearance was the nervousness that coloured his actions. He was afraid of something, and it had started in the dining room the night before. Whether the nightwatchman's murder had exacerbated this fear, I could not say, but it had certainly done nothing to relax him. We nodded to one another politely and even this small, friendly gesture seemed to alarm him.

Dr Carbonell was the next to appear. He came across as a more reasonable proposition than his cornery colleagues – even if he did insist on wearing his adventurous rigout down to breakfast. Of all the questions I had accumulated at Parham, the one that sounded loudest in my head was surely, *Why are you wearing that pith helmet!?*

I couldn't ignore the feeling that we were all waiting for the two big personalities to show their faces. There was still no sign of Lord Edgington or Elton Lockhart, and I had to wonder whether this was the path my life would take. Are little people like me destined to live our lives in the shadow of greatness, forever waiting for the opportunity to bask in the light? I decided to enjoy a muffin until that moment arrived.

Lockhart eventually came down, but he showed none of his usual charm and swagger. Without his entourage, he shambled into the room with his eyes cast to the floor. It was rather a disappointment if the truth be told. It was as if I'd bumped into a beloved actor like Ramon Novarro doing something normal, like buying a newspaper, instead of being chased by a mob of admirers. The most interesting thing that his arrival brought about was the sense of suspicion in the room. As soon as he entered, all eyes were on him, and it was easy to imagine who everyone's first choice of suspect would be.

The three girls and their mother made an appearance, but there was still no sign of my grandfather. I can only assume that he takes a secret stash of food with him whenever we travel, as he has been known to skip that most nourishing of meals entirely. I expected him to sweep into the room at any moment to declare, *There's no time for dawdling, Christopher. We have a crime to solve.* You'll be glad to know that I didn't have to sacrifice my breakfast, though, as I made sure to eat quickly, and he never came.

"Mother?" I asked when I'd consumed every crumb on my plate, had a second helping of buttered muffins and done the same to them. "Do you know where Grandfather is? I haven't seen him since the police arrived in the night."

She was still trapped listening to Eric Dullard... I mean Uhland! I believe he was in the middle of describing the most common grains of wood in seventeenth century picture frames, but whatever the topic, she was overjoyed to be offered an escape route.

"That's odd." She overacted just a touch. "Yes, that's very odd indeed. I haven't seen him this morning and we must investigate." She was already on her feet when she apologised to the supposedly renowned expert, and we hurried from the room.

"The man is like a carnivorous plant," I declared once we were out of earshot. "Instead of using his steely jaws to trap his prey, he mesmerises it with the tediousness of everything he says."

"That's not a very kind thing to say, Christopher," she replied. "And if he mesmerises his prey, surely a cobra would be a better comparison."

We went from room to room looking for our superior officer until the sound of books thudding and pages turning told me he was nearby. The police had removed the body from the Great Hall, but there were still a few officers milling about. I had to wonder whether Grandfather had told any senior detectives to take the day off, as the celebrated bloodhound of Scotland Yard would surely solve the case quicker than any normal man could – or perhaps they were having a break after a long night's slog.

Grandfather looked very much at home in the west library. Not only was it a large, elegant space that was filled from floor to ceiling with books on every topic, the place was a terrible mess. It was a more or less square room with a protruding bay window, much like the parlour we had just left, but the decorum of the rest of the house was absent. On one side of the room, a draughtsman's table was covered with plans, piles of papers and ancient, rolled-up parchments. On the floor, large stacks of books loomed, and I was not in the least surprised to see Delilah at her master's feet.

The desk itself was just as busy, although I couldn't say whether this was down to Grandfather's labours that morning, or it was always in such a state. As we arrived, he was reading a book on the history of Sussex and I noticed other volumes on famous British families, the industrial revolution, the history of smugglers in Britain and, for some reason I couldn't imagine, how to breed dalmatians. It was clear, even before he opened his mouth, that he had cast his net too wide.

"What do you think about this?" he asked, raising the book in his hand a little higher to show his source. "The former owners of Parham, the Barons Zouche, were so impoverished at one point that the house fell into disrepair, and it was clear that they would have to sell their family heirlooms in order to make up the shortfall." There was a wild look in his eye, and his voice wavered. In other words, he seemed even more eccentric than usual. "However, the baroness at the time decided that she did not want to lose the family gold – or for her undeserving heir to inherit it – and she appears to have smuggled it out of the house."

It was down to my mother to fashion a diplomatic reply. "That's very interesting, Father, but how is it related to Mr Stanton's death?" I would have asked this question a little more bluntly.

"It's got everything to do with his death." He scoffed then, as if it was most unreasonable of us to question his thinking. "If Baroness Zouche instead chose to hide the gold somewhere in this house, it must still be here."

He fixed his eyes on us and, when we didn't say, *Oh, how foolish of us not to realise what you meant,* he continued the explanation. "There are any number of potential hiding places here. Wherever she put the treasure could have been built over or blocked up. Alicia told us in great detail about the walls, fireplaces and windows that have been removed to reveal the original fittings. If one of our blessed experts had discovered what Baroness Zouche did, now would be the time to search for the gold."

He slammed the book shut and laid it on the table in front of him. The noise made Delilah shudder and – it seemed to me – shake her head despairingly. Admittedly, she was probably just cold.

"That's very… interesting," my mother repeated herself, "but what proof do you have that it was hidden here in the first place?"

"There's a priest hole!" he asserted in response. "The Bishopp family, when they were custodians of Parham Park, secretly converted to Catholicism. The room on the top floor, which is now the girls' nursery, was originally a chapel. Even the original owner was a Romanensian."

"I'm sorry, Grandfather," I finally interjected, "but what has a long-dead man's religion got to do with anything?"

"The priest hole, of course." He got up from his chair to stretch his legs. "It would be the perfect place to hide the gold, and it may have been uncovered in the work that is being done on the long gallery." I didn't need to tell him that this was an unlikely scenario, as it was clear from my silent reaction. "Very well, not gold then. But what about smuggler's booty?"

Mother stepped forward to reason with him. "Father, you haven't slept, and you're clearly overexcited."

"Of course I am!" He shook his head much as his dog had and kept walking. "I'm scraping the bottom of the barrel to leave no possibility unturned. And that's why I'm willing to entertain the idea that, when a gang of smugglers came here in the eighteenth century, murdered a man who had betrayed them, and left his body in the lake, they also hid their loot."

"What did they steal?" I asked somewhat reluctantly.

"Fifteen hundredweight of tea!"

"And what good would a very old haul of tea be to anyone today?"

"It would be no good at all." He huffed and puffed and tried to explain himself. "But whoever killed Mr Stanton might not have known it was tea and hoped to find something more valuable."

I could see that it would take a certain degree of delicacy if I were to get through to him, and so I stopped myself from saying the first thing that came into my head and sat down in an almost clear chair beside the window.

"Very well, I will listen with an open mind, but tell me this…" I paused to look about the room, which was as good a metaphor for his troubled mind as any great author could conceive. "…what made you come in here in the first place? Why are you searching back through history for a proverbial and perhaps even literal Holy Grail?"

He stopped his nervous movement, and his response sounded ever so sad. "Because I have to find some way of explaining what's happening!"

This plaintive cry disturbed Delilah in the cavern beneath the desk and she came to stand at her master's side. Mother looked just as worried about him and guided her father back to his seat.

"I'm fine, I'm fine," he promised. "I imagine you think that I have lost my mind, but I can assure you I've done nothing of the sort. The fact is, I made a mistake and I'm trying to put it right. I should have known that there was something more than theft at play. From what Alicia has told me, the Parham House staff have been unable to spot any gaps in their collection of valuables. I should have sniffed out the murderer in our midst, but I failed."

An uncertain hush fell over us and, for a few moments, the only sound was the beating of Delilah's tail against the desk as she put her head on her master's lap, and he stroked her obligingly.

"I don't think you're mad, Grandfather," I said to break the silence. "I think you're the smartest man I've ever met and, even when I question your behaviour and doubt your actions, I always know deep down that everything you do has a sensible reason behind it (except perhaps letting off pistols in your library at home)," I didn't actually say these last ten words, but he somehow knew I was thinking them.

"Todd and I were shooting in the library because it was too bright outside, and I wasn't in the mood to walk to the woods in search of shade." He said this in a matter-of-fact voice, which made the whole ridiculous situation sound quite rational. "But I appreciate your support, nonetheless." He turned back to his daughter. "And whether you believe me or not, Violet, there is method to my messiness."

Mother laughed at the lovable man who often danced through the realms of eccentricity, but never quite crossed over to the land of the absurd. "Very well. Explain your thinking, and we'll see what we can do to help."

She sat down beside me, and he started again. "I came here this morning in search of something to decode the enigma we are facing. Not one of the recent events at Parham are easily explained – be it the destruction of a vase, the reorganisation of a whole room's worth of paintings or the nightwatchman's death. We are working on the hypothesis that the killer wishes to steal something from the house and everything that has occurred is a prelude to that. But there are catalogues which detail every item in the building." He gestured towards the worktable on the other side of the room that I could only imagine belonged to the absent owner of the estate. "It is almost impossible to steal something without it being missed."

"So you're suggesting that whatever the killer wants has to be hidden somewhere?" I concluded.

"Precisely." It gave him no satisfaction to say this, and he looked off into space as though contemplating surrender.

Mother took her turn to respond. "I'm sorry, Father, but you're concentrating on the wrong things. For the moment, it doesn't matter whether some great treasure is waiting to be discovered. If it exists, the Pearsons and their workers are yet to find it, so I doubt that we will, either. What matters is the crime."

Her clear-minded approach was always refreshing, and it spurred me into action. "Mother's right. This is all a distraction. It's a curious one, I'll give you that. And if there weren't a dead man in the mortuary at this moment whose murder we must solve, I'd like nothing more than to work away here like a dray horse to find the solution."

"Very well." He would need some more persuading. "But how are we supposed to find the killer if we can't say for certain why the man was killed?"

"It's simple." Mother struck just the right tone of encouragement. "You'll do what you always do. You'll leave this room and consider the evidence we've already found. Then you'll move on to the suspects, and you'll concoct a plausible hypothesis for what happened before the revelation of who is to blame finally strikes you."

"You make it sound so easy," he said in cautious reply.

"And you always make it look so easy. Now stop your dallying and catch the killer."

CHAPTER FOURTEEN

There was one thing to do before we could get on with mother's plan. Although he couldn't be made to take a short nap, Grandfather insisted on getting changed out of the black evening suit he had worn to dinner and into his favourite dove grey morning wear. Todd was in his room waiting with the necessary outfit and, as soon as Grandfather had donned his second skin, it was as if everything was right with the world.

I was sitting on his bed reading over the Anderson file and didn't pay a great deal of attention until he was at the door and ready to leave, but I nodded and hmmmed at the right moments so that he at least thought I was listening.

"Clothes maketh me!" he said as he regarded himself in the full-length mirror beside his wardrobe. "Whichever scoundrel is responsible for last night's terrible deed won't stand a chance now. Eh, boy?"

I considered telling him that a woollen suit was unlikely to be instrumental in solving the case, but I didn't want to make him sad again.

"Where to first?" I asked instead, which led to a groan and a...

"Please, Christopher, speak in full sen—" But then something came over him and he changed his mind. "Actually, I take it back. You are almost a fully grown man, and you have every right to speak as you wish. As long as you don't make use of copious slang, we'll get on just fine."

"Thank you..." I replied uncertainly. "I think."

"As to the question of where we should go first, the answer is wherever our suspects are. I have an idea, and we'll soon find out whether it is correct."

He led off out of the room, and Delilah and I kept pace with him. Mother had gone to check on Alicia and would no doubt reappear before long to point out something that we had failed to observe. She was clever like that.

We spiralled down through the house to the lower ground floor to see a new side of Parham. There was a huge terracotta-tiled kitchen that Grandfather informed me had been in use since Elizabethan times. It was far larger and more orderly than the one at Cranley, with twin hearths and an enormous shelf on one wall displaying a selection of copper pots and dishes. As exciting as it was to see the maids and cooks at work, and to breathe in those heavenly scents, that was not why we had gone below stairs.

"I have a simple question for you all," Grandfather announced, and every last person there turned to look, from Mr Cridland who was sitting in one corner mending a gentleman's boot, to the Parham House cook whose cheeks were red from the steam of whatever pot she was bent over. "You will know by now that the nightwatchman was murdered last night. Can anyone here tell me why someone wanted to kill him?"

There were blank faces all around until a young scullery maid standing beside the sink broke out wailing. "No one could have wanted to hurt Michael, M'Lord. He was the best of men I ever knew."

The butler put his boot down on the floor and rose rather imperially. "I can confirm that, in the six years I have known him, Mr Stanton was never once late for work nor caused a single problem here in the house. He had no children but was a devoted husband, and I believe I speak on behalf of everyone here when I say that it is unfathomable that anyone would have laid a finger on him."

Grandfather thanked them both and turned to leave with an expression on his face which said, *Well, it was worth a try.* The visit was so perfunctory that I stayed where I was for a moment and felt I should offer something more.

"If anything should occur to you, you can find us here in the house…" I realised then that we rarely stayed in the same place for long and struggled to finish my sentence. "…somewhere."

There was a murmur of discussion as I followed my grandfather from the kitchen. Out in the corridor, we passed a glass room, a still room, a china room, and then stopped beside the silver room. There was a man inside with dark hair and broad shoulders polishing away to his heart's content. He stopped when he saw us, and I was sure that this was Graham Perugino. I had to wonder whether Grandfather had given more weight to the possibility that the half-Italian footman turned thief (turned reformed thief) was responsible for Stanton's death.

92

We nodded a greeting and were about to leave when the fellow called out.

"Lord Edgington," he shouted in a surprisingly high voice. "I know you will have heard stories about me, but I had nothing to do with the dead man. I was a stupid boy when I came to work here, and I quickly learnt my lesson. When Mr Pearson gave me a second chance, I seized it, and swore that I will never steal again."

This was all he managed to get out before Grandfather interrupted with a smile and a few short words. "I know you won't, Graham. You have no need to worry."

He waved and, as we continued along the corridor, I was still uncertain how he could be so... well... certain.

"If you even have to wonder," he said in response to the question I hadn't asked, "then you clearly don't know a great deal about me." I thought for a few moments and, when he could see that I didn't understand what he meant, he solved this brief mystery. "When I was a police officer, I often gave young thieves I had encountered second chances. There were those who ignored me and continued down the slippery slope that surely led to prison, but far more who appreciated the gift I had given them."

I would have argued that a grown man who steals was altogether different from the ragamuffin boys he used to scare back onto the straight and narrow path, but I was distracted by our surroundings. We'd come to a complex of rooms which led off the corridor at a right angle. I saw a gun room, and what looked like various storerooms, but Grandfather kept on to the furthest door, which was marked with a sloppily painted W that I soon learnt stood for workshop.

He did not knock but pushed it open and we walked through to a large space lined with deep shelves. At several tables in the centre of the room, the experts were studying significant items from the Parham collection. Six pairs of eyes turned to look at us and, if there had been any conversation taking place before we entered, it had come to an immediate stop.

"Lord Edgington," Eric Uhland said without communicating whether he was happy, sad or indifferent to our presence. "Here you are." He pushed his thick glasses up his nose to see us more clearly.

"As are you, Mr Uhland," my reinvigorated mentor replied.

"I thought I should discover exactly what it is you do down here before…" He allowed himself a long pause to let their imaginations run wild. "…I speak to you each individually."

"You're very welcome," gangly Mark Isaac said in his hesitant voice. "We certainly have no reason not to want you down here."

Uhland looked as though he would have preferred the boy to say nothing.

Grandfather began his slow walk around the room with his hands locked together behind his back. I imagine that benevolent Victorian industrialists would have done much the same thing when visiting their factories. He smiled at each nervous worker he approached, and the Horniman twins lined up before their table as though Lord Edgington was to inspect how clean their hands were or whether they'd washed behind the ears. I'm glad to say that he did nothing of the sort.

The only person who paid him no heed was Elton Lockhart. He had changed his clothes since we'd last seen him and now looked even more like the hero of a Georgian novel than he normally did. He wore high leather boots that were laced up to the knees, a long frock coat with a velvet collar, and every button on his outfit was made of polished bronze.

"What's this you have?" Grandfather asked in as vague a manner as possible, presumably in the hope of drawing an unexpectedly useful answer from our suspect. You know the sort of thing, *Ahh, the pressure is too much! Here's the chloroform I used on the nightwatchman. It's a fair cop, gov!*

Sadly, Lockhart didn't say that. He said, "We're going through the items that were purchased after the sale of Chatterton Hall in Yorkshire. It belonged to the Bishopp family who lived at Parham until a century ago."

This seemed to ignore the importance of the curious object on the table. It was a foot-long box of some sort with one side missing, and elaborate carvings all over. To me at least, it looked to be made of bone, though I couldn't say from which period of history the artefact came. In fact, I'd never seen anything quite like it, and I was ever so grateful that grandfather prodded him for more.

"I was referring to the fabulous item on the desk before you."

"It's Anglo-Saxon," Vyvyan with two Ys explained. "That's what brought us here. We're not so interested in dusty old portraits of royals and inbred aristocrats."

"We had our fill of those at home," her sister whispered loudly enough for everyone to hear.

I noticed that the others in the room were still listening, and even Eric Uhland had put his dry brush down to hear what the girls had to say.

Finding her voice now, Vyvyan moved closer to the table and knelt to admire the ancient treasure before her. "The whale-bone box tells a story of an all-powerful king who became a god."

"This really can't be of interest to Lord Edgington," Lockhart murmured.

Grandfather wouldn't let him get away with such evasion and jovially punched him on the arm to hide how eager we were to know more. "History fascinates me. I'm only too happy to hear about your work."

I walked over to them and bent down to see the strange pattern on the front of the casket. There were two lines of shapes that looked like normal letters but were just a little bit too pointy. I concluded from the information that Vyvyan had already provided that these were runes, and, as I couldn't imagine how anyone went about translating them, I looked at the pictures beside them instead.

Between the writing, there was a central figure of a man holding his blade up to the sky as beams of light shone down. Before him, I could see a pile of three dead bodies and a crowd looking on in awe.

"It's a fascinating piece, but we can't say the name of the hero on its main panel for certain," Dr Carbonell chirped up with just as much enthusiasm as Miss Horniman… or rather, the Miss Horniman with two Ys. "Personally, I believe that the story refers to the legendary archer Ægil."

"That's pure conjecture," Lockhart grumbled. "He doesn't have a bow, for a start."

Vyvyan ignored her grumpy suitor and continued the tale. "The inscription reads 'With the flood of light on the eve of Ēostre month, king became god and man a prince.'"

Dr Carbonell listened to her attentively, before stepping forward to point out a few more details. "If we look at the sides of the box, we can see his people bowing down in adoration. Even the animals seem humbled by his presence, and the light is pouring into him, as if he has taken on a great power."

"What's the eve of Ēostre month?" I asked, as I'd more or less understood the rest of what they'd said.

"Ēostre was the goddess of spring," Vyvyan answered. "The eve of her month was the March equinox. It was a time of celebration in pagan culture. In Scandinavia, a ritual sacrifice would be carried out that night, and they would ask the female gods to bless the harvest and usher in the spring."

I looked at the carved bodies at the hero's feet and wondered if they had been his sacrifice.

"What happened to this Ægil fellow?" Mark Isaac asked before I could.

Vyvyan's elfin smile grew wider. "We don't know. The back panel of the box is missing, and there are very few written sources that mention him. The only other tales that still exist concern a battle he fought and the time he helped his brother escape from a cruel king."

"It's just a box!" Lockhart said, beginning to show his temper. "It's lovely to learn about old myths and legends, but the fact is that this is just a broken old box and, while I wish it was in the British Museum, it isn't. It's been kept in a rich family for years and it looks as though it will remain that way for some time longer." He threw down the pencil he'd been holding and flashed his very white teeth. "Now, if you don't mind, I have a lot of work to do."

He pushed past us to reach the high shelves that were built into one wall. I could tell that he had no real reason to be over there, but he pretended to be busy by shuffling papers and unfurling parchments. Dr Carbonell looked on with something approaching disdain. I considered asking why the two men didn't get along, but then I noticed something on the shelves beside Lockhart. Hidden behind a number of other objects were two matching marble lions. I didn't know whether to shout about them or keep my mouth shut. Grandfather must have noticed them too and answered my doubt by not drawing attention to them in any way. In fact, he decided to make a fuss about something else.

"Actually, Lockhart, I do mind." He marched straight up to the handsome antiquarian and looked him in the eye. "I mind when any suspect wishes to divert my attention from a topic, as you are so clearly doing." He allowed this to sink in for a few seconds before issuing an ultimatum. "Come outside for a brief discussion, or I'll ask the nearest constable to arrest you, and the inspector will interrogate you at the nearest police station."

CHAPTER FIFTEEN

Our dog Delilah may be a wise and helpful companion, but she only has so much patience for the hard work that inevitably comes with any investigation. She had long since found something more interesting to do, but when Grandfather marched Elton Lockhart back along the corridor to the kitchen courtyard, she was excited to see us. She'd found a stick and evidently believed that my grandfather would have the time to throw it to her whilst questioning our first major suspect. This was, of course, entirely ridiculous, and so I did it on his behalf.

"Where is your famous arrogance this morning?" Grandfather put to the man once we were far enough from the workshop not to be overheard.

"You shouldn't believe everything that you read about me."

Lockhart's interviewer was unmoved and replied in the same direct manner. "You cannot put my knowledge of your bad behaviour down to hearsay or slander, my boy. You were arrogant last night when we first met you. In fact, you lived up to your reputation until you found out who I was. Like several of your colleagues, you've been more reticent ever since."

"A man has been murdered," said every suspect ever who needed an excuse for their nervousness around my grandfather – though in this case, it was Elton Lockhart who spoke. "What would you have me do? Strut about like I'm the master of Parham Park? Play hide-and-seek in the Long Gallery? Swim naked in the pleasure grounds just to show everyone what a rake I am?"

"I expect you to stick to your principles and be the person that you really are." Grandfather's voice echoed around the stone courtyard that was closed in on three sides.

Our potential killer turned to look up at the cloudy sky above us. It was the middle of March, and the spring was slowly coming into being. The days were getting warmer, and the fruit trees in the orchard would already be in bloom, but that didn't make Elton Lockhart any happier.

"What's the point when everyone has already made up their minds about me?" He peered back over his shoulder to make his point a little more forcibly. "I've no doubt that anyone here who knows who I am will suspect me of murder."

I wanted to say, *Who do you think you are, then?* but it wasn't my job to ask such questions. Sadly, no one had told my tongue that, and so I said, "Who do you think you are, then?"

He looked over as if he hadn't noticed me before and couldn't understand how I'd materialised out of thin air. "I'm Elton Lockhart, the man who was thrown out of my college when I went up to Cambridge because I inadvertently, quite accidentally, invited the dean's daughter up to my bedroom one night. I'm the person who was arrested without charge upon setting foot in Rome because—"

"Yes, thank you, Elton." It was Grandfather's turn to interrupt. "But the boy wasn't interested in the terrible larks you have got up to over the years, but who you are really." He glanced in my direction to ensure that this was correct, and I decided not to contradict him.

"Don't you see?" Elton spoke with both conviction and sorrow. "Don't either of you see? The truth doesn't matter. Perception is everything."

The same Charles Dickens quote I'd wanted to say earlier half formed in my head, but I still couldn't quite remember it.

"I see that you're finding excuses," Grandfather told him. "I'm here to question you about a murder, and all that concerns you is your public image."

Lockhart raked the ground with his foot like an angry stallion before accepting defeat. "Very well. Ask your questions."

"Did you know Michael Stanton for any reason other than his work here?"

He looked even more contemptuous than normal, and I thought he might simply walk away. "Who's Michael Stanton?"

Grandfather offered him no respite. "The man who was killed last night. Did you know him before you came here?"

"No." There was such conviction in Lockhart's responses that I found myself wanting to believe him.

"Is there anyone who can testify to your whereabouts at half-past two in the morning?"

He closed his eyes as if the question was too much to bear. "As it happens, there is."

I think that his response even shocked my grandfather. "Oh, really?"

"Frances was in bed with me." Though Lockhart only whispered his answer, his honesty made my grandfather rock on his heels.

"You were awake together when Stanton's screams travelled about the house?"

He looked at me then, and I willed him to say yes, but nothing is ever that simple.

"No, we were asleep. But she was there with me; I swear she was."

"You mean she was there when the pair of you fell asleep. As you weren't conscious at the hour in question, you cannot say where she was. Just as she cannot say whether you were downstairs taking an innocent man's life."

Lockhart turned one way and then the other, evidently unsure of the best response to my grandfather's argument. A younger Christopher would have felt terribly sorry for the man, but this wizened cynic couldn't help but question whether it was all just an act. Shouldn't internationally renowned rogues like Elton Lockhart possess a fraction more resilience than to fall to pieces at the first suggestion of guilt?

"You're right," he said in that same quiet but forceful voice. "I have no alibi – no one to vouch for my whereabouts. And that is what frightens me."

I felt that, had this been a normal interview – sitting somewhere comfortable to work our way through questions in an orderly fashion – we would have started it differently. I wished to ask about his background and what had led him to Parham House, but we'd gone straight to the biggest questions and that set the whole process off balance.

Curiously, Grandfather did nothing to address this. "If you could steal anything from this estate, what would it be?"

It was evidently not the question our suspect had been expecting, and he exhaled a brief laugh before attempting to answer it. "I'm not a thief."

"I didn't ask whether you had the scruples to take something. I want to know what you would take." He didn't couch his words in unnecessary babble; he was as blunt as could be.

"Fine. I'd take the cup."

"What cup?" I asked because I have to say something from time to time, and this seemed as innocuous a comment as any other.

"There's an eighth-century bronze chalice which is inlaid with silver and gold. It features pictures of both pagan figures like Ægil, Woden and Ēostre, but also Jesus and Mary. I've spent most of my time here studying the Anglo-Saxon artefacts, and that is surely the most precious and unique."

"But how did they come to Parham? They seem quite out of place alongside the courtly Elizabethan portraits and suits of armour." Two questions in under a minute? I was positively babblative.

"I told you before. They were in a private collection in a house that belonged to the Bishopp family who once lived here. In order to retrieve those items, your friends bought up the contents of Chatterton Hall and employed me and my colleagues to assess their age, value and their historical connection to Parham."

"And how did the Anglo-Saxon artefacts come into the possession of the Bishopps in the first place?" Grandfather asked.

"Because the dig that uncovered them was on their land in Yorkshire. They only allowed it on the condition that any valuables would be handed over to them. They did rather well out of it."

I remembered something that Dr Carbonell had mentioned at dinner the night before and made a simple connection. "And you were involved in that dig?"

"No, it was before I was born, but I have worked in Yorkshire a few times on similar excavations." At that moment, he switched from being a suspect in a murder investigation to something more like an educator. His eyes burned with an almost fanatical love for his subject. "You see, there is so much we still don't know about our distant ancestors – so much we still have to learn. The Anglo-Saxons fascinate me even more than the ancient Egyptians or some of the far-eastern civilisations I have studied because there are so few written texts about them, and our knowledge relies heavily on what we find through archaeological work."

"You've been to Egypt?" I may have focused on the wrong information, but this excited me more than I can say. I'd recently been reading about the curse of Tut-Ankh-Amen's tomb and, well, it was all quite thrilling.

"I've been to many places, but Britain is where my heart lies. I

102

could never turn my back on my home entirely." There was something very final about these words, as though he believed this patriotism stood as proof of his good character.

The interview wasn't over yet, and Grandfather moved on to our wider group of suspects. "So you and Frances Horniman are *courting*?" He pronounced this final word very carefully.

"Frances and I are close friends. Her sister and I are equally fond of one another."

It was hard not to be a little scandalised by this. I'd met several people by this point in my life who believed that marriage was just a trap. They said that we should be free to love whomsoever we please, regardless of class or background. However, I had never come across anybody who was "close friends" with two sisters at the same time. I didn't know where to look.

"And how do they feel about one another?" Grandfather asked most pointedly.

Lockhart was back to his disbelieving best and set off around the courtyard under an indignant cloud. Delilah and I instantly scampered after him so as not to miss his reply, but Grandfather stayed right where he was.

"The twins are here of their own accord," Lockhart eventually shouted back to his questioner. "I have never forced them to accompany me anywhere. As I said, we are fond of one another, and any rivalry that exists was there long before I found them." He spoke as though they were fascinating relics he had turned up in a muddy field.

Grandfather smiled as though he understood more than Lockhart was willing to say. It unnerved our suspect, who walked a little quicker, but only in a circle around the central axis the detective provided. I felt more than a little silly to be wandering after the man and, from up on the higher floors of the house, I'm sure it looked as though we were playing a school-yard game. On instinct, I looked to the upper windows and caught a glimpse of the eldest Pearson girl. It was only for a moment, but I just saw Veronica's face before the curtains were pulled over and she disappeared from view.

"And what of your colleagues?" Lord Edgington sounded more confident than he had. We were finally getting to the topics that mattered most.

"What of them?"

"Do you have any reason to believe that one of them would be capable of theft and murder?"

Lockhart stopped walking, and I was happy not to have to follow him any longer. "Surely it's manslaughter," he suggested. "Who would murder someone with chloroform?"

"Someone who knows that it is just as likely to lead to death as it is to incapacity. However, I take your point." Grandfather rarely felt the need to correct himself, but he did so now. "In which case, do you have any reason to believe that one of your colleagues would be capable of endangering a man's life to achieve his goals?"

Lockhart didn't have to think for long. "Not one of them is what you might call normal. Uhland is presumably insane if he can't see how incredibly boring he is – though I sometimes wonder whether he knows it only too well and uses it against us. I swear that I fall into some kind of trance every time he speaks. I end up agreeing to whatever he wants just to stop him talking."

"And the others?"

"The sisters are equally driven as any of the men here. They're not just here to be with me; I can tell you that. They've got the determination to make a name for themselves in this field, and I'm sure that they'll manage it."

"What about Dr Carbonell?" I asked, hoping to learn of the relationship between them. "He doesn't seem too fond of you."

Lockhart kicked at the cobbles beneath his feet with the heel of his high leather boot. "Oh, it's very hard to live up to dear Raymond's example. I've known him since I was a boy, and I believe he's just as disappointed in me as my parents are."

"Is there any particular reason why he would show such hostility to you?"

He regarded me through one eye whilst facing the house. "There are a thousand reasons. Where would you like me to begin? Should I tell you how I stole his fiancée? Would you like to know about our time at university together when I had the ill grace to study the same subject as him and, to begin with at least, charmed our teachers in a way that dear Raymond couldn't? Or perhaps I should reveal the fact that my father took his mother as a mistress and made no attempt to hide the affair from either of our families."

Grandfather showed no sign of unease at these sordid revelations. Instead, he clicked his heels together and, with a half-smile on his lips, declared, "I don't think you can be blamed for that last one. I've never met Viscount Lockhart, but if the truth be told, I haven't heard much to recommend him."

"Quite! And with that in mind, it's no wonder that I turned out as I did." Lockhart walked on, as if a magnetic force were pulling him forward.

Grandfather hadn't quite finished with him. "I'm starting to wonder whether you are your own harshest critic. For a man who is supposedly so brazen and strong-willed, you have a habit of feeling sorry for yourself."

Our suspect paused before the entrance to answer him. "You know, it's not always pleasant being a villain." He was as much a contradiction as my grandfather had implied. A mess of emotions burned inside him like the gases at the centre of the sun. "Sometimes, I would prefer to evade the spotlight and be myself rather than the person that everyone wants me to be. Now, if you've no further questions, my work is calling."

He turned and was through the door before either of us could say another word. Delilah released a short bark, as it was obvious he'd slipped away too soon.

"What did you think of all that then?" I asked when I reached my companion.

"I think it was a very good performance, and he avoided answering any number of difficult questions."

"I agree." I realised that this was a rather empty response and so followed it with another. "He clearly has something to hide."

"Indeed." Grandfather whistled to his dog, and the three of us walked back towards the building. "The question is, what?"

CHAPTER SIXTEEN

I'd seen a few uniformed officers that morning, but I'd yet to spot any detectives who could be leading the investigation, so it was about time that one of them appeared.

"Superintendent Edgington," a jolly inspector in his fifties called to us as we reached the ground floor. "I've found something you'll want to see." He beckoned us along the corridor to the staircase that led to the upper levels of the house.

"Inspector Kirk," Grandfather began. "Allow me to introduce my grandson."

"There's no need for an introduction, sir." Kirk was clearly one of those officers who still regarded Lord Edgington as an essential member of the Metropolitan Police – though he had retired some eighteen years earlier. It was a much bigger surprise that he was an admirer of mine, too. "I know all about your young assistant's brilliant crime-solving brain. It is an honour to meet you, Mr Prentiss."

"And you," I told him, and all thoughts of the brooding suspect we'd just interviewed went clean from my head.

"Now, what have you found for us?" Grandfather asked as we came to a corridor with a run of bedrooms to which I'd paid little attention until now. They were smaller and simpler than my grandfather's, though still three times the size of my little box with a bed in it.

"From what my men have ascertained," Kirk told us as he walked through the second door, "this room belongs to a young lady by the name of Frances Horniman. My men have found something which may point to her guilt." Based on the way he drew out revelations to build up our hunger for more, he was from the same school of police work as Lord Edgington.

He led us through the comfortable, carpeted space and knelt down beside the head of the bed, which was as neat as could be with a woollen Welsh quilt tucked in all around the mattress. We stood over him to see what he would produce and, having put on a pair of gloves and run his hand along the gap between the bedframe and the wall, he pulled out a small bottle.

"I put it back to show you exactly where it was found," he said to explain this theatrical flourish. "There's no label on it, and I didn't get too close, but it smells like strong stuff to me."

Grandfather had already donned the necessary protection and accepted the dark brown bottle. He pulled out the stopper and, rather than lift it directly to his nose, allowed the smell to waft out of it before sniffing the air.

"Well done, Inspector. This is very likely the chemical that killed Michael Stanton."

I caught a sweet scent in the air as the vapours from the bottle spread about the room. It was pungent even at a distance, and I could quite understand why grandfather hadn't got too close to the open container.

"Does this make her the likely suspect?" Kirk scratched his perfectly round head and asked the question that it was normally my job to put to the expert.

"What do you think?"

The inspector looked at me and, in turn, I adopted an expression which I hoped said, *Yes, what do you think?* I could have been more honest and adopted an expression which said, *Don't look at me! I haven't the foggiest,* but I didn't want him to be disappointed by my limited prowess as a detective.

Even when addressing such grim topics, there was a cheeriness to Kirk's voice. "I'd say on the face of things that it's bad news for Miss Horniman." I was about to jump in to correct him when he did it himself. "However, there is nothing to say that she was the one to put it here, and the killer may well have hidden the substance in her room in order to incriminate her."

"Very good, Kirk." Grandfather liked nothing more than taking a novice officer under his wing and, while Kirk was no spring bunny, he was a good deal younger than the former superintendent.

"Of course, there is always the possibility that Frances hid the bottle here herself, knowing that we would think that someone else was trying to make her look like the culprit." I was aware that any such thinking could trap us in a spiral of hypotheses from which it was impossible to escape, but I thought it bore saying.

Grandfather showed his agreement, and Kirk had a question to put to us. "Do either of you know anyone here who has a bone to pick with Miss Horniman?" Despite his relaxed manner, the inspector had his wits about him.

"As it happens, we do," I confessed. "Perhaps it is not serious enough to frame her up for murder, but Frances's sister Vyvyan – Vyvyan with two Ys, that is... Well, her sister Vyvyan seems to be quite jealous of her. The pair of them are forever trying to outdo one another. Even at breakfast this morning, they were tussling over a croissant."

"Which isn't to mention the young man they are both trying to win." Grandfather wore a critical expression, which I believe he reserved for instances when I had mentioned food.

Instead of responding to this, Kirk opened his mouth to raise another point. "I wasn't certain whether to remove the evidence or not."

"You're right to consider the best options," Grandfather replied. "I think it would be best to leave the bottle here and refrain from saying anything to the suspects about it. The killer may slip up and alert us to its presence and, if she's innocent, Frances may find it and do the same herself."

Kirk showed how impressed he was by my grandfather's thinking, but I had something to add.

"I think it would be even smarter to replace that bottle with an innocent container of water and then test its contents and check the exterior for fingerprints. That way, if the killer plans to use it again, no one will come to any harm."

The two men were shamefaced not to have thought of this themselves, and Grandfather replied with a mumbled, "That does make a lot of sense," before the inspector changed the subject.

"Lord Edgington, do you still feel that the main suspects we must consider are the men and women who are working on the valuables in the house, rather than the general workmen, the staff from Parham or even the family who own the place?" I'd been longing to ask this question myself, but Grandfather would only have replied with a disparaging comment, so I was glad that Kirk had posed it for me.

"I do, though we should still consider every possibility. To that end, I have instructed a few of your men to carry out investigations into the backgrounds of other members of the household, as well as Mr Stanton's. But the fact remains that I do not consider the murder an isolated incident. Were one of the servants or labourers to attempt to steal something, it would be a rapid, opportunistic affair. The events we came here to investigate started weeks ago. I still think that the criminal has unfinished business – that he has learnt some significant information about the place which has made him adopt a slow, patient approach. Both of these factors point to the suspects I have identified. I may live to eat humble pie, but I say it is the small group of antiquarians upon whom we must focus our attention."

"Very good, Superintendent." The inspector placed the bottle in the inside pocket of his cotton jacket and gripped the bed to get to his feet. "If there's anything you need, don't hesitate to ask. I will find out whether my men have made any progress and report back to you when there's something to report."

I wondered whether he'd been an inspector for long as he pulled at an imaginary hat on his head and nodded.

"Nice fellow," I said as we watched him go.

"Christopher, please speak in full—" Grandfather stopped himself before he could say any more. "I'm sorry. I'm so sorry. It's a force of habit."

He sat down on the bed and fell into silent reflection for a minute or two, upon which I eventually decided to intrude. "I've been thinking about Lockhart."

"Oh, yes?"

"Yes. He clearly wishes for us to feel sorry for him, and I find that strange."

He clapped his hands together and got to his feet. He must have decided upon our next move, but I was still thinking about the enigmatic suspect.

"It is a similar case to the situation with the twins, isn't it?"

"Is it?" He was giving nothing away.

"In the sense that we could get trapped in an endless cycle of thought."

"Could we?"

As we left the room, I decided to stop leaving pauses in my speech. "Yes. You see, the poison might have been left in Frances's room because she used it. Or it might have been put there by Vyvyan because she wanted to incriminate her sister. Or it might have been put there by Frances because she knew we would suspect Vyvyan's

110

involvement and so on and so forth."

"And how does that relate to Lockhart?"

I felt more confident now. "Well, he might be acting hard done by because, underneath his bravura, he really does suffer the attention he receives as the *enfant terrible* of his field. Or he might be putting on an act to make us think that is the case, when, in truth, he just wants to convince us of his innocence. Or perhaps he really is guilty, and he's playing a role to gain our sympathy."

Grandfather paused at the top of the stairs, and his moustaches bunched together. I believe he was quietly impressed. "And that, Christopher, is the dilemma that comes with being a detective. We must look beyond what people say to know the truth."

"How are we supposed to do that? Is there really a way to be sure when someone is lying?"

He looked conflicted as he searched for a new maxim to impart. When this failed, he said, "There is no one infallible way to know, Christopher. If there were, our job would be very easy. But there is a piece of advice you would do well to remember."

"Is there?" Now I was at it!

"Yes, it's as Charles Dickens said in 'Great Expectations'." I found myself mouthing the words at the same time as him. "'Take nothing on its looks; take everything on evidence. There's no better rule.'"I couldn't believe it. I'd been trying to remember these very words all day long, and he'd plucked them from my brain. "So what you're saying in response to my complaint that I have started to question everything is that I must continue to question everything?"

"That is correct." He started off down the stairs. "You have got to the crux of what it means to do our job, and for that, I applaud you." The subsequent gesture was made all the quieter by the white cotton gloves he wore.

I decided to stop asking such abstract questions and focus on the case before us. "Very well. With that in mind, what should we do next?"

"I would say that was obvious." He did not turn back, but I have no doubt that his expression was both mysterious and a little superior. "It's time we engaged in a spot of treasure hunting."

CHAPTER SEVENTEEN

There are many things in life which people might consider obvious. The day of the week is generally quite difficult to mistake, though I do so on a thrice monthly basis. Most people can tell the difference between a greenfinch and a heron, too, unless they happen to be under a good deal of pressure. As for treasure hunting in the middle of a murder investigation, I would say that was the opposite of obvious. I would say it was… Well, I'd say it was… unobvious.

Grandfather was a man of his word, though, and he scouted the house for clues. We started in the state rooms, which turned up very little aside from the aforementioned portraits and the like. It did give me the chance to brush up on my history, at least, as my mentor decided to name every royal he spotted hanging there.

"To our right is James I. Over there is his son Henry Frederick, who died of typhoid before he could inherit the crown. Behind you, you'll find Henry VIII's son Edward, who managed to become king for six and a half years, but he died young because of a nasty cough."

It was less than fascinating to hear name after name reeled off to me, and it reminded me of my history classes at school. And yet Grandfather managed to make the past even more depressing by detailing the manner in which each person had died.

"Shouldn't we talk about the lions we saw down in the workshop?" I put to him, mainly to have an excuse to interrupt.

"What is there to say about them?"

I thought this was fairly obvious. "They were supposed to have been stolen but have turned up without fanfare."

"Which suggests that it is another of the killer's games. Much like the broken vase, the shifting paintings and perhaps even the chloroform in Miss Horniman's room. There is very little we can learn from their rediscovery, as any one of our suspects could have put them there."

"But don't you think…" I replied irritably, before realising that I didn't know what else to say.

"Very well, Christopher." He was still looking at a portrait of… someone royal. "You've convinced me. The next time I see a police officer, I will tell him to fetch the lions and dust them for fingerprints.

There won't be any, of course." He gave a short laugh as though the very idea was ridiculous. "Our culprit is far too clever not to have worn gloves."

When we'd been through half of the rooms on the ground floor, I decided I'd had enough. "Grandfather, might it not be a better idea to ask someone for the location of whatever treasure you hope to find?"

"Can I be of help?" a voice said from further along the main corridor where we stood. Alicia Pearson appeared to have regained her confidence over the course of the morning. She looked quite formidable as she stood with her three daughters and my mother at her side.

"We're looking for—" Grandfather began, before having second thoughts and hurrying over to speak in a lower voice. "We're looking for any works of art that were bought from Chatterton Hall."

"That's easy enough." Young Veronica turned on her heel in a businesslike fashion so that our mothers grinned at one another, and we all paraded after her.

She led us out of the south library, along a broad corridor and through the Great Hall once more, all the way to the Great Parlour where we'd had breakfast that morning.

"So that's why!" Grandfather declared as we passed through a door that was set back in the wall. "It is one of the few rooms I've yet to visit."

He looked around with quiet reverence, much as I had when I'd spotted the table laid out with baked delights. In my defence, I'd like to think that the only reason I hadn't taken much notice of the wonders on display there was that my stomach had assumed control of my very brain and forced me to seek out sustenance before I could do anything else. Which, now that I think about it, is a fairly feeble excuse.

"I suppose you have heard about our most recent acquisitions?" Alicia began as she showed him to the longest wall in the room. It was between two banks of windows and was covered not just with portraits, like much of the house, but elaborately decorated ceramics, silverware and various carpets and tapestries. "We didn't necessarily want such a selection, but to restore the paintings that had been taken from Parham, we had to buy the lot. These are the ones that our experts in the workshop below have already examined."

Grandfather stood nodding before the grand display. "I'm

114

impressed. I really am. Will you leave all these pieces here, or is it a temporary arrangement?"

The girls had already become bored and gone off into a corner to play jacks. Alicia came to stand next to him. "My husband and I like to put pieces that we acquire on display to see if they fit. It may sound strange, but it sometimes feels as if the house tells us what's appropriate and what isn't. There's a portrait in the Saloon which we must have tried in fifteen different places before we found the right one."

I stood at the end of the line beside my mother, and we made the right sounds as our eyes tripped over the great range of artefacts. It wasn't long before we were all looking at the same thing. The bronze, gold and silver cup stood quite alone on the top of a small marquetry cabinet.

"It's exquisite," Mother said, just as enchanted by the ancient piece as I was.

It was not merely eye-catching and ornate; it had an indescribable glow in the light of midday, as the sun broke through the tall windows along the southern wall. I felt it calling to me to drink from it and, if Alicia had told me that it was the real Holy Grail, I would have believed her in an instant.

"It may be the oldest thing in the house," she said instead. "Eighth or ninth century, so Elton Lockhart tells me. We've ended up with an interesting collection of Anglo-Saxon pieces. Everything from jewellery and daggers to coins and plates. I can't say that we would have thought to buy them if they hadn't come here, but they do hold a certain charm, and I'm sure we'll find a place for them."

"Grandfather hung one of his Gainsboroughs in a cloakroom in our servants' quarters," I said, as I enjoy vexing him.

"Only because it reminded him so strongly of his least favourite uncle," Mother said in her father's defence.

I was half expecting a slap around the back of the head for my impertinence, but, oddly, Grandfather did not appear to have heard.

Alicia directed our attention to a few of the oldest pieces. "As you surely know, choosing the best place for our possessions in a house like this is a painstaking affair."

"You must post a guard here," Grandfather said, quite out of the blue. His voice was serious and there was that same intensity about him that I'd witnessed in the library. "I mean it. You must post a man here night and day until we catch the killer."

"You think this is it, then?" I moved to stand next to him and looked at the chalice more closely. There was the likeness of Jesus on one side, just as Lockhart had attested, and the mix of Christian and pagan imagery stood out even to someone like me who knows very little about history, religion, art or metals. "This is why someone was bothering Alicia and why Stanton was killed?"

"I can't say for certain, but there's a good chance." He turned away from the cup at last and began to lay out his theory. "Let's say the killer attempted to knock out the nightwatchman in order to take this cup. He misjudged how much chloroform to use, or Mr Stanton simply had a negative reaction to it, which brought about his hallucination. The killer realised the risk he faced and escaped before anyone came to investigate the screams."

"The only problem with that," I was quick to add, "is that he could have waited until Stanton was in another part of the house. The nightwatchman's rounds surely took him all over the building."

He raised one finger as if he had a categorical explanation to this, then changed his mind and looked uncertain. "Or... Or perhaps that was the killer's intention, but Stanton doubled back on himself unexpectedly. Perhaps he'd forgotten his cup of tea in the Great Hall or heard a noise and returned to investigate."

As much as I enjoy challenging my grandfather's theories, Mother is just as good at it when she so wishes. "Very well. But it still doesn't explain how he hoped to get away with it." She walked up to her father with all the confidence I dream of possessing, and her friend looked rather impressed. "If he was going to steal the cup, he would still have to get it out of the house. It's one of the most conspicuous artefacts here. Someone would have seen that it was missing."

Grandfather was growing increasingly agitated. "What else makes sense, though? I was saying to Christopher just this morning that the killer must have a large prize in mind to go to so much effort. This cup has history, immense value and even a little mythology attached to it. It's the obvious choice."

It wasn't that his claim lacked credibility, but I felt that he was ignoring the issue in order to have something solid upon which to base our investigation.

"Are these all the items that came from Chatterton Hall?" I asked Alicia when it seemed we had met an impasse.

"I'd say this is one third of them. There are still a lot down in the workshop which have to be examined, and Clive insisted that we display the swords and knives in the Great Hall. But the most valuable things are here before you."

There were three detectives in that room – four if you include Veronica who had been listening to every word we said – and every last one of us looked perplexed.

"We may well be approaching this from the wrong angle," Grandfather admitted in a mournful tone, and I waited for him to offer another solution. Instead, he stared at the painting on the wall directly above the cup. It was a portrait of a man standing beside an apple tree, and I very much doubted it would help us solve the case.

When no one else had anything helpful to say, my mother spoke. "Father, I believe that you are falling into the killer's trap. You keep getting distracted by the mystery that he's presented when, to catch him, all you need to do is focus on your normal process."

"Mother's right." I sounded incredibly eager considering the hole in which we'd found ourselves. "We've only really spoken to one of the suspects. There's still so much left to do."

He remained silent for some time and looked back and forth between the cup, the various Elizabethan, Jacobean and Carolinian portraits and the girls playing their game. In quite the least encouraging gesture imaginable, the great Lord Edgington shook his head morosely and reluctantly left the room.

CHAPTER EIGHTEEN

We walked back through the Great Hall, and I inspected the blades on the wall that Alicia had mentioned. They were arranged in order of length with big, impressive swords at the bottom and little poky daggers at the top. (I am sorry. I still don't know a lot about weapons, even though I've seen what they can do many times.) Such displays were common in the houses where our investigations had taken place, and I still say, if you don't want people to be murdered, don't provide so many options for a would-be killer. It's only common sense.

"Chrissy," someone pssted to me as we crossed the hall. Well, she actually said, "Pssst, Chrissy," but I'm sure you understood what I meant.

In a moment, Veronica was at my side. She kept her eyes straight ahead as we walked, though I don't know why.

"Hello," I whispered because I couldn't think of anything else to say.

"I've been watching the suspects, and they are all acting very suspiciously. That boring man Eric is very angry with his assistant for some reason. And Elton Lockhart's twin floozies seem to hate each other for some reason. And, for some reason, the man with the silly explorer's hat doesn't like Elton Lockhart or the boring man, though I don't know how he feels about the others."

She may not have worked out the reasons for any of this, but she'd observed just as much as I had about the interactions within Parham's group of historical experts.

"It sounds as though you've been very busy."

"Oh, I have. I've barely stopped detecting all day."

I appreciated her unselfconscious self-confidence. My grandfather was equally assured, and it had served him well in life.

"My sisters have done what they could to help me," she continued. "But I'm unconvinced they have what it takes to go into this line of work. Lavinia is always too nervous to do one thing for very long, and Dione forever wants to play games. They're simply too immature to be of any help."

I believe that I'd already learnt my lesson that week when it came to treating children as anything less than geniuses in the making and so, instead of patting the young girl on her head and telling her to keep at it, I thought I might ask her opinion on the case.

"Have you formed any ideas on who might be the killer?"

Far from being happy that I'd asked her, she put me in my place. "I beg your pardon, but I haven't finished telling you all that we have done yet. We spoke to various members of staff who knew Mr Stanton best and tried to find out as much as we could about him."

"Oh, really?" I was excited by the prospect that she had uncovered some previously unknown chapter in the victim's life. "What did you find?"

"Not very much. Cook told us that he kept to himself but liked a flutter on the horses. Our nursemaid thinks he has a wife in Worthing who he sees on a Sunday afternoon. And Lavinia remembered the times he cooked us little pancakes whenever the adults were out on a cub hunt and there was no one else awake."

"Ah. I doubt that will lead us to his killer." We'd reached the main corridor again, and I stopped as I assumed she would be following her mother upstairs.

"Of course it won't. But I've got some questions to ask you before I get on with my task." She had a formal air about her now and opened her notebook to consult a page that mainly consisted of long rows of question marks with the odd sentence written in between them. "First, has Lord Edgington identified the killer yet?"

This was a more difficult point to answer than one might assume. "I don't believe so, though it's never totally clear what my grandfather is thinking. He doesn't usually trust me with his secrets."

She put a large cross at the side of the page and whispered to herself.

"Lord Edgington doesn't know what's going on," she said before looking back up at me. "Question number two, is chloroform easily obtained from a chemist's?"

I was a little taken aback. "I'm sorry?"

"Don't be." She closed the book again and looked a little concerned. "It's a simple enough question. Nanny says that the chemical that killed poor Mr Stanton was called chloroform. What she didn't know was whether it can be bought from a shop like a chemist's or perhaps it has other uses and can be bought at an ironmonger's."

She'd got me there. I couldn't imagine providing much of an answer, but there was one thing I did know. "The Dangerous Drugs Act of 1920 placed controls on a lot of such potent substances. It means that you couldn't buy it for medical purposes without at least registering your name and more likely having a certificate from a doctor."

"Oh," she replied, and her face crumpled with disappointment.

"However, that doesn't mean someone couldn't buy it for other purposes."

She was immediately happy again. "The ironmonger's!"

"I can't say for certain, but it's possible that people in certain industries could obtain it more easily. And there's always the chance that the killer bought it before the law changed and held on to it."

"This is wonderful, Chrissy! Thank you," she said rather loudly and received a frown from both our mothers for her trouble. In response, she looked more sombre and, with a wink for me as soon as no one was looking, trailed after her sisters towards the east wing of the house.

"She may be doing a better job than either of us," I told my grandfather when I caught up with him. "Have you considered the possibility that the bottle of chloroform could lead us to the—"

He interrupted before I could finish my point. "Yes, Christopher. Of course, I have."

"So is it possible that it can be obtained without too much—"

"Yes, of course it is, which just adds to the complexity of the case before us."

He was still in his blue funk, but it could have been worse. I find that he is often at his best when things are at their bleakest. It would surely only be a matter of time before he had a revelation, and then the world would look sunnier once more. Well, that was what I hoped, at least. And when we arrived back outside the workshop, I was amazed to discover that we agreed on something.

"I think we should talk to Dr Carbonell first. Perhaps we'll finally understand his attitude towards Elton Lockhart."

Grandfather held the door closed as he answered. "That's a very good idea."

"Really?" I struggled to hide how much this tickled me. "Are you sure you wouldn't rather talk to Mark Isaac, who we've learnt nothing about, does not seem to be related to any of the other suspects, and is a fairly innocent-seeming young man?"

"No, I think we should talk to Dr Carbonell."

I still wouldn't believe him. "What about another person whose name we haven't actually mentioned yet? Perhaps someone I would never consider as being in any way related to the case? The housekeeper, Mrs Evans, for example? Or perhaps our very own footman Halfpenny, who has been noticeably absent ever since yesterday?"

He was not impressed. "No, boy. I think that a brief conversation with Raymond Carbonell is just what we need." He opened the door for me and, as I wandered past him in a daze, added, "Oh, and I've given Halfpenny, Cook and Dorie the afternoon off to paint in the grounds of the estate. It turns out that I might have brought one or two more members of staff with me than were required." This was a rare admission of fallibility and was further evidence of his strange mood.

When we walked into the centre of the workshop, everyone stopped what they were doing to look at us. I found it curious that expert bore Eric Uhland was always the most nervous in our presence. He immediately became anxious and walked around his table to put a frame on the floor before picking it back up again to return it to its original position. The others froze, clearly expecting an announcement, and Grandfather was not one to disappoint – or turn down the chance to speak to a captive audience.

"The case is progressing nicely, and I feel confident that our understanding of what happened last night is becoming clearer with every passing hour." I must say that he was not one of those people who are so fond of their own voices that they have to drone on forever. No, it was more that he wanted other people to be fond of his voice, and so he made the most of such dramatic moments. "I will admit that the path we are exploring is a serpentine one, but you will note that our focus has once more turned to the people in this room." He paused to let the implications of this rattle around their heads. When he spoke again, his voice was even more powerful. "We will start by interviewing Dr Raymond Carbonell."

With this, he turned and left the room. I waited for Carbonell to grab his hat and follow. I don't know if he was afraid of being sunburnt without it, but I could have told him that such a fate in Sussex in the middle of March is as likely as an elephant strolling past on his way to the opera or a creature from another planet crash-landing in search of hot cross buns.

In a line, we followed Grandfather into the kitchen courtyard and away from the house. We reached the lawn around the property, but he didn't stop there, and he didn't look back. He had the confidence to know that we would stay with him. We came to a path that skirted the wall of the courtyard and, even when we got to where he'd evidently decided we were going, he didn't peer over his shoulder once.

He stopped beside a large, elongated pond – or perhaps it was a small lake. It had a cover of floating water lilies, which I could imagine being quite beautiful all abloom in summer. For some reason I could not define, though, I found them terribly claustrophobic. For a moment, I imagined myself falling beneath the surface, down into the depths of the water, unable to escape as the roots and weeds took hold of me. So that was a nice way to start an interview.

"I brought you here because I thought you might be more comfortable talking to us away from the house," Grandfather told our next suspect when he'd had a good chance to admire the beautiful-cum-deadly surroundings. There was a rather picturesque dovecote on the other side of the pond, and two mallards were gliding about in line with it.

Carbonell pulled the peak of his helmet down a little lower, though it was so tightly fixed in place that it barely moved. "I would have been more comfortable if you hadn't singled me out in front of everyone. I would have been more comfortable if I'd never come to Parham House in the first place."

Whereas Uhland and his assistant had looked nervous and – let's call a knave a knave – guilty all day, Carbonell had looked… well, it's hard to describe. I would say he appeared somehow hurt or perhaps worried. It was as if he knew he had something unpleasant to do, but he really didn't want to go through with it. I hope this means that my skills at interpreting body language are improving because it turned out that was just how he felt, and Lord Edgington had noticed it too.

"You cannot hide any secrets from me," that wondrous wizard of mesmerism, prestidigitation and conjuration (or, Grandfather, as I call him) declared.

"You read minds now, do you?" Carbonell leaned against the wall to regard his inquisitor.

"No. No one can. But I can see that there is something you are not telling me and, if you don't say what it is, I will assume that you are concealing your guilt and have you arrested for theft and murder."

Both Grandfather and I knew that the law did not work like that, but I can't imagine that Carbonell was quite so sure.

He took a deep breath before replying. "I haven't the first idea what happened to the nightwatchman. And I don't know about anything that has been stolen from Parham House. In fact, I doubt that I can tell you much that has any bearing on your investigation."

He had a pleasant, slightly plummy voice that reminded me of my favourite teacher from when I was at school. Just like my teacher when we'd investigated the death of my headmaster – a rite of passage that most boys surely go through in today's violent world – Carbonell looked nervous.

"What a beautifully constructed reply." Grandfather took his white gloves off and neatly folded them together to put in the pocket of his morning coat. "I'm sure that you were telling the truth, as you chose your words so carefully, Raymond." He was a few inches taller than our witness, who was now slumped against the garden wall so that Grandfather's stare seemed all the more aggressive. "However, you gave too much away at dinner last night, and I know that you have something more to say."

The normally calm man showed his temper for the first time. "That was before anyone was murdered. That was before my words could send a man to the gallows."

"In which case, I'll assume you're talking about Elton Lockhart, and I'll arrest him instead."

"No." He shot back up to his feet and held both hands in the air. "I may not approve of the person he has become, but Elton and I were friends once. I wouldn't wish that upon him. It's simply not right."

"If he did nothing wrong, he has nothing to fear." Guess who said this! Go on, guess! No, it may have sounded like just the sort of thing that Grandfather would put to a witness, but it was actually me doing my best imitation of a competent detective.

He turned to me, holding his reply in for a few moments so that the sound of the wind in the oak trees filled my ears. "That's just the thing, Christopher. Elton has spent his life doing wrong. He was told from an early age that he was the black sheep of the family, and he's been doing his best to fulfil that role ever since."

I wouldn't let him avoid the question so easily. "That doesn't make him a murderer. If there's something you know about him, you must tell us, if only so we can rule out the possibility that he's connected to the crime."

His agitation had reached its peak. He turned once more to look over the water and finally gave in to our demands. "The main reason I haven't told you is because anything I say will sound prejudiced against him. The man seduced my fiancée and didn't even have the grace to marry her. He has been an incurable verruca growing on my foot for over a decade, and so, if he is the one who tried to steal from the Pearson family last night and ended up poisoning a man, it would not surprise me in the least."

The effort expended in launching this broadside left him a little breathless, and he paused before continuing. "Elton Lockhart thinks only of himself. The three driving principles he holds to are lust, avarice and self-interest, and hang the consequences."

I was moved by the force of his words and would have encouraged him to say more. Grandfather, on the other hand, was unimpressed.

"Yes, yes. I'm sure he's a black-hearted scaramouch, but I've known many such people in my life, and they don't all turn out to be murderers. So what's different this time?"

Carbonell put two fingers to his lip as if to pull the words from his mouth, but he still wouldn't answer, so I tried to help him along. "Last night at dinner, just before Lockhart stormed out – he got upset because of something you said." He looked away, but I kept talking. "You implied that some people consider him a thief. Now tell us why, or we'll call Inspector Kirk, and he will get the answers from you."

The fact that Kirk seemed like a genuinely soft-hearted soul was irrelevant just then. Carbonell had been on edge until now, but the acceptance that he had to say what he knew sparked something within him, and he was able to breathe again.

"No matter what I might think of Elton, I shouldn't have said anything, and I've since apologised. I was angry at the way he acted, but I should have been more discreet." He pulled his cream linen shirt tighter over his trousers and finally explained his thinking. "I don't know the whole story, but there was something of a scandal at a dig we were on in the Yorkshire Wolds. We were excavating the site of an Anglo-Saxon cemetery. It was an immense undertaking with tens of people there, but it was only from the area Elton oversaw that things went missing."

"You mean he robbed a grave?" I asked, unable to hide my shock.

Carbonell gave a soft laugh. "That's one way of looking at it, I suppose. Though the warriors we were exhuming had been dead for over a thousand years. There were twenty of them in all, and three quarters of them were uncovered with armour, shields and their own possessions. However, the ones that Elton oversaw lacked certain elements that we'd not only expected to find there, but which the marks around the body suggested had recently been removed."

"He stole from his own excavation?" Even Grandfather sounded surprised by this. "To what end? Are we to believe he wished to sell the bounty?"

The specialist on military antiques lost his smile and looked a touch perplexed. "I really can't say, and I should tell you that Elton denied it when the accusations were put to him. He said that someone must have got there before us or come in the night when the graves were half dug. I thought it a plausible explanation until you arrived." He picked over his words to choose the right ones. "The fact is that Elton takes his work most seriously, and he would have gained more from revealing his finds. The impressions around the highest-ranking soldier suggest that a box similar to the one you saw this morning was stolen. If it was complete, it could reveal so much about the myths and society of the day. I assumed at the time that Elton would have wanted to share that with the world."

"And now you're not convinced?" I put to him.

"I wouldn't say that. If a local ne'er-do-well had caught wind of what we were doing there, he might well have poked about to find what he could. The problem for Elton was that it was only his graves that were looted, and so people started to talk."

"Could one of his assistants have been responsible for the thefts?" Grandfather was clearly thinking a few steps ahead as he said this, and

I could see what that might mean for the current case.

A frog poked its head out of the water for a moment before returning to the blackness with a splash. It gave Carbonell a chance to consider the question.

"It's possible. And that's why I feel guilty for mentioning the suspicion that fell on Elton. There was no real evidence to say that he was to blame, and so I held my tongue when our colleagues accused him. Despite the past we share, I've always assumed that his devil-may-care demeanour was the reason that people speak so negatively of him, rather than any proof of his ill deeds."

He was so careful with his delivery, and I wondered how he could be so forgiving. I must have made this fairly clear from the way I looked at him, as he soon explained his feelings.

"I did hate him once. I despised him, in fact. After he stole my Eliza from me, I wanted to murder him." He looked down at the ground as he said this, then continued in the same calm manner that rather typified him. "To be quite frank, I nearly lost my mind at that moment. It was as though I'd been split in two, and I doubted I would ever put myself back together."

"Yet you managed it somehow. That must have taken great resilience." Grandfather spoke wistfully, and I wondered whether he'd ever had a broken heart. His life before he met my grandmother was a mystery to me, but he was twenty-eight at the time, and I could only assume he had fallen in love before then.

"I was a wreck for several years before I realised that Elton no longer meant anything to me. He took the woman I was supposed to marry and upstaged me in my career, but that wasn't what prevented me from regaining my happiness. I was miserable because I'd given up on life, and so I returned to the job I loved and tried to forget the past."

When I'd first met Dr Carbonell, he'd seemed so controlled and competent. It was odd to have a glimpse of what lay beneath the surface. Just like the big pond by which we stood, there was a great deal more happening there than one might first think. While that is surely true for most people, I was still fascinated by what he'd revealed.

"I have more questions for you," Grandfather said in a detached voice as his feet shuffled in the dry earth. "Did you know any of your other colleagues at Parham before you came?"

"I'd crossed paths with the twins before. They're two real characters. It's a shame they're in thrall to a man like Elton Lockhart. They're intelligent women and they know what they're doing here."

"What about Uhland and his assistant?"

Carbonell rolled his shoulders as if turning the page of a book. "I don't know either of them. I believe Mark Isaac is a talented painter, though his work here is fairly menial. Uhland has a reputation for fastidiousness, but I haven't worked with him before."

"And Parham House?" Grandfather asked to conclude his run of questions. "What brought you to this particular assignment? It seems far from the civil war battlefields of your youth."

"The truth is..." He leaned forward as if to impart a secret. "...I came here because it pays well. The Pearsons have been very generous, and the remuneration is a great deal better than universities and museums tend to offer. It's mainly old suits of armour and rusty seventeenth century weaponry I've been hired to examine, but I've turned up a few gems, too."

"I have one final thing to ask," I told him.

"Go ahead." He looked back along the path we'd taken, and I wondered whether he was as hungry as I was.

"In light of what happened here last night, do you really think that your childhood friend stole from the dig in Yorkshire?"

Until this point, he had been purposefully vague on the matter. I assumed he would hedge his bets again and avoid anything definite, but he turned back to me and declared, "Yes, I believe he probably did. Elton's sense of morality is very different from most people's. Perhaps he did it for money or to further his career somehow. If that were the case, he wouldn't hesitate to sabotage his own project. He has an unwavering belief in himself, and I very much doubt that he would allow the law to be an obstacle to his insatiable sense of ambition."

CHAPTER NINETEEN

Dr Carbonell shook our hands and returned to the house ahead of us. I leaned back against the wall and watched his languorous stroll down the path. I knew that Grandfather was lost in his thoughts, and I wondered what he made of the oddly emotional interview, but I had my own questions to put to him.

"My first thought was that Dr Carbonell was lying to incriminate his rival, but if so, all we have to do is ask Lockhart or one of the twins and they'll tell us what happened on their dig in Yorkshire."

"Yes, and he was hardly excessive in his condemnation of the man. He may have connected the debonair archaeologist to a possible theft, but he didn't accuse him of murder or push for us to think the worst of him. I can only conclude that what he told us was verifiably true – which we, of course, will verify."

He smiled at me then and, disapproving of my slouching pose, pushed me up to my full height. I couldn't help laughing at the old stick in the mud, and we began our short, undemanding trek back to the main house.

"What we don't know is whether Carbonell has really forgiven the man who betrayed him," I pointed out. "Isn't it possible that he has created a situation that would incriminate Lockhart in order to exact his revenge?"

I could hear the muffled sound of our footsteps on the soft ground for a few paces before he replied. "I suppose it's possible, but there are more obvious ways to go about it. And the two have evidently continued to work together, no matter their differences. Whilst it's clear that Dr Carbonell would rather have nothing to do with the man, his words made sense to me. He suffered a great deal, and I know from my own experience that the only way beyond such pain is to put it behind you."

"What about the Horniman sisters?" I asked. "Their names keep popping up, but we've yet to interview them on their own. They were presumably at the dig where the artefacts went missing, and the chloroform was in Frances's room. They don't appear too fond of one another and have been fighting over Lockhart. It's all very well his saying that the two sisters are accepting of their bohemian arrangement, but perhaps everything that has gone on here will come down to the rivalry between them."

"It's possible," he said noncommittally. "However, for the moment, I'm willing to set aside the personalities involved to focus on material concerns. If this whole investigation comes down to theft – if everything that called us here, and everything that has subsequently occurred, is leading up to the removal of a particular object—"

"I thought you said that the cup had to be the prize?"

"It is a strong possibility, though that might be what our culprit wishes us to think." It was curious to discover that Grandfather's previous certainty was tempered with a dash of realism. His mix of self-assurance and doubt left me quite rudderless.

"Then how do you intend to identify the killer's plan?"

"The library where you found me this morning doubles as Clive Pearson's study. He has written the most incredibly detailed logs of every item that was in Parham when they purchased the house and every item that has been bought since. That is where I will discover whatever it is that the killer was planning to steal last night. What Dr Carbonell told us only makes it more likely that we are on the trail of a thief who is yet to steal the item which he came to Parham to find."

"That sounds painstaking (and tedious)." I actually said these last two words, and he tutted accordingly.

"It may be a time-consuming task, but police work is not all about running after criminals and putting suspects to the sword. A detective's greatest tool is occasionally a sledgehammer but, more often than not, it is a fine-tooth comb."

I was wondering what terrible crime I'd committed to deserve to spend hours poring over dry auction catalogues, historical documents and old journals to find the provenance of every last item in Parham House when he offered me a stay of execution – or at least a lighter sentence.

"I will ask Todd and your mother to help me. They will be capable substitutes while you are busy interviewing witnesses. I would start with the sisters, but Eric Uhland and his assistant might be more important than we have yet come to realise."

I was taken aback by his plan. "Do you really think I should interview them on my own? Isn't it possible that you would notice something terribly important that I will only miss?"

He replied in an acerbic tone. "No, Christopher, I do not believe that to be a risk. You will conduct the interviews and then report back to me in detail on what you discover. Do you understand?"

This answer gave me a jolt of confidence, and I responded in the affirmative. "Yes, Grandfather. I will do my best."

I must confess that I was excited to be setting off on my own. I barely noticed the sweetness of the bird song or the very nearly spring sunshine on our skin as we walked; my head was full of questions. Above all, I hoped that my time with the Horniman twins would at last help me make sense of their beloved Elton Lockhart.

Although Dr Carbonell had described for us the man that Lockhart had once been, his perspective was informed by all that had passed between them. Vyvyan and Frances, meanwhile, knew the man there today – the man whose enigmatic personality had been at the centre of the case since I'd first seen him in the Great Hall the day before. I was convinced that, whether Lockhart turned out to be the killer or not, the solution would revolve around him in some way.

Grandfather kept on towards the front of the house, and I walked to the entrance beside the kitchen. Inspector Kirk was standing in the courtyard, smoking a cigarette, which he stubbed out when he saw me, as if he'd been caught by a superior.

"There's no need for that," I told him as I drew closer. "You have every right to enjoy your break. I'm sure you've been quite overwhelmed. There is always so much to investigate in a murder inquiry." It felt a little strange to speak like this to an experienced officer, but he clearly appreciated it.

"Thank you, Mr Prentiss." These two words alone made me feel quite grown up.

"Please, call me Christopher."

He bowed his head courteously, and I sensed that he was a little nervous.

"The truth is, Christopher, it's only the second time I've had to deal with a case like this. The first was a simple husband-and-wife situation with fingerprints on a knife and a full confession. I can't honestly say I have a clue how to catch a clandestine killer." For a moment, he sounded a lot like me. "My officers keep looking at me as though I should know what we're supposed to do next, but I'm at a loss."

"You're doing very well," I assured him before deciding that it might put his mind at ease if we were to focus on the facts that had so far been established. "Perhaps you can tell me, if you don't mind, what you've discovered about the dead man. I don't suppose anything so simple as a grudge or a wronged lover could explain his death?"

"Sadly not." This only made him look more glum. "From all we've discovered, he was a popular member of staff here and a loyal husband. His wife has an alibi for last night, too. I believe we can rule her out as a suspect – especially as she'd have struggled to get upstairs in her wheelchair. So that's another dead end."

I tried to cheer him up. "No, no. It's not a dead end. You mustn't think of it like that. It's a potential explanation eliminated, and that means we are one step closer to finding the right one. With every hour that passes, it seems more likely that the killer's real motive has not yet been revealed."

"Well, in that case, I can tell you that there were no fingerprints on the lions or the bottle of chloroform. So that's two more possibilities eliminated. What should we do next?" He was his jovial self once more.

"As it happens, I was about to interview the Horniman sisters."

"How interesting. I don't suppose I could…?" He didn't need to finish the question to make me squirm.

"I… Well…" I would eventually have to start a sentence if I wished to reply. "I can't think of any reason why you shouldn't join me (even though this is the first interview I've ever conducted alone, and I'm already terrified that I'm not cut out for it)." Don't worry, I did not say these last… however many words and, from the cheerful expression he wore, I could only think that Kirk hadn't guessed them.

"After you, sir," he said with a wink as he held the door open for me.

He took a more theatrical bow this time, and I reluctantly moved past him into the lower floor of the building. I cursed myself for not telling him that an experienced detective like me (ho ho) can only work at peak efficiency when free from unnecessary observation.

As we walked along the corridor to the workshop, I pondered upon the best strategy for interviewing the twins. My first thought was to talk to them together so that the friction between them would spark and lead to any number of revelations. Then I wondered whether it might not be better to separate them and ask the same questions back and forth, one after another, in different rooms so as to find out who was lying and who was telling the truth. In the end, I decided to make it up as I went along.

"Could I speak to you both, please?" I asked when I stuck my head into the room.

Dr Carbonell was back at his table leafing through old documents beside a rusty sword, but there was no sign of Lockhart or young Mark Isaac. Eric Uhland, meanwhile, was sitting on a stool on one side of the room with his eyes closed.

They sprang right open when he heard my question. "What have I done?"

"Not you, Mr Uhland," I replied. "I was referring to Miss Horniman and... well, Miss Horniman."

Vyvyan was the smilier of the two and immediately came to the door. "I'm happy to help. What about you, dear sister?"

Frances was evidently more reluctant and dragged her feet as she crossed the room. I opened the door for them to go through and, out in the corridor, Inspector Kirk looked excited that he would get the chance to see me in action. There was only one problem... Well, that's not true. There were any number of problems, but one was particularly evident at that moment.

"I don't suppose anyone knows the right place to host an interview?" I asked, and Frances huffed a little and led me to the gun room.

"Perfect. If you don't mind waiting in there," I said, whilst already eyeing the next door along in the hope it would suit our purposes.

Frances stayed behind, and I motioned for her sister to go next door. It turned out to be a very small boot room, so that was no use. The silver room was chairless, the glass room was occupied by the half-Italian footman (who, as Veronica had told me, was forever polishing something) and the china room was just what we needed.

"I won't be a minute," I told Vyvyan and then ran back to her sister, who Inspector Kirk was keeping company.

"Of course, I'm a great admirer of the works of Tchaikovsky," he said very seriously, and I had to wonder how they had got onto this subject so rapidly.

In my absence, Kirk had also found the time to set up three chairs, and the interview of the first Horniman sister was all set to begin.

"Thank you for talking to us, Frances." I cleared my throat as I sounded terribly squeaky. "I'd like you to start by telling me all you know about…" I was going to say *Elton Lockhart,* but it occurred to me that she might include some details that I had no desire to hear. "Or rather, I'd like to know about… whatever you can tell me… about…"

It really wasn't the start that I'd imagined. The fact that, in place of my grandfather, I was accompanied by a serving police officer made the experience both more and less stressful. On the one hand, the imperious Lord Edgington was not there to be condescending or roll his eyes in despair, but it was somehow worse that Kirk expected me to be good at interviewing people.

I was far better at jumping in with the odd question than leading the discussion, but I knew that I couldn't delegate anyone else, and so I gave it a second go.

"…your sister," I said a fraction more firmly than before. "Tell me why you don't get on with her and the extremes to which you would go in order to get your own way." My voice came out as someone else's. The sentence was cold and clinical, and nothing like me. I did not mind it one bit!

"Vyvyan is an enormous pain. She's been following my example our whole lives." She did not need to explain her joke, but she did it anyway. "I was the first-born daughter, you see? She's copied every single thing I've done ever since."

I looked at the inspector as if to say, *Well, that's suspicious, don't you think?* When he didn't understand, I turned back to our suspect.

"So she followed you into this world of historical investigation, and she fell in love with Elton Lockhart, just as you did?"

She made no attempt to contradict my easy conclusions. "That's right. She is infuriatingly unoriginal in her thinking." She pushed aside her long blonde fringe and revealed more of her striking features. The shape of her eyes put me in mind of an Arabian princess from a fairy tale, though her colouring could not have been more different. "And she really takes the biscuit with Elton. It's bad enough that we work together, it really is, but…" She was seething by now and had to stop talking to calm herself.

134

I was about to enquire into the nature of her affair with Lockhart when she spoke again. "None of this means that I had anything to do with the dead man. You do know that, don't you?"

Her confidence fed into mine, and I didn't stutter or even hesitate as I replied. "We'll be the judge of that." I exchanged looks with Kirk once more and, this time, he was ready and replied with a knowing frown. "Mr Stanton's death may have had nothing to do with your sister, but perhaps your feelings for your boyfriend aren't quite as simple as you've suggested. Perhaps you hatched a plan for revenge."

Unimpressed, she sat back in her chair. "Give me one moment to make sense of what you're saying. Is it your idea that I plotted revenge on Elton because I'm so in love with him that I want to see him suffer?"

I wouldn't let myself be cowed by her hostile tone – no matter how much this whole experience unnerved me. "I'm saying that you may not be as accepting of the situation in which he has placed you as you wish us to believe. Over time, love can turn to resentment and then hate if it is not properly fostered. From the way that Mr Lockhart has described the situation between the three of you, it is ripe for jealousy." I considered adding a neat metaphor to make my point further, but I got confused between roosting birds, sewing seeds and making beds, so I decided to leave it there.

She turned away indignantly to look at the glass cases on the wall where the Pearson family's hunting rifles were stored. This was the only answer she would give, and so I moved on to another topic. "From your surname, and the fact that you can afford the low-paying occupation to which you've devoted your life, I assume you are related in some way to the Horniman tea dynasty."

"What a detective you are!"

"Have you and your sister been funding Elton Lockhart's work over the last year?"

Her eyebrows jerked a fraction higher before she answered. It was only for the briefest moment, but it told me I was asking the right question.

"We may have assisted him in some respects, but our father did not object. We come from a family of explorers, historians and anthropologists. If it wasn't for that spirit of adventure, Daddy would never have established the Horniman Museum and expanded British knowledge of foreign culture and the peoples of the world."

Or perhaps this was not the right question. She sounded as if she was reading from a pamphlet that had been distributed around her family to ensure they all said the right thing.

"What about your dig in the Yorkshire Wolds?"

There was another flicker of surprise on her face, but I wouldn't get my hopes up just yet.

"What about it?"

"What went wrong there? I've heard talk of important historical artefacts going missing. I'd like you to tell me what happened."

Her eyes strayed to the other side of the room this time, where more ceremonial and historical weapons were on display on the wall. It was unlikely that such items were ever used, but that hadn't stopped Graham Perugino from keeping them shiny.

"I wonder who told you that. You do realise that Raymond Carbonell has a similar feeling for Elton as I do for my sister. He and Elton once fell in love with the same woman and Raymond did not emerge the victor."

"That's one way of describing it," I was quick to reply, "but both men told us that the woman in question was Dr Carbonell's fiancée and that his supposed friend stole her away from him in a less than admirable manner."

Each time I told her something new or went against her expectations, her body seemed to register it like a bead pushed along an abacus. This time, it was her mouth that dropped open rather mechanically, though she tried to ignore the importance of what I'd said.

"Quelle surprise, Elton is a rotter. If you think I had any other perception of him, then you're clearly more naïve than you look. It's not his saintliness, but his brilliance that made me fall in love."

That beautiful word sounded wrong falling so contemptuously from her lips. I hadn't imagined her using such a term for whatever existed between her and Lockhart (and Lockhart and her sister).

"That's all very well," Inspector Kirk intervened, and I was happy for him to do so, "but you haven't answered Mr Prentiss's question. What happened at the dig in Yorkshire?"

She eyed the inspector disdainfully, like a child who has been caught fibbing. "I suppose it won't hurt to tell you. It's all a matter of public record anyway. When we uncovered the graves of what we believed were the highest-ranking soldiers who had been buried there after a battle, the valuables we had expected to find with them were gone. The earth had been disturbed and there was clear evidence that something had been removed. It seemed to me that they had been stolen the night before we attempted the excavation."

"And so Mr Lockhart may have been the one to take them?"

She was unmoved by the accusation. "Mr Lockhart, or any one of a hundred other people who were nearby that night. The fact that Elton was in charge of that area of the excavation does not prove that he was to blame. If it hadn't been for some simple-minded locals making a fuss, there would never have been a problem."

"I see," I said in the way that Grandfather often does and which I hope would suggest I understood some deep and meaningful truth. "It is evident that you hold Mr Lockhart in the highest esteem. Can you tell me what would happen if he were to throw you over for your sister?"

"I would murder them both in their beds!" Her wide eyes were fixed upon me. Her breathing halted and, for approximately five seconds, she didn't move a muscle... until she laughed. "Isn't that what you want to hear? You believe that one of us has been conspiring to wreak havoc, first by interfering with the household, then by killing that poor nightwatchman. But the truth is that, if either Vyvyan or I were responsible, we would have gone about it in a far cleverer way."

"I truly appreciate your candour." I paused to let her think the worst. "However, I don't believe it is wise to go before a judge and claim that you couldn't possibly have committed the crime because you would have done a better job of it. You could just as easily make a mess of things to deflect suspicion onto someone else."

"Well, we didn't. I haven't done anything wrong. My only reason for being here is Elton and because I'm fascinated by the work he does. The man is a visionary. If you had seen what I've seen, you'd understand why my sister and I would happily follow him to the ends of the earth."

"What slavish obedience." I allowed one more pause for good measure. I once met a musician who told me that the rests between notes were just as important as the sound of the instruments, and I'd often noticed that grandfather cultivated the silences in our interviews.

"Of course, being so devoted to another person means that you might not just follow him but do whatever he bid. Would that extend to theft and murder?"

"Yes, it would," she replied, to shock me again, but I was ready for the reversal this time. "I would do anything he required because he is a great man, but that does not mean I have ever broken the law for him. The truth is, Elton is no devil. One of the few things upon which Vyvyan and I can agree is that, despite what people like to say about him, he is a compassionate human being. He is simply not beholden to the outdated rules of society as more limited individuals are."

"Surely if he were such a good man, he would commit to one of you and not play with your feelings so callously." I didn't mean to sound quite so angry, but their attitude had got under my skin and this torrent burst from me. "You may believe yourself a muse to a great man, but if that man is taking advantage of you, then he doesn't deserve your loyalty."

"You wouldn't understand," she replied, turning away once more.

Beside me, Inspector Kirk rubbed his hands together as the atmosphere crackled.

"I'm sorry, Frances," I said, changing the tone of my voice and, hopefully, the mood in the room. "I don't wish to upset you, but I'd still like you to tell us where you were when the nightwatchman was attacked."

"I was in my bedroom asleep." She evidently considered how much information to offer at this moment before adding, "I did not wake up from the sound of the screams that others heard."

"I'm sorry if it's an indiscreet question, but were you alone?" I persevered.

She looked uncomfortable as she glanced at the inspector, then back at me. "That's right. Elton stayed up late working last night."

"I see." I was aware that this contradicted what Lockhart had told us, but I wasn't ready to reveal this just yet. I debated whether to mention what we'd found in her bedroom and soon made up my mind. "So you were alone at the time of the killing. No one can provide you with an alibi and, when the police searched your room this morning, they found a bottle of chloroform hidden between your bed and the wall."

It was worth it just to see her reaction.

138

"I…" Panic gripped her, and she had to breathe in deeply before she could reply. "It's obvious what happened. The real culprit hid it there to incriminate me. I've already told you that I would be a far more efficient killer than whoever has been causing trouble here. Why would I hold on to the murder weapon?"

I was willing her to ask this and had the answer already prepared. "Because you hadn't achieved whatever you hoped to and felt that you would need it again."

She was shocked once more, and I felt rather wonderful (and perhaps the tiniest bit guilty) to have turned the tables.

"I don't need to—" she began, then cut herself short. "Or rather, I don't know what the killer intended, but I know nothing of chemistry and haven't a clue where one would obtain such a substance in the first place."

"Thank you, Miss Horniman." I could have pushed her further, but I smiled and looked innocent instead. "If Inspector Kirk has nothing to ask you, I think we can finish the interview there."

"That's fine by me," the inspector replied. "I believe we've covered the most important points."

"The truth is that we only wished to speak to you to rule you out for good," I lied. "In fact, we have another suspect in mind, and it's unlikely we'll need your help again. Thank you for your time."

"You're most welcome." Frances looked nonplussed just then, as if she was uncertain whether to believe me.

"Unless, of course, there's something you'd like to tell us?" I added with my eyes as wide as can be.

"No, no." She was up on her feet and eager to leave.

"Very good." I pretended to look thoughtful for a moment and considered my final question. "If I may ask you one last thing before we speak to your sister. I was wondering whether you believe she will tell the truth."

"I beg your pardon?"

"The truth, Miss Horniman; can your sister be trusted to tell it, or might she perhaps lie to push the blame onto you?"

Her cheeks flushed, and she looked shy for the first time. "Oh, I wouldn't say that. Vyvyan and I fight like furies, but we are sisters nonetheless."

She straightened the leather tunic she wore over a crisp white blouse, looked at us both in turn and fled from the room without another word.

Kirk waited until we heard her footsteps fade along the corridor before saying anything. "That was marvellous work, Mr... Christopher. Really – fabulous stuff." He paused before continuing in a more hesitant tone. "I must admit that I have some questions for you."

"Really?" Whatever strength of will I'd shown in the interview had drained away by now, and I was back to my nervous worst, afraid of what the more knowledgeable officer might ask. "I suppose you had better fire away."

"My first doubt was, were either of you speaking the truth?" He didn't move for a moment as he awaited my response, and I was quite relieved that he hadn't chosen a more difficult question.

"I was certainly economical with the truth at times and, when I told her we have another suspect in mind, that was only to see how she would react."

"You were marvellous, sir."

I'm certain that I was blushing. "I wouldn't go that far, but if she is the killer, and she believes she is no longer a suspect, she might well make an error that will provide us with the proof we need to stop her."

"What a clever ruse!" Kirk loudly joined his hands together. "But was she straight with you? Do you think that she really meant what she said?"

"That is the key question," I told him. "And one I hope to resolve when we speak to her sister." I stood up from the rather tatty dining chair and placed it against the bare wall. "Come along, Kirk. We have another interview to conduct."

CHAPTER TWENTY

I will readily admit that I enjoyed being admired. Though our suspects were both tight-lipped, and it was a struggle to extract their secrets, Inspector Kirk looked at me throughout as though I were working some kind of magic.

To begin with, Vyvyan gave us much the same picture of events as her sister had. We raced through everything she knew about the dig in the Yorkshire Wolds, moved through her love for her sweetheart, and came to the key point of difference.

"You were not alone in bed?"

"No, of course I wasn't. Elton was with me all night. In fact, we were awake when we heard the screams from below. I assumed a servant had stubbed his toe on a piece of old furniture. There's certainly enough of it about."

"What were you doing up so late?" I asked and immediately regretted it.

"We were…" Her wicked grin grew. Now that I knew them better, it was not just Frances's beauty mark that helped me tell the twins apart. Vyvyan had a certain enthusiasm and audaciousness that her sister lacked. "We were conversing into the early hours." A wicked grin became a wicked laugh. "Elton has quite the most brilliant mind. I could converse with him for hours on end and never grow bored."

"I'm sure he has," I said, to push away the more salacious thoughts that had invaded my brain. "But let me be quite clear on the matter. Elton Lockhart spent last night with you, not your sister."

"My sister, indeed! He has really very little interest in Frances. She likes to think that he might one day love her in the same way he does me, but she is a drab, dull little thing, and Elton has never shown a great deal of affection for her. I'm sure that he will get rid of her altogether before long, the poor creature."

"In which case, can you explain why, when we asked Mr Lockhart where he was last night, he didn't mention you?"

She was not alarmed by the question and waved it away with one hand. "To protect my honour, of course. He is a terribly thoughtful man and would not want to besmirch my name, even though I don't give a fig for what people think of me."

"I truly appreciate your candour," I said once more, but this time I was the one who was flustered. "And what of your sister?"

"What of her?"

"Yes, precisely. Or rather, I mean to say…" I was babbling and needed to find my thread again. "Do you believe that Frances could kill to achieve her goals? Would her jealousy drive her to such an act?" I really couldn't say how Frances's jealousy could have led to Mr Stanton's death, but I was happy just to have finished a few complete sentences.

The idea apparently appealed to her. "I don't see why not. There is an aggressive side to my sister that few people have seen." Her eyes truly sparkled at that moment and then she released a musical laugh. "Or perhaps that is what any sibling would say."

I turned to Inspector Kirk, who looked just as uncertain as I felt.

Vyvyan was enjoying herself, and the smile never left her face. "I'm sorry, gentlemen, I really don't know whether my sister is a callous killer or not. All I can tell you is that we don't always see eye to eye, but I have no reason to believe she would kill a man. Now, if you have asked all your little questions, I have an awful lot of work to complete."

She did not wait for an answer but rose to sally from the room.

"I can make neither head nor tail of those two young ladies," Kirk confessed as we remained in our seats in the china room.

"At least one of them must be lying about who was where last night," I eventually muttered as I attempted to extract some meaning from what we'd heard. "Whether it is one of the sisters or their boyfriend, I cannot say."

"I think they like to shock," the inspector concluded as he put his chair back where he'd found it. He had certainly looked shocked when Vyvyan had described the arrangement between herself, her lover and her sister. I can't say that I found the situation particularly easy to understand, either. Just imagine how Lockhart would feel upon visiting their parents at Christmas!

"That is certainly true."

He shook his head in bemusement. "People pretend to live their lives in a brave new way, but in the end, their main objective is to scandalise those around them."

"I believe that is often the case, Inspector. I've met several such people and, for all their desire to change the world, they don't appear to be very happy in what they're doing."

"Too true, Mr Prentiss. Too true. And now, if you don't mind, I'm going to take my lunch at home with Mrs Kirk, with whom I am very happy indeed." He winked at me and walked away muttering to himself.

Alone with my thoughts, I was both excited by what we'd uncovered and baffled by the whole case. Even if we'd caught someone lying, it didn't seem to be directly related to the matter of Stanton's murder or the moving portraits and reappearing lions. It felt as though I were trapped in a labyrinth and everything that looked like an exit was really a cul-de-sac with a person at the end of it chattering away about how hard done by he was.

I wandered upstairs to the main part of the house in a daze. On my way, I saw the butler ironing the day's newspaper. Mr Cridland bowed to me as if this was a perfectly normal thing to do and continued his task. For a moment, I wondered whether I was hallucinating. I looked at the cover of the paper but, sure enough, it was The Chronicle from that morning, the nineteenth of March. The headlines said that the House of Commons was *still* debating the Zivoniev Letter (four years later) and that Mrs Keith Miller had successfully completed her flight from Croydon to Australia. I very much doubted I would have imagined such details and, accepting that in this strange house newspapers were ironed, I continued on my way.

If you'd like to know just how out of sorts I was, I should tell you that it had gone two o'clock, and I'd barely thought about lunch yet. Thankfully, when I got to the west library, there was a selection of sandwiches, pies and quiches for everyone to consume without having to stop what they were doing.

Todd was sitting with some variety of catalogue in front of him, Grandfather was at the draughtsman's table looking over plans and schematics, and mother was on a leather Chesterfield with three books open on her lap. No one noticed me as I came inside, which was fine, as I was busy thinking. I helped myself to a few cucumber sandwiches and drifted upstairs to my cupboard to do something important.

I've often found that focusing too closely on a problem only makes it more difficult to solve and so, rather than dwelling on the Parham House enigma that no one could crack, I returned to the old file that grandfather had lent me.

The gambler, Martin Anderson, was still dead, and his baby boy was still missing. I continued to digest the story that Grandfather had annotated. There were reports from various officers and witnesses involved in the case. I read a statement from the old couple who lived near the site of the murder and the woman who was believed to be Martin Anderson's sweetheart when he died. The police left no stone unturned in the search for his missing son, but he had disappeared without a trace.

Inspector Edgington, as he was known at the time, even interviewed "Holy" Jeb Dixon, a famous gang leader who'd had dealings with Anderson. Although he confirmed that the debtor had been murdered when he couldn't pay back a sum of money, he knew nothing that could explain who would have taken the child.

The case remained open for months, and it was clearly one to which grandfather devoted great care and attention. In addition to the formal report was a long account of his reflections on the case, which I assume had been transcribed from his private notes. The most interesting part of it was a list of theories that he'd compiled. They included the possibility that the poor boy, who was believed to be in his father's arms when the man was killed, had been sold to a baby farmer or left at a convent. There were, of course, more gruesome possibilities, but it was my grandfather's conviction that, not only would the criminals with whom Martin Anderson was involved have drawn the line at killing a child, there was no evidence that little Daniel was dead.

All that was known about Anderson's last day was that he stayed at a nearby inn with his son and left in the early hours. He'd been in the area for two nights before he was murdered and had paid for his lodging on arrival. The real mystery was why whoever killed him had taken the boy. It was ever so tempting to open the envelope with the solution in it, but I was determined to solve it myself. I was just reading the report of P.C. Robbyns, who had found the man's body and proved an invaluable assistant to Inspector Edgington, when I heard a disturbance through the pipes in my room.

I couldn't quite make sense of what was being discussed, but a tone of immense agitation was unmistakable, and I was sure that it was Grandfather's voice I could hear. I immediately pushed the papers onto the bed beside me and raced from the room. His calls seemed to fill the house, as though he were shouting into a canyon. The commotion had disturbed Delilah, who ran out of the room of whoever had last been spoiling her and down the stairs after me.

I heard a new voice clearly as I reached the ground floor. My mother sounded as though she were saying, "That sore bunion!" which told me precisely nothing.

Delilah and I ran to the library, but there was no one there. I took a piece of flan, as I was still a little peckish, and then our capable (when she felt like it) hound sniffed out her master. We followed the corridor around to the Saloon, where the French windows had been left open, and I spotted my mother and grandfather in the distance outside.

Delilah sprinted off ahead of me, and I did my best to catch up. Perhaps sensing that I would always be approximately three minutes behind everyone else, Grandfather looked back over his shoulder just as I emerged from the house.

"Do hurry up, Christopher," he called, without explaining why I should do any such thing.

Vibrant yellow daffodils were growing here and there in the long grass on either side of me, but there was no time to think of such things as I dashed through the Lion Gate towards the walled garden. Todd and a uniformed officer were already some way ahead of the others, but Delilah would soon catch them and get to wherever we were going before everyone else.

The wall that I was following hemmed in a series of outbuildings and the large courtyard beside the house. I took the next gate in the wall as a few stray beams of sunlight found a way through the shifting pattern of clouds overhead. It was one of those very British days which couldn't decide whether to be mild or Siberian, but by the time I'd reached the others, I was hot from running.

The garden was the definition of a well-organised mess. Bushes, grasses and shrubs waiting to bloom were crammed in together in the flower beds alongside fruit and vegetables of all varieties. I instantly imagined what that quintessentially English space would look like in a few months' time, when an endless spectrum of colour had been splashed across it. For the moment, though, there was something else blooming in the walled garden – something sad and quite out of place there.

Another constable was waiting for us at the entrance to the first glass and brick greenhouse that, judging by its age and modern design, the Pearsons themselves must have installed. There were four of them in all, standing in a neat row like tents in a campground, but we were not there for anything so jolly.

Alicia was walking back and forth in the centre of the garden, and my mother went over to see her as I followed Grandfather into the greenhouse. Of course, I knew what had happened before I saw him. I knew that the casualty list had doubled and that our conception of the killer's plot was about to be blown apart. I flicked through the names of the people I had met over the last day, wondering which of them I would find with garden twine around his neck or a trowel through his heart.

Peculiarly, Elton Lockhart was at the top of the list and, as I walked along through raised beds that were beginning to sprout, I pictured him lying dead where Todd was now standing.

"It's Mark Isaac," my grandfather revealed. I recognised the distended face of the young man slumped in the corner and thought, *Oh. I would never have picked him.*

CHAPTER TWENTY-ONE

"We didn't even think of interviewing him!" Grandfather lamented as the officers inspected the scene. "Really, Christopher, what has happened to me this week? I've gone about this investigation in entirely the wrong fashion. I've gone against so many of my foremost rules because the puzzle that the killer has set me has taken charge of my brain, and it will not be evicted."

"I believe you have answered your own question, Grandfather. We've fallen into his trap. He's distracted us, just as he planned. I wouldn't be surprised if we were to return to the house to find that whatever he was after has now disappeared."

This did little to soothe him. He dropped his head into his hands and, perching on the side of a planting box, looked quite distraught. He would never normally have expressed such doubts in public, which goes to show how much the case had affected him.

Mother had presumably done what she could to comfort her friend as she now appeared in the doorway. "That poor young man," she whispered, and I finally understood that she hadn't been talking about bunions back in the house.

I stood next to her, and we examined the dead body from a suitable distance. Eric Uhland's assistant was only a year or two older than I was. He was a student, and I realised that, had I gone to university as my parents had intended, I could have found myself in his place. Which, when you think about it, is a rather selfish way of considering his death. *There but by the grace of God go I* has always seemed a bit mean to me.

The constable who had been charged with going through his pockets finished his fruitless search and stood back from the body.

"How was he killed?" I asked, though I could see a splash of blood behind him on the concrete floor.

Grandfather's right-hand man spotted what I'd failed to see. "He's sitting a little bit forward from the wall and there's a stain just visible on his breast pocket. I'd say that someone stabbed him through the back."

The constable knelt again and pulled Isaac towards him to discover what had done the damage. Sure enough, we could see a metal spike sticking out of him, its shaft well buried in his flesh. It reminded me of what had happened to Martin Anderson in Grandfather's old case file, but I didn't see how the similarity would help us.

"I know nothing about him," Grandfather complained one last time as I caught sight of something and moved closer to look.

On the dead man's hands were flecks of paint in various colours. There were reds and gold, purple and green. This was hardly surprising, as we'd heard he was a talented artist, and his supervisor was an expert on portraiture – a well-respected expert if his own praise was to be believed.

"What should we do now?" I asked, desperate for guidance.

The constables didn't look as though they knew the best course of action and, even if Inspector Kirk hadn't gone off to have his lunch, he was in thrall to the crime-solving lord and unlikely to take charge.

"I don't know what we should do," Grandfather eventually replied, looking as though he no longer had the energy to hold his head up, let alone devise a plan. "I'm quite at a loss."

I wasn't the one to take him to task for this attitude but, luckily, my mother was.

"I beg your pardon?" She was not the first person to use this expression to good effect that day. "Are you really about to give up?"

Grandfather looked stunned that anyone would question him. He gazed back at his daughter but said nothing.

"After you've spent your life telling me that the foremost rule of a detective is to persevere when all appears lost, do you feel so sorry for yourself that you aren't going to examine the scene of the crime even though there is a killer on the loose and a mystery to solve?"

"Darling, you don't understand what—"

This was possibly the worst thing he could have said to her. "I don't understand?" She had to gasp for breath. "Am I, whom you raised to believe that playing with dolls was not a sufficiently cerebral challenge, expected to believe that you, who chose to give me a police baton and magnifying glass as presents on my fifth birthday, are giving up?"

"Not in so many…" Grandfather didn't have the courage to finish his sentence, but at least her words had sparked him into life.

Mother had said all she wished to and stared at her father until he stood up again, brushed the traces of earth from the back of his

148

jacket, and got to work. He bent down to examine the man who had been dead for approximately half an hour, if I know anything about the recently deceased.

"I can see that the blow was delivered with some force," he began, presumably to have something to say, as this was true of most murders where a sharp, or indeed blunt, instrument had delivered the fatal blow. "From the location of the wound, and the position of the body, I would imagine that he was not killed here, but closer to the entrance of the greenhouse."

A rosy-cheeked constable had been guarding the door and was evidently listening as I heard a quiet, "He's right!" before he pointed at what I could only imagine were traces of blood on the ground.

"Which means that he was not expecting the attack." Grandfather became more animated the longer he spoke, and now moved down the long aisle to take in more of the scene. "It's also possible, however, that, in dragging his victim out of sight of the doorway, the killer stained his clothes. We must take note of any of our suspects who have changed since we last saw them."

"Afraid not, gov," the same helpful constable responded as he held up a large white gardener's apron that was stained with a thick red streak on top of the usual marks from leaves and earth. "Looks like he covered himself up before moving the body."

Grandfather clicked his fingers in disappointment, and I thought to ask a pertinent question.

"Why did he decide to move it in the first place?" I had hoped I might summon an answer to my own question, but nothing came to mind.

Grandfather glanced around the room without speaking, and it would fall to my mother to fathom a solution. "It seems to me that he wanted us to find his victim, but not too quickly. Wouldn't you say, Father?"

He clicked his fingers again but more optimistically this time. It really was impressive that he could invest so much meaning in a simple gesture. "That's just it. Having committed the crime, he would have needed time to get back to the house. But as you say, Violet, he wanted us to know what he'd done. There are several gardeners working here, and one of them reported what he'd found when he came back from his lunch break."

"But why would he want the body found?" the constable asked, and we all turned to look at him. He instantly went a shade greener about the gills, as he realised that no one had expected him to contribute to the conversation.

I thought my grandfather might have taught him the importance of only speaking when it's necessary – as that is the kind of thing he always tells me. He was nicer than I expected, though, and went to put one hand on the young policeman's shoulder.

"Yes indeed, why?" He gave it an appreciative squeeze, then began to pace in his usual contemplative manner. "Of course, the question of *why* is the very thing that has perplexed me since Alicia first explained the situation here yesterday. Why would the killer creep about, moving things around? Why would he steal something with no great value when there are priceless treasures on display? Why kill a boy who, as far as we know, had little connection to the rest of the group?"

"You're taking it for granted that Eric Uhland isn't the killer then," I told him. "If you're looking for an explanation, why don't we start with him?"

Grandfather clicked his fingers yet again. Three times in quick succession was a little excessive in my book, but it would be his last of the day, so I could let him off.

"That is exactly what we will do, Christopher. Let us interview our final suspect."

CHAPTER TWENTY-TWO

I imagine that Mother was tired of missing out on the excitement of the investigation, as she left Delilah to look after Alicia in her place. I'm sure our hostess appreciated the dear creature's cheery disposition, and at least it kept Delilah out of the house.

"Chrissy," my name carried across to me from the far corner of the garden as we left the greenhouse and turned towards the orchard. "Chrissy, over here!" I recognised Veronica's voice and soon saw her waving from a window that appeared to have been cut into the garden wall.

"See whether she knows anything, my boy," Grandfather muttered, as he put his arm through Mother's, and they commenced their slow stroll back to the house. "We'll go to the workshop first. Catch up with us there."

With her father's crisis of confidence apparently now over, Mother smirked at his superior tone. He was a dear mad fellow, and we loved him to pieces. It was only fair that, just shy of seventy-eight years old, he should be allowed to indulge his eccentricities from time to time.

Not wishing to miss the interview with our new chief suspect, I hurried to see what the girls were doing. Their mother was sitting on a garden bench, hugging Delilah on one side and Dione on the other. It was hard to know who appreciated the attention more between the little girl and the golden retriever. The owner of Parham House looked quite stoic as she peered in my direction. If I had known her any better, I would have promised that everything would work out for the best, but instead I gazed back at her as sympathetically as I could.

Behind her was a rather appealing sight in the midst of all that woe. I had never seen such an elaborate Wendy House before, but I had to assume that was what it was. It was flush with the brick wall that surrounded the garden and half-covered with the same species of yet flowerless wisteria that grew on the southern façade of the main building. The playhouse really was ever so pretty, with two portholes and a balcony on the first floor and contrasting brick lintels over the lower windows. I was certain that I would have greatly enjoyed playing there when I was younger, and I can't deny that I still felt the pull to venture within.

The first thing I saw inside was Lavinia lying on her back on a small sofa with her hand to her head, but the interior of the miniature house was also quite remarkable.

"Don't mind her," Veronica told me from her position on a bare wooden gallery above my head. She had to lean over the railing as the ceiling was so low and, even aged twelve, she could no longer stand at her full height. "My sister doesn't have the stomach for dead bodies. She once had to leave halfway through our trip to the opera because she was scared of the Valkyries. She's nothing like me."

To prove this, she bravely shot down from the platform on a rickety staircase. The main area held a Welsh dresser covered with small china figurines of clowns, animals and elegant ladies. There was a fireplace for the winter and not a great deal else.

"Have you found the killer?" she asked in a whisper, presumably so as not to disturb Lavinia any more than she already had.

"No, not yet," I confessed. "But Grandfather is here, and it will only be a matter of time. He may not be having his best day ever, but he's especially effective after he's calmed down from one of his poultry-flutters."

She became wistful then and gazed through the doorway. "How fascinating. Dione is much the same, but I thought that such behaviour was restricted to the under-tens."

I considered telling her that I'd known many adults who would get into a flap when things didn't go their way. Indeed, several murderers we'd apprehended had taken such behaviour to a violent extreme. The world would be a much better place if we learnt from an early age to inhale deeply, take a good look at ourselves, and realise how silly we were being when flustered – though it might put mystery novelists and police inspectors out of their jobs.

"Have you discovered anything important?" I asked, having long since decided not to underestimate the intelligent young lady before me, even if she was dressed as Captain Hook at the time. I should probably have mentioned before that Lavinia was wearing a Peter Pan costume and Dione had wire and tissue-paper wings strapped to her back.

152

"That's difficult to say. But I spotted Raymond Carbonell hanging about the place. He was walking away from the duck pond a little while ago, presumably around the time that the last man was killed."

Lavinia released a tortured groan, and I hurried to set her mind at ease. "I'm afraid that's not proof he was to blame. He was over there talking to my grandfather. I can't really say why Lord Edgington thought it necessary to take him so far from the house. To tell the truth, I struggle to understand half of the things he does."

"Adults are strange," Veronica said with a note of resignation. "Eric Uhland was in the garden as well. But he's often over here. He was given permission to use one of the old wooden sheds for his work."

"I don't suppose you saw him carrying a metal spike at any point?"

Veronica shook her head, and her sister covered her ears.

"No, there was no spike. I saw the twins going for a walk towards the lake, though. Why they would spend any time together when they argue so much is a mystery to me. If I didn't like Lavinia and Dione, I would simply stop talking to them."

I was about to ask her about Mark Isaac himself when her mother suddenly called out. "Veronica, Lavinia, you must come now, please. I've made a decision."

Despite her distressed state and general lethargy, the middle child quickly followed her older sister out of the Wendy House to obey their mother. I had no wish to intrude but went after them all the same.

"Children, I don't believe it's safe for you here any longer. You'll go with your nanny to a hotel in Worthing and stay there until Lord Edgington has finished his work."

Dione only extracted one important detail from this announcement. "You mean that we're going to the seaside? I like the seaside."

Veronica looked less happy on the matter and began to complain as I slipped away through the orchard and back towards the house. I heard a shout of, "But I'm twelve, Mother. I'm not an infant anymore." I could only assume that such appeals would fall on deaf ears, and it appeared that my young helper would not be the one to solve the case after all.

I hurried along past dipping pools and curious stone sculptures before reaching the path that followed the wall around the property. I reached the workshop just as Grandfather and my mother arrived there. It was deserted, which wasn't the worst outcome we could have imagined.

Grandfather immediately walked over to Uhland's table where Mark Isaac had been working the last time we'd seen him. He touched its surface and rubbed the paint that came away on his fingers. I looked at the breastplate of a suit of armour on the opposite desk before examining a pile of coins in Lockhart's corner. They did not seem particularly relevant to our investigation, but then Mother found something more useful.

"There's a note on the floor." She pointed but didn't bend down to touch it. "It says, 'I'll see you in the garden after two o'clock.' It may have been on this table but fallen off when the door opened, and the breeze came inside."

I walked over to her and peered down at the scrap of paper, but Grandfather stayed right where he was.

"It has the same flecks of red paint that are visible on the tabletop," Mother continued. "Do you think—?"

Grandfather interrupted before she could make any supposition of her own. "I think we'll have to ask each suspect for a sample of their handwriting."

"Surely only Uhland would have left such a note without putting his name to it," I concluded. "We saw no sign of any interaction between Isaac and any of the others. He assigned to help Eric Uhland as part of his studies."

"That may all be true, Christopher. But until we talk to the others, it's impossible to say whether he was doing extra work for Dr Carbonell, carrying out a clandestine task for Elton Lockhart, or he'd struck up a friendship with one of the Horniman twins. There are many possible explanations, and we will rely on facts alone to determine which is the right one."

"Fine, but you must admit that there is a good chance Uhland knows something." I moved around the table to address him as he picked up the note and put it safely in his waistcoat pocket.

Grandfather walked right past me but turned around as he got to the door. "I will admit that he is the first person to whom we must now speak." He motioned for his daughter to follow him and then disappeared outside. So that was anticlimactic.

CHAPTER TWENTY-THREE

With a little help from Mr Cridland, who had finished his ironing and was now busy filling ink wells, we found Eric Uhland in his room in the service buildings. The gatehouse with the pretty white clocktower, which we'd driven through when we arrived, was terribly grand to be used for servants' quarters and a laundry range, but that's what it contained. It was also where Grandfather's staff had been sleeping and, while the rest of the experts were lodging in the main house, Uhland and Isaac had chosen to be there. I very much doubted that sleeping in those cell-like rooms with neighbours packed in close on either side could be more peaceful than the arrangements in the main house, and I was already suspicious of our next suspect.

"Good afternoon, Mr Uhland," Grandfather began. "I'm afraid something terrible has occurred."

"What is it?" Uhland was washing his hands in a small sink in the corner of the room when we arrived. From his tousled grey hair and the state of the bedclothes, he appeared to have had a nap. "What's the matter?"

My mother was terribly good at choosing the right words to suit any occasion and even Grandfather deferred to her at this moment. "It's your assistant Mark Isaac. One of the gardeners found his body in the greenhouse and reported it to the police on duty. We believe he was murdered within the last hour."

"Murdered?" If he was to blame, he was a better actor than I would have predicted. For a man who showed alarmingly little emotion in conversation, his face was suddenly a picture of distress. "But why would anyone hurt Mark? He had no connections here, and he was a thoroughly nice person from what I knew of him."

"What did you know of him?" Grandfather said to get the interview started in earnest.

I would like to say that Uhland turned pale on receiving the news, but he was a bloodless chap at the best of times. He leaned against the plain white wall and practically blended into the background.

His eyes darted about as he attempted to answer. "He was a promising student at the university where I work."

"And where would that be?"

He cleared his throat in that infuriatingly self-important manner of his. "I work at both Leeds University and the Leeds School of Art." I wondered whether he was a touch embarrassed not to be affiliated with one of the loftiest British universities, seeing as he had told us so pompously of his renown in his field.

"So Isaac was a student of history?" Mother put forward and Uhland squirmed again.

"No, no. He studied fine art, but he was a quick learner and had a real appetite to know about my work. That's why I agreed to his coming here with me to *Parham Park*." He pronounced these last two words proudly, breaking his usual monotone as if the prestige of the estate burnished his own reputation.

"Had you worked on previous assignments together?" Grandfather was resting on the bedside table. There was only one chair in the small room and that had been offered to my mother as, I can only assume, women's legs tire more easily than men's. That's a joke, by the way. Some of the strongest people I know are women and they can go any length of time without needing to sit down.

"No, no." Our suspect was just as nervous as he'd looked when he'd discovered that he was dining with a famous detective. He kept threading his fingers together to flex them, then reversing the movement, only to repeat it again. "I've only known him for a short period, and this is the first time I've involved him in my work."

"Do you know anything about his background?"

"Well, I know that his family are from the north. I believe his father is a merchant of some description. I don't remember what he sells. I doubt it is pertinent to the case." Even when answering basic questions, he sounded arrogant. Alongside his sheer lack of charisma, it was an unbearable combination.

"You're an expert on paintings, isn't that correct?" Grandfather often asked questions to which he already knew the answers in order to unsettle our suspects, and he was doing it now.

"Yes, and Elizabethan art in particular. That was why I was so excited to be in Parham House. I would never have been able to access the pieces I was brought in to assess if they had remained in Chatterton Hall. I jumped at the chance when I heard the news that they had been sold."

There was a flash of excitement in Grandfather's eyes. "So you specifically asked to come here?"

If Uhland realised that this information might cast him in a bad light, he hid it well. "That's right. I wrote to the Pearsons to offer my services when I heard about their plans."

"And why did you feel you needed an assistant?" Mother asked, and he took a step or two back from us. She was a softly spoken woman, not known for striking fear into people, but it was clear that something had put the wind up him.

"In a perfect world, it is always best to have… assistance and, indeed, assistants." He sounded like me, waffling on when I didn't know what to say. "Mark was a bright young man, and I thought he could learn a lot by observing me."

"Did you give him any special tasks to fulfil?" Grandfather's question instantly recaptured Uhland's attention.

"I would not use the word special." He seemed to relax just a fraction as he saw the opportunity to bore us on a topic he knew well. "I did ask him to analyse a few key works from the collection to see whether he might detect signs of later amendments that had been made. It is also true that I gave him the responsibility of collecting paintings from the storeroom beside the workshop and, indeed, returning them when they were not required. In instances when he… blah blah blah. Drone, drone, drone!"

At some point, I stopped listening to the blue boring stodger. He had sent me into a trance, and I had to wonder whether it was a gift he had developed for such occasions. Just imagine for one moment that he turned out to be a savage killer who travelled the length of Britain with his work, murdering left, right and centre to obtain the portraits he was studying; how effective would it be to debilitate any person who came to suspect him by inspiring in them a feeling of pure, unadulterated ennui? I know this might sound farfetched, but you were not in that bedroom with him.

"Have you ever been arrested for a crime?" Grandfather asked to shock the man and wake me up.

"A crime?" Uhland sounded as though someone had stamped on his foot as he replied. When upset, he became even more pompous. "I'm an historian, not some seedy malefactor. I have never been convicted of a crime, and I resent you even asking such a question."

Grandfather shifted his weight but kept his eyes on his prey. "I would have thought that was a very fair question in the circumstances. I am a detective; you are a suspect in the murder of your associate. It is only natural I should wish to know of your criminal past." He was ever so good at making such phrases sound quite innocent whilst going out of his way to imply the opposite.

"Very well. Then the answer is no. I have never been convicted of a crime."

I wasn't the only one to notice that he had repeated the same exact phrase.

Grandfather practically jumped upon it. "Which I take to mean that you were suspected of committing one but not convicted for it?"

He looked back and forth between the three of us. Mother couldn't hide a fraction of a smile, but Grandfather remained quite sombre.

"I…" He needed a deep breath before continuing. "You can ask anyone I know, and they will tell you of my fine character and excellent reputation."

"However…" I said when he wouldn't.

"However, if you search back through my long and storied career, you may uncover an episode in which a misunderstanding between a colleague and myself led to certain…" He sought a phrase that would not sound too bad. "…negative perceptions of my behaviour. It was quickly resolved, and no charges were forthcoming."

For a man who had, but moments before, been extolling his excellent reputation, this was something of a fall from grace. I had to wonder what he had done to get himself in such a situation, but Grandfather seemed to know instinctively.

"I can imagine what sort of allegations they would be in your line of work. Were they true?"

It's an odd thing to see such a limp, uninspiring person become incensed. You expect a firework to go off, but instead there's the brief sputter of a match lighting.

"They said that I'd confirmed the identity of a painting, the provenance of which was disputed, in order to gain from its sale at auction."

"What was the painting?"

"It was a miniature by Nicholas Hilliard." He took his thick glasses off at this moment to polish them. "He was a favourite of Queen Elizabeth's."

Grandfather evidently wasn't comfortable perching on that table, so he rose as he replied. "Yes, thank you. I know who Nicholas Hilliard was. Did you inflate the value of the painting?"

Uhland emitted a second short flare of anger. It was another real squib. "I've already told you; I was innocent." He put his hand to his head and rubbed both temples in small circles. "It is really very taxing to have to listen to this."

"It is really very taxing to be murdered," I said without meaning to but, as I'd started, I decided to keep going. "Tell me, why were you and Mr Isaac the only ones who refused rooms in the main house?"

"I am not the most sociable person, and I decided it would be better to have a little more peace and quiet."

"Yes, that's what the butler told us, and it would make a lot more sense if you were actually on your own here. I know what our staff get up to together in their quarters every Friday night. It is less than peaceful, and this is not a place I would choose to sleep."

"I wasn't to know that, though, was I?" He had a saggy face for a man of around fifty, and his chins wobbled indignantly. "Are you suggesting that my choice of bedroom is a sign of my capacity to kill a young man of whom I was actually rather fond?"

"Come, come, Mr Uhland." Grandfather stepped forward and put both hands on the man's broad shoulders. It was good to see him back to his intimidating best. "There's no need to be upset. I'm certain that you want us to find the person who is responsible for murdering your assistant."

He hesitated before answering. "Well, of course I do, though I would rather you did so without sullying my very good name."

It was funny how desperate he was to remind us of his flawless reputation – even if we'd learnt that it was not as flawless as he'd first suggested and, in actual fact, flawless was the wrong word altogether. While he'd made a career for himself in academia, it was hard to believe that there was no smoke without at least a spark or two.

"Of course you would." Grandfather was suddenly more expressive. "So the next thing you must tell us is whose handwriting this is." He poked two gloved fingers into his waistcoat pocket and extracted the note before placing it on his palm to show Uhland.

The ever-so-respected yet dubious expert donned his thick glasses to read it in a whisper. "'I'll see you in the garden after two o'clock.'" He gulped noisily before saying anything more. "Well... you see... How can I put it?"

"Who wrote the note?" I can be quite impatient at times with unhelpful witnesses.

He was shaking as he answered. "As it happens, that was me. I wrote it for Mark a few days ago. I left it on his desk in the workshop."

"And what exactly were you doing in the shed in the garden?" I growled again.

He did well not to collapse out of fear of his steely interrogator. "Nothing suspicious in the slightest." His hands linked and decoupled once more. "We simply needed somewhere to store our materials."

Mother looked particularly impressed by my work, whereas Grandfather smiled magnanimously. "Mr Uhland, you'll be happy to know that you've told me all I need to for the time being, and we will not bother you again until later."

This only made him more nervous. "I didn't kill him. I didn't kill poor Isaac."

"You have been most helpful." Mother's tone was light and cheery like her father's. "Now you mustn't worry about anything else, as we will solve the case in no more than a pig's whisper."

The two of them led Eric Uhland to the exit and left him there, which meant I had to squeeze past to get through the door. "Thank you, Mr Uhland. You've been a great help."

CHAPTER TWENTY-FOUR

If the truth be told, I wasn't clear what had just happened, but the two other members of my family were overjoyed.

"Oh, what a pompous prig," Mother declared once we'd passed through the stable yard, away from the clocktower. "I do hope he turns out to be the killer. I've rarely met such an immediately disagreeable individual."

"Oh?" Grandfather's eyebrows worked their way up his forehead in jerking increments. "I thought he was rather wonderful. His thoughts were transparent on his face, and he entirely failed to hide his secrets. If only all suspects were so easy to manipulate."

Mother smiled for a moment before presumably remembering the sad situation that had led us to Uhland's spartan room.

"You were wonderful, my darling," Grandfather told her, and then he turned to me. "As were you, my dear grandson. And you were right in your identification of Mr Uhland as a genuine suspect. I will always listen to you from this moment forth."

I did not believe this but thanked him, nonetheless. "Thank you, Grandfather." You see?

His good cheer faded in an eyewink. "And now, I'm even more convinced that the answer to everything that has happened lies within Clive Pearson's catalogue of the treasures of Parham House."

I was concerned that he was sticking so closely to this one idea. "Don't you think we should investigate avenues that lie beyond the potential theft?"

"You're absolutely right, Christopher," he said, sticking to his promise (for the moment). "And here comes Inspector Kirk to help us do just that."

I couldn't tell what marque it was, but the little black car that rolled in behind us looked like a Box Brownie camera on wheels. It was hard to imagine the inspector driving any other vehicle. There was something comical about him – though he'd never told a joke in my presence – and a man like him deserved a funny little car.

"I'm so sorry," he called as he hurried out to us, with pie crumbs flying in all directions. "I should never have left. I don't know what I was thinking."

"Don't worry, Inspector," Grandfather told him. "I very much doubt that you could have done anything to disrupt the killer's plan."

"But a second body?" Kirk said in dismay. "I can't believe it. I've waited half my life for another murder to investigate, and then I get two in the space of a day."

"Hang around long enough and you might get a third," I replied in a whisper that was meant for me alone. Of course, Grandfather's ridiculously fine-tuned ears caught my comment, and he dispatched a frown in my direction.

"Perhaps you should have a look at the scene of the crime while my family and I continue our study," he told the inspector instead of swatting me about the back of the head.

Kirk must have heard the details of what had happened from his subordinates, as he turned towards the gardens with a nod.

"Is that really it, Grandfather?" I sounded disappointed, which was exactly how I felt.

"Is what 'it', Christopher? I do wish you would be less vague in your speech."

"Is that all you're going to do?" I replied. "Another man has been murdered, and your only course of action is to return to your previous occupation?"

Something in his bearing reminded me of a superior priest I'd once known. "What would you suggest, boy? Supposing that one of our main suspects was involved in Isaac's death, is he likely to admit it if we interview them again? Except for Uhland, they have no apparent connection to the man, and if they do, the inspector and his officers will discover it. I intend to dedicate my time to something which is beyond their remit."

"I'm sorry, Christopher." My mother walked over to show that she cared – even if she didn't agree with my ideas. "I'm afraid that Father's right. Mark Isaac must have discovered something that he was better off not knowing. To stop the killer, we must prevent him from carrying out his plan. And to do that, we must work out what it is he wants."

I was amazed by their singlemindedness, especially as Grandfather had always taught me that we must not become fixed on one solution to a crime when a million different possibilities exist. I opened my mouth to tell him just this, but he had already turned away. I wanted to ask whether Uhland really was the killer, or whether someone had placed the existing note we'd found on Isaac's worktable to get him to the greenhouse. I wanted to, but the words refused to come.

I might well have followed them to the library and stared at descriptions of old portraits and vases until I fell asleep, but then something reminded me that there was a job I could still do without them. The sound of the Horniman twins squabbling nearby underlined the fact that there was a whole parallel case to investigate, which my grandfather had largely ignored.

For one thing, I'd caught Lockhart in a lie. He'd claimed to be with Frances when Mr Stanton was killed. Frances said she was alone, and Vyvyan said she was with Lockhart. At least one of them was dealing in falsehoods – unless the antiquarian had got his paramours' names muddled. I once called our dog Mother by accident, so I concede that it's easily done.

Rather than confront them on the matter, I followed the women's voices back towards the gardens. They were on the other side of the wall from me at first, but I ducked through the doorway beside the clocktower and pursued them at a distance. I couldn't make out what they were saying, but there was a lot of poking, shoving and barging going on, and they clearly weren't happy with one another. From what I could tell, they blamed each other for… something and were angry because of… that same thing. I didn't risk getting any closer in case they spotted me.

They didn't walk towards the garden as I had expected, but turned away from the house and through a number of trees that were spaced out around the walls of the orchard. It was now much easier to hide, and I ran a little faster to crouch behind one of the beeches. To be totally honest with you, I was hoping I might overhear a confession, but when had we ever been so lucky on one of our cases?

"I'm not going to argue around in circles," Vyvyan (or possibly Frances) complained.

"You're only saying that because you know I'm right," Frances (or possibly Vyvyan) replied. It was not so easy to tell them apart from behind, especially as they had changed their clothes since I'd last seen them.

"You are never right, Frances." Ah ha! I was correct after all. "You live in a state of perpetual fallacy."

There was some more pushing at this point as the debonair and intelligent young women reverted to childish ways. They stopped when they emerged from the trees and came to an immediate halt.

"Oh, I'm sorry." Frances evidently wasn't expecting whatever she found there. "We're looking for Elton Lockhart. I don't suppose you've seen him?"

I ran to another tree trunk so as to get a better view. My grandfather's elderly footman, Halfpenny, was sitting with our maid, Dorie, and our cook, Henrietta, on the banks of a much larger lake than the first I'd visited. Each had an easel and canvas before them, and there was a large supply of art materials laid out on a table nearby. They looked just as bewildered by the intrusion as the sisters were to find them there.

"Mr Lockhart?" Halfpenny replied, scratching his sideburns and having a good think as he did so. "That wouldn't be the chap who roams about the place in riding boots looking like a hero from one of Mrs Radcliffe's novels?"

This reference must have proven a little dated for the sisters, but Frances shrugged and confirmed the general idea. "Yes, that's the chap. We've been looking for him for some time. There's been another murder, and we'd like to make sure that he's all right."

Dorie, who had been concentrating on the easel in front of her, turned to glance at the newcomers. "We've had nothing but peace and quiet until you two came along," she said in her typically gruff manner.

"Then we're sorry to bother you." Vyvyan looked embarrassed, and the pair of them walked off towards the walled garden, squabbling once more as they went.

I angled myself around the tree to make sure they didn't see me and, once they'd left, broke my cover to find out what our faithful employees were doing there. They had returned to their painting but, after a few seconds, an enormous laugh broke from Cook.

"Silly girls," she said, though I couldn't understand what had inspired such a comment.

"They haven't the brains they was born with," Dorie added.

Halfpenny just grinned, and I looked about the scene, hoping to interpret what had just happened. The only unusual thing I noticed was a fourth unfinished canvas that was lying on the ground not so far from them. It was enough for me to fill in the blanks.

"You can come out now, Mr Lockhart," I called, which shocked the painters for a moment, until they burst out laughing again.

CHAPTER TWENTY-FIVE

"Master Prentiss," our dear old footman said as he climbed to his feet. He was a formal sort and was never truly off duty. "We weren't being cruel, it's just that—"

"I asked them to do it," Lockhart had been hiding behind a small summer house on the other side of the lake. It was made of the same sandstone as the main building and had three elegant French windows on the front with white wooden muntins. None of which is important, of course, but I think it is a testament to the wonders of that remarkably diverse estate that even the lake was artistically embellished.

"I thought as much," I told the suspect as he strode closer. "Were you hiding from the Horniman twins?"

He sat down on the steep bank that led down to the lake and took up his canvas. He held it in his hand as he searched around for his brush and palette in the long grass.

"Something like that, yes." He gave a rather boyish laugh and explained. "I hope you don't think poorly of me, Christopher, but after all that's happened, I needed time to think. It's rather difficult to do that when everyone expects something from me."

By the end of the sentence, his amusement had gone, and he looked exhausted. I sat down on the ground next to him and, although the grass was still a touch damp from that morning's dew, it felt good to stretch my legs out in front of me and lean back on my elbows, as if I were on my summer holiday. At first, I didn't even want to talk, and it occurred to me that I knew just how he felt.

"I must admit, it is tiring to always be moving and never get the chance to stand still," I eventually told him, though this was perhaps insensitive within earshot of our hardworking staff. "I think it's important to do nothing from time to time."

Lockhart replied with a silent nod. He looked across the lake to where a clutch of herons was standing in the water in front of the far bank. Just behind them, there was a line of tall trees with nests dotted about them. There must have been thirty birds visible with who knows how many more in the making. I'd never seen such a large heronry. My grandfather was happy when a single pair had made their home at

Cranley one year, even if they remained childless.

It was just this sort of unfocused thinking for which I rarely had the time, and I enjoyed the silence that punctuated our conversation.

"I understand why you lied now," I told him. "Why you said you were with Frances, and why Vyvyan said she was with you. It was only Frances who was telling the truth, though, wasn't it? She said she was alone when the nightwatchman died."

"Ahh…" He didn't look at me but selected a pot of paint from the box beside him and poured out a blob of dark green. "I was hoping you wouldn't realise. (You see, I was the one who killed him.)" Fine, he didn't say this second sentence, but the fearful look on his face suggested it for half a moment before he explained. "The truth is that I hoped you'd ask Frances whether I was with her, and she would say yes out of loyalty."

"My grandfather taught me too well for that. I would never say, 'Were you with this person?' to confirm an alibi. I simply asked her where she was, and she didn't know that she was supposed to lie. Vyvyan, on the other hand, saw an opportunity to help you and claimed that you were not only together, but awake when the chloroform got the better of Mr Stanton and he screamed the house down."

"Foiled again! I knew I should have said Vyvyan and not her sister," he said with a frown. "Does this mean you're here to arrest me?"

I admit that I briefly questioned whether I'd made a mistake in not bringing a constable with me. "I don't actually have the authority to… Even if I'd been planning… Or rather, no. I'm not here to accuse you of the crime again. I think I know why you didn't tell us the truth in the first place."

"It's those girls," he said in a sad voice to confirm my theory. "You know, when I met them last year, I thought I was in heaven. They are the two most intelligent, beguiling and brilliant women I've ever encountered, and I couldn't choose which I liked best. And then they told me that I didn't have to choose, and that they were both so in love with me they would willingly share. That was the moment I passed through heaven and entered a whole new realm for which there isn't a name. I couldn't believe my luck, but it didn't last long."

His usual slickness was absent as he offered a glimpse at the amazed, perhaps even naïve being at his core. "When I'm alone with

168

either of them, it's normally rather wonderful. But as soon as the two of them are together, they fight over me like chickens with a bag of grain. I thought I'd found the ideal situation that any man would want but—"

"I don't want two sweethearts," I was quick to interrupt. "I would not only settle for just one, I'd honestly prefer such an arrangement. All my favourite interactions with people have occurred when there are two of us alone together. Whether it was with my mother, grandfather, or the girl I once kissed who soon stopped returning my letters, those moments would have been different if a third person had been there to spoil it."

He threw his brush down, and his impetuousness returned. "You don't understand, man."

"Yes, I do," I snapped. "You are like a little boy who has been left to stuff his face with cake and now wants everyone to feel sorry for him because he's feeling sick. Believe me, Lockhart, I understand."

He turned to look at me face on. "Have you ever been in love, Christopher? Have you ever felt as though your insides have turned to fire and you'll have to jump in a lake to soothe the pain?"

I was about to mention my first and only kiss again when I realised that the correct answer to his question was "No. As a matter of fact, I haven't. I've met several very lovely young ladies, but as they were suspects in murder investigations or they'd recently lost a loved one to a madman's knife, the chance of love passed me by." I reflected on this for a moment before adding another thought. "My brother, on the other hand, has fallen in love any number of times. With each girl he meets, the result is a little more calamitous than the last. He claims to have given up on love entirely now, and I hope that is true, as he will surely end up dead or in gaol if he returns to his former ways."

"That is exactly it, Mr Prentiss. You are wise beyond your years. If only people like me and your brother could know in advance just how stupidly we will act around the fairer sex, then maybe there wouldn't be so many problems in the world."

I couldn't totally follow this logic and, aware that he was still feeling sorry for himself, I decided to return us to the more pressing issue of where he had been in the middle of the night.

"You told my grandfather that you were with Frances, and you weren't. Vyvyan told us you were with her, and you weren't. So where were you really when Stanton was killed?"

He breathed out as though he'd taken a drag on a cigarette and then seized his brush to dip it in oily green paint. "I was alone. It's as simple as that. I told the twins that I needed to stay up all night working, and then I hid in my bedroom as soon as they'd gone to sleep. I just wanted some time to myself, and so I lied to them. I knew that, if I'd told them the truth, they would have tried their hardest to convince me otherwise, and so I lied."

"That doesn't explain why you wouldn't admit it when you spoke to my grandfather. He's a more understanding man than the stories about him in the newspapers suggest."

He shook his head, clearly frustrated by my lack of comprehension as he dragged the brush across the canvas in order to create the outline of the trees in the distance. "You're not listening. I'm telling you that I lied because of them. Two lies and two twins to match my two faces. I lied to them by saying I would be up late working. I lied to Lord Edgington because I didn't want it getting back to Vyvyan and Frances that I'd lied in the first place."

There was something unusual about his painting. It wasn't quite the world in front of us, and yet it was unmistakably the same place. It was as if he was viewing the world through a different kind of lens from the rest of us, and it made the shapes before him hazy and imprecise. I don't know a great deal about art of the modern day (or of the past, for that matter), but I liked what he'd created.

"That surely wasn't the only reason," I replied just as soon as I stopped being distracted. "You lied to Grandfather because you needed an alibi. You couldn't admit to being alone, as you thought it would land you in trouble."

He stabbed his brush into the paint again and then flicked a splash of green onto his composition. "Very well, there was that, too. It's just as I said at dinner last night; people don't know who I really am. They want me to act up and play the scoundrel. I imagined that a man like your grandfather would think badly of me no matter what. I was sure I would be the first name on his list, and I couldn't risk that, so I lied." He leaned forward to wash off his brush in a small glass jar before selecting a grey from his palette to blend into the block of colour he'd already painted. "Send for the inspector, if you must, because I'm tired of lying. But most of all, I'm tired of having to explain myself."

I wouldn't let him escape so easily and was ready with my next question. "I will not trouble you much longer, but there is something I must know. You admitted that you stole Raymond Carbonell's fiancée, and he told the same tale. He also said that he holds no ill will against you. Can both things really be true?"

He held his brush up to measure the distances between the different parts of the landscape before him. "You know, I think it probably is. For all that has passed between us, my old friend generally treats me rather well. Better than most people, at least. I suppose he's like a brother in that respect. He wasn't happy after all that business in Yorkshire when I was erroneously accused of theft, but for the most part, he's been a good egg. I was beastly to him when we were younger, but he must have come to see that if Eliza – that was the girl's name – if Eliza was so willing to betray him, then it was a good thing she did it before they were married."

He stopped his work for a moment and bit his lip. "I've never felt so guilty about anything in my life as I did in that moment. It took him two whole years to recover after he called off the engagement. He really was in a terrible state but, for some silly reason, he never truly blamed me for what I did. If the truth be told, I wish that he had. It's a lot easier to feel I'm in the right when someone's screaming his head off at me. I'm used to adversity; it's kindness that confounds me."

Elton Lockhart was as much a puzzle as the one that the case had presented. He was a famously debonair rake who had a girl (or two) in every port and had travelled the world in search of adventure. And yet, there he was before me, his eyes glistening as he recalled the harm he had done to a former friend. He was clearly a complicated character, and I didn't know what to make of him.

To fill the fragile silence, I chattered about nothing. "I've come to see over the last few years that it is a mistake to assume that other people's lives are easier than our own. I've met dukes who believed their servants lived an idyllic existence and poor men who would kill to spend a night in a palace. I don't think you can be truly content unless you're happy with who you are."

For some reason, this made him more animated. "You've hit the nail on the head there, Christopher. That is human existence, neatly summarised in three short sentences. I'm tired of feeling sorry for myself. Tired of complaining because two beautiful women are fighting over me. I'm a bad person, and I don't deserve either of them." He pushed the palette and canvas off his lap and stood up in one quick movement. "Thank you. I truly appreciate everything you've said." He seemed to direct this comment not just at me, but at the three painters further up the bank.

With a cheerful look on his face, he turned and ran off through the trees as fast as his feet would carry him. I sat there in something of a daze, now confident that the man I had just bored with my thoughts on life, love and human existence was either a psychotic killer or a thoroughly misunderstood individual.

CHAPTER TWENTY-SIX

I realised after he'd left that I hadn't asked him a single question about the death of Mark Isaac, but that would have to wait. First, I had some art appreciation in which to indulge. It was an odd feeling to go from the intensity of the previous conversation to a friendly chat with the staff from Cranley Hall.

"Oh, that's very good, Halfpenny," I told our footman, and he tapped his canvas proudly. His painting was a surprisingly accurate depiction of the scene before us.

"Yours too, Henrietta," I said as I moved on to see the work she had done. Her use of colour was very impressive, and I felt that she had either been given some tips by my grandfather – who liked to consider himself something of an artist – or she'd ignored those tips (because he wasn't very good) and found a style of her own.

"And Dorie, what can I say?" I looked at the maid's composition and struggled to know what I thought of it. On the one hand, she had a good eye, and her use of perspective was strong. However, I was less sure how I felt about the sea monster peeking out of the lake to eat the herons, or the dragon in the sky overhead.

"I like to imagine what the world would be like if we were overrun with monsters," she explained.

"Well, it is certainly very creative. Well done."

My grandfather must have lent them his collection of art materials, as there were boxes of paints, bottles of turpentine, and brushes spread out on the table and the ground beneath it. It was nice to see them enjoying themselves, and I once again questioned whether their master brought so many members of staff with him wherever we went so that he could give them a break from their everyday duties, or he simply enjoyed being pampered.

On the way back through the garden, I went to see whether the Pearsons were still there, but the Wendy House was empty. I did find Veronica's notebook on the dresser inside, which I decided would be safer back in the nursery. I read it as I followed the path for what I hoped would be the last time that day. It was full of wonderful lines like, "As Raymond Carbonell is presumably a Doctor of History, would that have made it easier for him to purchase chloroform, or would one have to be a Doctor of Medicine?" and "How many dead bodies are required before a series of murders can be described as a massacre?" and "Why was Eric Uhland calling Mark Isaac's name from the greenhouse shortly before he died?"

I was almost back at the house when I read this last one, and I immediately felt light-headed. "Grandfather!" I called, though he could have been anywhere, and it was silly to think that he might—

"Quick, boy." He stuck his head out of the library window to interrupt my thoughts. "Come in here immediately. I've found the very thing for which we have been searching. It wasn't the cup! I should have known it wasn't the cup."

He pulled the sash window closed, and I ran up the steps to open the door to the Saloon. In thirty seconds, I was there alongside him, but he was not alone. Mother, Todd, our hostess Alicia and our dog Delilah were gathered around the desk in the library where Grandfather was sitting before a large, framed painting.

"I knew it." He positively beamed up at me. "I told you, and you wouldn't listen."

"It's incredible, Lord Edgington," Alicia told him. "It's a real needle in a haystack, and you found it."

He pretended to be humble. "Really, it's nothing. Anyone with even a passing interest in Elizabethan art would know that this painting is not an original Robert Peake. I had noticed it before, of course, but assumed that it was an acknowledged reproduction."

I did not know the implications of anything he had just said, but I examined the painting in front of him through the eyes of a detective. It was a handsome portrait of a man standing beside an apple tree. He wore a shimmering gold doublet and pearl-white breeches. I'm really not the person to say with any authority, but judging from the composition of the picture, I didn't believe he was a king or prince but rather an important aristocrat.

"So, boy?" The old mastermind continued to grin at me. "What do you say now?"

"I say that there's a strong chance Eric Uhland is to blame for Mark Isaac's and, most likely, Michael Stanton's death."

"Oh," was all he could muster in reply and, rather than asking why

174

I would think this, Mother explained their discovery.

"We've come to the very same conclusion. Do you see what this is?" Thankfully, it was a rhetorical question. "The painting is a copy."

I came around the desk to view it from the right angle and it looked much like any of the other paintings on display in Parham House.

"You must focus on the type of paint that was used, Christopher." Grandfather spoke as if this was quite obvious. "Robert Peake the Elder, not his son or grandson, was famous for the bright colours he used in his paintings. He was a much-admired painter in the court of both Queen Elizabeth and her successor James I." He kept stopping as though he hoped I would fill in the relevant information. I knew as much about Robert Peake the Elder as I did about Robert Peake the Younger, which is to say, nothing at all.

"He was known for his paintings of not just royalty but courtiers and aristocrats of every stripe."

"Yes, but how does this help us solve a murder?"

Delilah looked a little sorry for my ignorance. Alicia smiled for the first time that day and Mother took me by the arm.

"You'll have to show him, Father," she said, moving me aside to make space to pull back his chair. "Explain it just as you did to us."

He went along with her plan and, having once more drawn my attention to the vibrance of the painting on the desk, which I believe I recognised as coming from the parlour where the recently acquired items were all on display, he led me to the Great Hall.

We gathered in front of the largest painting in the room, which showed a young man in elaborate dress with a feather in his hat. He was seated on a great white steed and had a whip in one hand and reins in the other.

"You'll remember that this is a portrait of Henry Frederick, the Prince of Wales," he assured me, and I chose not to contradict him. "Look at the colours, Christopher. Look at the detail."

I felt as though I were back at school again, in that I didn't have the first idea what anyone wanted me to say or do.

"I'm trying," I promised.

"What do you notice?" Mother asked, and she and Alicia looked hopeful that I would unlock the secret.

"This was also painted by Robert Peake." This was the only clue

Grandfather would provide, and then he stepped away from the painting.

Equally reminiscent of my time at school, it was clear that no one would give me the answer, and so I decided to have a good think. I walked a bit closer and craned my neck as I examined the design on the skirt of the prince's riding clothes. There were miniature scenes of a sunrise contained within it, and both his outfit and the immense fabric saddle upon which he rode were bordered with intricate patterns in gold, green and blue.

"It's magical," I said, as the beauty of the work before me was quite stirring. "It's almost as if it gives off a light. As if there is a bulb or flame behind each element of the portrait."

"He's got it!" Grandfather clapped his hands together – but he did not click his fingers. "That's the very thing, Chrissy. The very thing that told me that the painting in the library is not an original Robert Peake."

Rather than mumble a whole lot of nothing in his direction, I dashed back to the library to compare the two pictures. "I do see the difference," I said, as I lifted the frame to look at it in the light that came through the window behind me. "It doesn't have the same vibrance. The recreation of the scene is effective, and it is surely a thousand times more accomplished than anything we could paint, but there is something missing."

At first, Grandfather seemed troubled that I had denigrated his artistic skills, but he soon recovered. "That's the answer, Chrissy. Although, it is not just the vibrance, but the colours themselves. It is one thing to copy a great painting that is several hundred years old, and another altogether to recreate the materials that would have been used at the time. In the days of Elizabeth and James I, brightly coloured paints were an expensive commodity. They were created with the finest pigments that were collected from around the world. What we have before us may have been painted on an antique oaken board that resembles the canvases of the era. And it may use the same brush strokes and techniques that Robert Peake used, but the colours are less dazzling than the ones from his time. To make up for it, the artist has used slightly duller hues so as to give the impression that the painting has faded and dulled over time, but it's an amateurish trick and any expert would have spotted the difference."

I was pleased to see him back to his normal self and happy to form a conclusion at last.

"Eric Uhland is our culprit," we said at the exact same moment. Well, that's not quite true. Grandfather spoke half a second before me so that it sounded as if I were copying him.

Our hostess was not entirely convinced. "You haven't explained why he killed his own assistant, or why he did all those strange things that occurred before you arrived."

Alicia sat down in a leather armchair near the desk and prepared herself for Grandfather's interpretation of events. Though she was calmer than I had seen her until now, there was a certain strain in her voice which suggested that it would take some time for her fear to subside entirely.

Grandfather waited until we had all settled and watched his audience keenly to see how we would react. "Since we got here yesterday, I've had the sense that someone was creating a diversion, but I couldn't tell why. The broken vase and disappearing lions were not important enough to attract an art thief's attention, and the movement of the pictures in rooms across the house was evidently designed to confuse. As nothing of great value was missing, my mind turned to the possibility that the culprit wished to substitute one of the treasures on display for a forgery."

I finally understood why he had been so keen to hide away in the library with a pile of books rather than interview our suspects with me. I listened attentively as he explained his discovery.

"I knew that, by consulting the information that Clive and Alicia had compiled on the collection here, I would eventually be able to spot a discrepancy, and when I read Robert Peake's name, I had a sense of what must have happened. Let us imagine that Eric Uhland – who was previously suspected, lest we forget, of providing exaggerated valuations of certain paintings – came here knowing of the treasures he would find. He studied his selected artwork in detail in the workshop, and then, with the forgery created, he went to the Great Parlour last night to exchange it for the real one."

"We know that Uhland kept his distance from the other experts," I said, enjoying the way in which Grandfather could make even the most oddly shaped pieces of a puzzle fit together like two hands intertwining.

"He was painting his forgery the whole time. And then, as he attempted to make the switch last night, Stanton caught him in the act."

"That's it to an extent," Grandfather corrected me. "Uhland presumably had Isaac's help in the exchange, and they would have been looking out for the nightwatchman. What they couldn't prevent was his coming into the room whilst they were in the middle of their work. So one of them stood in the Great Hall and placed the dosed cloth over his mouth and nose when he entered. I can't imagine that they intended to kill him, but chloroform is an incredibly unpredictable substance, and it's just as likely to lead to hallucinations as it is to knock a man out for any length of time."

"It's such a tragedy," Alicia said, remembering her dead employee. "Mr Stanton was ever such a kind man. He used to make the children pikelets if they woke up in the night after a bad dream. There came a point at which I believe they started feigning nightmares just to enjoy his treat, but he was truly generous to them."

"I'm afraid that he was unlucky. Another man in his physical condition would not have reacted like that. Whatever sympathy I might have had for the killer's mistake was forgotten when he killed again, though."

I thought I'd have a guess of my own then and, as it had been a while since he'd had anything to do, Todd started mixing celebratory cocktails.

"Uhland told us that Isaac studied fine art, not history," I said. "I thought it was strange at the time, but it makes sense now. He was the one who forged the painting. And that must be why they stayed in rooms away from their colleagues and used a shed in the walled garden."

Grandfather confirmed my theory with a slow, silent nod. "That's correct, Christopher. Well done. I've already asked the inspector to send his men to search for the original painting."

"It also explains the note we found in the workshop." I was pleased with his praise and apparently hungry for more. "Uhland told us that he'd written it days ago, but he couldn't prove it. Isaac would have thought nothing of meeting him in the garden if that was where he'd been working on the painting. When he got there, Uhland called him over to the greenhouse and did the deed. Veronica heard him from her Wendy House and made a note of it in her book. It's a shame the dying

178

man didn't yell out in agony, or she would have heard that as well, and we'd have caught his killer all the sooner."

"You have enterprising children just like mine," Mother told Alicia before amending her comment just a fraction. "Well, at least one of mine. I still don't know what to make of Albert."

Grandfather waited for her to finish before concluding his tale. "I believe that the most perplexing elements of the story have been resolved."

"Wait just a moment," Alicia interrupted. "There's still something I don't understand, and to be quite honest, it's the same thing that confuses me in every detective novel I've ever read. Why, when the criminals knew that the great detective was here to catch them, did they continue with their plan and end up in even hotter water than if they'd simply walked away?"

It was plain on Grandfather's face just how eager he was to explain this new complexity. "In this case, at least, my arrival only precipitated events. They decided to exchange the paintings as soon as possible so that I wouldn't notice the difference. My arrival also meant that there was someone here to fall for the trap they'd set. They wanted me to believe that there was a thief on the premises who was planning to steal something significant in order to distract from the real crime of forgery. Don't forget that Uhland works in the history department of Leeds University, which happens to be in Yorkshire. He would have heard of the accusations against Elton Lockhart during the excavation of the Anglo-Saxon cemetery that was really not so very far from where he lived. Uhland expected me to think that Lockhart was the thief, which shows that he truly underestimated me."

"That's all well and good," I interrupted as Todd brought round a tray of ice-cold shandygaffs, "but it doesn't explain why Uhland killed Isaac. If they were working together, why did he have to die?"

He turned in his chair and his gun-metal-grey eyes were visible even with the light streaming in behind him. "What was the one thing you noticed about the pair of them last night?" Happily, this was another rhetorical question; they really are my favourite kind. "Even when our attention was focused on the overdramatic Mr Lockhart, Uhland and Isaac were on edge. As soon as they heard my name, they turned into different people. It's all very well planning an audacious crime, but it's quite another when you realise that you have to carry it out under the watchful eye of a renowned detective."

"They were both nervous," I replied with little enthusiasm. I would have told him that this wasn't enough to justify murder, but then I found the thread he'd been weaving and followed it. Sorry, I don't know anything about weaving, and I fear that metaphor may have fallen apart somewhere in the middle. "But Mark surely suffered most. He was a capable young man with a promising future. It was one thing to copy a painting, and quite another to put himself at risk to steal the original."

I'd been perched on the desk until now, but the chance to exercise my imagination and flex my brain muscles made me want to stretch my legs too, so I stood up once more. "When everything went wrong, and they had to knock out Mr Stanton, Isaac must have been terrified. If he'd threatened to go to the police to tell them that Uhland had planned the crime, it might well have got him killed."

Grandfather didn't say anything at first but rose from his seat. "That is the very solution I had in mind. Well done, Christopher. Of course, I couldn't have solved this case without a significant amount of help."

I was about to remind him of the part my mother had also played, when there was a knock on the door. Delilah was up on her feet and eager to discover whether it was a friend or foe, but Grandfather set her mind at ease.

"That will be him now."

The door opened, and there was jolly Inspector Kirk. "We found the stolen painting, just as you predicted, Superintendent Edgington. There was also an unfinished portrait, which makes me think that Uhland and Isaac had other crimes in mind. Should I bring the suspect in before I take him to the station?"

"Please do, Inspector." Grandfather walked around the desk to stand in front of it as Uhland was escorted into the room. He was already shackled and would not look up at the trio of brilliant detectives (fine, the duo, and me) who had caught him. It was sad to see such a knowledgeable and well-educated man end up in that state. No matter what he had done, I couldn't help feeling a modicum of sympathy for what would now befall him. The compassion I could summon on his behalf may well mark the difference between killers like him and ordinary, decent people.

Grandfather started a didactic speech but gave up halfway through when it was clear that it would have no effect on the prisoner. Uhland trembled and looked pathetic. He opened his mouth to speak once, but no words would come, and all he could do was shake his head at his wretched fate. The seeds he'd sewn had brought the roosting birds home to make the bed and— No, that's still not quite right.

"Fine, take him away, Kirk." Grandfather looked at the man as though it were painful to do so. "I hope that I don't have to see him again outside of a courtroom."

As Uhland turned to leave, he looked straight at me, and his desperate stare would stay with me for some time. I could feel his fear, and it was most discomforting.

"It's all so hard to believe," Alicia told us as the door closed and Kirk led him to his waiting car. "I wonder what drove him to crime."

"I'm afraid that there's unlikely to be any grand ideals behind his actions," Grandfather responded. "He was simply greedy and wanted to make more money than he could through his regular occupation."

My thoughts had been gathering in my head like water in a sink, and the time had come to pull the plug. "Even when we interviewed him, I never truly imagined that someone like him would turn out to be the killer. He was just so…"

"Boring?" Grandfather suggested. "Yes, I thought the same thing, but then perhaps he knew that was the case and hoped to get away with it. If there is one group in society that is easily overlooked, it is the terminally dull."

CHAPTER TWENTY-SEVEN

I can't describe how much I enjoyed telling the other suspects that the killer had been found. Yes, the mood of celebration was marred by the knowledge that a promising young forger had been senselessly murdered, but I enjoyed the relief on the faces of the other experts. Dr Carbonell took my hand to congratulate me on a job well done.

"Really," he told me when I found him still studying various helmets, gloves and swords in the workshop, "you have achieved the seemingly unachievable."

I could hardly ignore the part that others had played. "I didn't do it alone. Grandfather worked his usual magic. My mother is a wiz at spotting discrepancies in the evidence, and the eldest Pearson daughter was the one who overheard Eric Uhland calling Mark Isaac to the greenhouse. I only knew about it because she'd written it down in her notebook."

"Then it was a group effort." He had a warm smile, and I was glad he had not turned out to be the killer. "What could be better than that?"

"Indeed!"

He must have noticed my curiosity in the items laid out before him, as he followed my gaze and asked, "Would you like to lend me a hand, Christopher?"

"Would I? Or, rather, yes. I would."

He pointed to a particularly rusty lump of metal and instantly communicated his enthusiasm for the subject. "This may not look as if it is of any great value as it is missing its blade and any jewels it would have once held, but this is the oldest piece I have examined. We have very few Anglo-Saxon weapons remaining to us, and so even pieces like this tell us a great deal." His eyes swept over the sword pommel and the stub of a blade underneath it. "Much of our knowledge of such weapons comes from ancient texts like Beowulf, and so it's always a thrill when a real one emerges from the earth."

I looked at the scrolling lines on the hilt of the weapon. There were leaves and figures etched into it with great skill and, for a moment, I felt the same excitement that he clearly had.

"It helps us understand a little better the men who would have wielded these weapons over a thousand years ago." He spoke as if he could travel back through time, and I knew then what his job really entailed.

"It's fascinating."

We both leaned in to marvel at it in silent appreciation. It was nice to meet a man who was keen to share his love of his work, though, after some time spent talking to him, I realised this was not the only reason he was happy to have me there.

"May I tell you something, Christopher?"

"Of course, go ahead."

To be fair, he'd already gone into great detail about his fondness for such ancient weaponry and some of his experiences in excavations across Britain. He even had me write down my observations on a few of the more unusual pieces on the table.

"Before I do, let me say that it has been a curious feeling to be considered a potential murderer. I don't know whether, during the course of your work with your grandfather, you've ever been a suspect, but I cannot recommend it." He was clearly still perturbed by what had gone on that day, and I thought I would have to prompt him for more, but then he came back to himself. "So what I wish to impart is that, for much of my adult life, I have tried my very best to be a good person. I suppose that is the reason I found it so difficult to contemplate…"

"That we might think of you as the killer?"

"Well, yes." He was so forlorn at that moment that I was glad to be able to set his mind at ease.

"Grandfather never rules out a suspect until it has been categorically proven that he could not be guilty – and even then, he still keeps him at the back of his mind, just in case." Fine, to begin with, I didn't do a very good job of setting his mind at ease, and so I changed tack. "But except for your falling-out with Elton Lockhart, which ultimately had no bearing on the case, we didn't come across anything that could incriminate you."

He put down the piece of armour he'd been discussing and smiled again. "I already assume a lot of guilt in life. I felt awful for suggesting that Elton was responsible for the thefts in Yorkshire, and the idea of you thinking badly of me as well was too much to bear."

A short, inappropriate burst of laughter broke from me. It is not often that I feel mature, but I saw then that this capable, knowledgeable man was just as uncertain about the world as I was.

"You know, he spoke well of you," I told him. "Lockhart, I mean. We sat talking beside the lake earlier, and he clearly feels terrible about what he did. I know you were good friends in your youth. Perhaps you will be again one day."

The gloomy atmosphere broke, and he became more animated. "Thank you, Christopher. I wish we had met in more pleasant circumstances, but I think you are a very wise man (for your age)." To my surprise, he did not say these last three words, or even imply them. He spoke to me as an equal, and I can't tell you how much I appreciated it.

Although I greatly enjoyed this conversation, I must admit that I was curious to see what decision Lockhart had come to since our meeting beside the lake. I said goodbye to Dr Carbonell and found his old friend in the Saloon with Frances and Vyvyan on either side of him. It came as something of a shock that all three were smiling. As I approached the sofa where they were sitting, there were no shouted threats between the sisters. They weren't pulling on Lockhart's arms, either, and no one was screaming.

"Christopher, I want you to be the first to know," he called when he saw me. "I'm getting married."

I was stunned into silence, terrified that he was about to announce he was a bigamist.

"Elton asked me, and I said yes!" Vyvyan was full of the joys of young love, and I released the breath I'd been holding.

Yet more surprising was the fact that Frances looked just as happy.

"They'll be married before the summer comes." She looked at her sister with something approaching love. "Spring weddings are always best."

"Congratulations," I told all three of them. It seemed rude to ask how they had come to this arrangement but, fortunately, Lockhart was happy to explain.

"It's all thanks to you, my boy. You gave me the talking to I needed. You see, though I may like to shock and bewilder, I'm a mossbacked fellow at heart. All I really desire is to settle down in a pretty house in the country somewhere with the woman I love and, when the time comes, to have children of our own, who I will take out on expeditions so that they can make me feel old." The laughter roared out of him and right through his companions. "I'm tired of being a libertine."

The key question was how he'd decided which of the two women he wished to marry, but I definitely wasn't rude enough to ask that.

"I'm sure you think this is all very strange," Frances inferred from my mute reaction. "You see, the thing is, the three of us have been miserable for months. I knew from the beginning that Elton and I weren't suited to one another, but I was captivated by the world in which he lives."

He looked at her with that mischievous grin and made a promise. "I swear that I will be a far better brother-in-law than I would be a spouse."

Vyvyan did pull on his arm then but more correctively than possessively. "Which had better not be true in our case."

"Of course not, my darling." His charm switched on like an electric vacuum cleaner and she was trapped. "I will be the best of husbands. You have my word."

"I really couldn't be happier for you," I told them and turned on my heel before they started kissing. It was only when I reached the door that I realised I'd forgotten to tell them what I'd gone there to say. "I've actually got some good news of my own to tell you. We've caught the killer."

I watched the joy spread from face to face. Lockhart jumped up from his seat and ran over to congratulate me. I'd rarely seen such a happy chap. With my tale told, I walked back to my bedroom, passing a number of happy faces along the way. The staff of Parham had no doubt been unsettled by the murders, and they looked particularly grateful for the part I had played in capturing the culprit. There was a spring in the step of every maid and footman, and even the chalk-faced butler, Mr Cridland, had a touch of colour in his cheeks.

Now that Parham's puzzle had been pieced together, I could turn my attention back to the Anderson file. Perhaps it was overly ambitious to think I might solve two cases in one day, but I was willing to try.

I started with P.C. Robbyns's own account of finding the dead man, whom he described rather poetically as being "as cold as a pebble on a beach". He talked of how he went to the neighbouring cottage for help, where an old man – "grubby looking with white stains all over

186

his clothes and false teeth that slipped as he spoke" – answered the door. He was with his frail wife, who reacted as though the house was under siege and "had a face that seemed to scream without making a sound". He asked them to keep an eye on the dead man's body while he sent word of the killing to his superiors.

Upon reading this, I realised that it was not an official police report, so much as a general account Robbyns had written at my grandfather's request. I don't think most officers include such descriptive language and so many unnecessary details in their paperwork.

Finding no answers, I moved on to the interviews Grandfather conducted with the dead man's associates. There was a woman way in Marlow who, though she'd been Anderson's girlfriend, had never attempted to be a mother to Daniel. It seemed unlikely she had plotted her boyfriend's death in order to gain custody of a child in whom she had little interest.

There were distant relations who hadn't seen either father or son for months. Anderson's old drinking friends were just as in the dark as the police over what had happened, and even his acquaintances from racecourses and gambling dens hadn't a clue where the child could have gone.

After months of such disappointment and a period of doubt that his investigation would ever bear fruit, Grandfather received information from a criminal interned at Newgate. The man had committed a violent robbery and would never know freedom again but, before he was locked up, he'd been a member of the gang who had lent Martin Anderson money to gamble. This convict claimed that his boss was so angry with the debtor that he'd not only sent men to kill him but taken his son, too.

Young Inspector Edgington arranged an unofficial rendezvous with the gang leader, "Holy" Jeb Dixon, at the docks in Limehouse. Dixon was a slippery character who had been arrested twenty times without ever being convicted. Grandfather assumed this meant he had powerful connections somewhere but, whatever the reason, his name held a certain cachet, even among other thieves.

When I read the page that described their meeting, I was certain that the thug was going to gloat over what he'd done and taunt my grandfather for not being able to prove it. But Dixon was not the monster I had imagined when I'd first read of him, and I believe my grandfather was a touch in awe of the unusual character.

Dressed in the simple garb of a puritan priest, Dixon stood beside the water with his hands out. Grandfather said in his account that, just for a moment, the hardened criminal looked truly holy as he denied any knowledge of what had happened to baby Daniel, even whilst admitting that the father's murder was a result of his actions.

"The man I sent lost his temper and killed Anderson, but if I thought that he'd killed the child too, he would have faced the consequences," Dixon continued. "I regret the father's death, but I'm no savage. I would tell you what I know."

Inspector Edgington was back where he had started. There was still no explanation for how the little boy had disappeared. And yet, almost fifty years later, Grandfather insisted that he had solved the case based on the information in that file. He had also given me a sealed envelope containing the solution, but I wasn't ready to admit defeat.

I was trying to make sense of all this when the bell rang for dinner and, having quickly dressed for the occasion, I went downstairs. I was pleased to see that Veronica and her sisters were back from the coast, though at least two of them were unhappy with this development.

"I wanted to stay at the seaside. We were only there for a few hours," Lavinia complained to their mother as she inspected their clothes at the foot of the stairs.

"It's unfair," Dione added with a surly stamp of the feet. "I like the seaside, Mother. It very much agrees with me!"

Alicia did her best not to smile at the little scamps' protest, and Veronica soon calmed them down.

"It's even better being here, though." She put her hands around her sisters' shoulders and urged them on towards the dining room. "We're hardly ever allowed to have dinner with grown-ups, and it's happened twice in a row. Besides, I'm sure that Lord Edgington will tell us all about how he caught the infamous killer of Parham House."

The promise of excitement evidently soothed them, and the eldest sister looked back over her shoulder to smile at me.

I waited for her mother to draw the younger girls away before approaching her. "If I ever become as good a detective as my grandfather and I need an assistant, I will come back to offer you the job."

She smiled for a second and then looked uncertain. "That sounds as though it would be quite exciting, but I don't think my parents would agree." And with that, she sauntered after her family into the dining room.

The mood in the house that night had changed. With the removal of the odious Eric Uhland, a great weight had shifted from our shoulders, and it was clear just how relieved everyone was with the outcome. Elton Lockhart was particularly ecstatic and even sat next to his old friend, Dr Carbonell, whereas the Horniman twins were capable of holding a conversation without any veiled insults or sniping, which still came as a surprise to me at least.

Dinner was served to us by a mix of Parham and Cranley staff, and both houses' cooks had a hand in the dinner. This meant that the simple but delicious roast partridge main course was served with a curious dish made of tapioca, leek and nutmeg. Henrietta also made a pickled herring and devilled egg appetiser to complement (if that's the right word) an apple and parsnip soup. Happily, she made up for these choices with an exquisite Alsatian-style gingerbread loaf to finish.

All in all, the boisterous and dynamic conversation helped us to get through the more eccentric food we consumed, and the jovial atmosphere continued late into the evening. Once dinner was over, the girls even decided to entertain us with a song. They were far more willing this time and performed the first verse in unison before each girl stepped forward to sing alone.

> **"If the world were ruled by girls,**
> **What a difference there would be.**
> **The country and town would be upside down,**
> **And a wonderful change we'd see."**
> **Veronica was the first to sing a solo verse and smiled at**
> **me conspiratorially as she did so.**
> **"If ladies were policemen,**
> **The plunder would quickly begin,**
> **The villains would murder and burgle and steal**
> **For the pleasure of being run in."**

Considering the number of accomplished women I had met in my life, I could only think that, in such a scenario, they would achieve more than merely titillating criminals, but the girls sang the song with great heart, and I had no intention of interrupting. When it was over, Grandfather rose from his place at the end of the table to congratulate them before their nanny came to take them to bed.

It was the perfect end to our last night in Parham, and despite the terrible events of that day, I believe we all went to bed with a feeling of contentment and bonhomie.

CHAPTER TWENTY-EIGHT

Why did I wake up in the middle of the night once more? There was no scream to disturb my slumber, no gunshot or even the creak of a floorboard. So what was it that made me sit bolt upright as though someone had attached me to an electrical wire and run a hundred volts through me?

It was pitch black like the night before. I decided not to wake my grandfather, like the night before. And when I found myself out in the corridor, with the darkness stretching before me like a physical presence that felt almost unpassable, the place was silent. Except it wasn't. There was a sound in the stillness. It was faint, but I could hear a noise like a whisper at the point where the stairs led up to the top floor. I could hear a muffled breath.

I hoped that my eyes would adjust so that I could make out who it was, but the only light was from a frosted window at the end of the corridor, and if anything, my eyes seemed to find new sources of blackness rather than distinguishing between the shapes before me. I wanted to run straight at whoever was there, but I knew that the moment I moved, everything would change. I finally found the courage to shuffle one foot forward a few inches, and with that done, I did the same with the other.

I managed to move along the corridor a good two feet before the hidden figure came to life. The shadows whirled around one another like clouds in a stormy sky and he came into view. He was only there for a moment before he disappeared up the stairs, but it was enough to send me off on his trail. I should have realised he was only going to trap himself up there. I could have easily called for help, but instead I sprinted after him without considering the consequences.

I shot up the first set of stairs and caught a glimpse of him where they turned back on themselves. I'd only been to the top floor once to visit the girls in their nursery, and it occurred to me that they could now be in danger. I'm sure this propelled me forward just that little bit faster and, while I had no idea what I would do if I caught the man I was chasing, I was determined to do so.

The moonlight penetrated the long gallery through two of the doorways that led off it. I could see the stretch of the hallway where the floorboards had been taken up and the ceiling panels removed. The runner had come to a stop just before it, and a sense of exhilaration coursed through me as I realised that there was nowhere for him to go. Even if there was a priest hole up there, as my grandfather had described, it would do the fugitive no good to hide.

"I don't know why you're running, but I've caught you," I said, sounding both overconfident and oddly childlike, as if this whole thing was a game.

I thought he would turn to look at me, but he lingered where he was for a few seconds, and I approached in the same slowly shifting manner as before. Once again, stillness was followed by a burst of activity as he jumped across the first gap in the floor to land on a beam. I stood and watched as he picked his way from one to another, slowly moving away from me.

"Don't!" I called out, partly for his own sake and partly because I had no desire follow him.

I knew in an instant that there was no choice, but the way he moved was so confident that I doubted I would be able to cross the space so easily. Despite the loose clothes he wore, there was an assuredness to his movement. I tried to follow, jumping in halting steps like a child playing hopscotch. Beneath the beams, there were holes in some places and wooden boards in others, and I feared falling to the floor below and breaking my legs in the process. I'd made it halfway through the unfeasibly long room when he stopped once more and pulled his black cloak or coat or whatever he was wearing around himself. There were no more doors through which to exit, or even a window for him to climb out onto the roof. There was no escape, which is why, glancing back at me for a fraction of a second, he jumped.

I was certain he would scream out in agony, but it didn't happen. He barely made a sound. By the time I reached the spot from which he'd leaped, there was no sign of him through the hole, but I could hear footsteps beating down the corridor where I'd first seen him, and I knew I'd missed my chance.

My head was a muddle of sleepiness and hazy ideas. Grandfather was certain that Uhland was the killer. So who was I chasing? Or rather, why would he run away? I questioned whether it could be one of the servants – the half-Italian fellow who had already been caught stealing and not learnt his lesson after all. That didn't explain why he had run, though. He could have made up a story and sent me back to bed.

There had to be a reason, but so little during our stay in Parham had felt solid or substantial, and it was hard to know what to think. As I navigated the bare beams and got back to the part of the gallery that didn't instantly give me vertigo, I began to notice flaws in the grand conclusion that we had formed the previous afternoon. I hadn't intended to question Uhland's part in the deaths; we knew he was a criminal, and the chances were that he really was to blame. But the very enigma that Grandfather had identified – the series of strange occurrences that had brought us there in the first place – was surely at odds with the forgers' need for discretion.

I rushed back down the stairs and almost lost my footing in the darkness. No matter how fast I ran, it wasn't going to help. The figure had disappeared and, even if I woke everyone up, there was no way of saying who I had seen up there. I stared along the corridor once more, but it was lifeless now, and just as gloomy as when I'd left. I listened without moving for so long that the silence seemed to bung up my ears until the noise of a door opening unblocked them.

"Christopher?" a voice asked in a harsh whisper, and I had to question whether my grandfather could see in the dark. "Christopher, what are you doing out here?"

"There was a man," I replied, taking a few steps closer. "Well, I assume it was a man, I can't say for certain. He was here in the darkness. I suppose the sound of him on the stairs woke me up and, when I came out to see what was happening, he caught sight of me and ran. I gave chase, but he managed to escape. I can't even say in which direction he went."

I could hear, if not see, my grandfather looking around, and he tightened the belt on his dressing gown before walking over and taking my arm. Without another word, he led me down the staircase to the ground floor, and we descended as quietly as church mice.

Much as when I'd left my room a few minutes earlier, I had that same feeling of promnesia – of living through the events that had already taken place – but something was different now. I had my grandfather beside me, which meant that, no matter what I might find, everything would be all right. It was almost as if I had travelled back to the moment before I found Stanton's body, only this time, my mentor was there to help me.

Once again, I felt that familiar tug towards the Great Hall. There were candles on the sideboard in the hallway and they cast strange patterns of light up the walls. Floral arrangements that, in the daylight, looked homely and inviting were transformed into an unholy manifestation, writhing with fifty tentacles. I tried not to look at them but kept my eyes on the path that led to the heart of the house.

The body before me had fallen in almost exactly the same spot as the night before, but this time the figure lying there was a woman. I couldn't tell at first if it was Vyvyan or Frances, but her bright blonde hair was splayed out around her head like a sunburst. That wasn't all I noticed, though. I could see blood on the floor in front of her and all over her hands that now lay limp beside her chest.

Grandfather bolted forward to look at her, but I hesitated. I think that it was the knowledge of what I would find there that held me back – the realisation that I couldn't bear to see one of those spirited young ladies lying dead in a pool of her own blood. Whatever he discovered was so appalling that he had to look away. I'd rarely seen my grandfather turn from the macabre scenes we had so often witnessed, but it was too much, even for him.

"It's Frances," he tried to say, but his voice was little more than a croak.

"Is she—?" I began, but I couldn't finish the question and he couldn't bring himself to answer.

CHAPTER TWENTY-NINE

There was no sign of the knife that had cut through her, but there was an empty bracket halfway up the wall of weapons. I finally walked over to see my grandfather, but I didn't hold out much hope of consoling him.

"This is my fault," he said before cursing under his breath. His gaze had fallen to the ground, and it would be some time before he could bring himself to look up from the glossy pool. "You were right all along, Christopher. I was arrogant – I became fixated on what the blighter wished to steal, instead of thinking about who else he might hurt."

"Don't be so hard on yourself, Grandfather. You were trying to save people by identifying the killer's plan. Arrogance doesn't come into it."

I looked about the room to see what might have been stolen, and he must have noticed as he jerked his head in the direction of the Great Parlour. Instead of staying with the body, I walked across to the neighbouring room. It was nerve racking as so much of our time there had been leading up to this moment. There was no guard on duty, which in hindsight seems an oversight, but as far as anyone knew, we had caught the killer. I turned on the light and it immediately glinted off the Anglo-Saxon cup, which was still on its stand beneath the wall of artefacts. The Robert Peake painting, or at least the copy that Mark Isaac had produced, was still there, too. In fact, I could make out no obvious space in the collection and was about to turn around when Grandfather called to me.

"Christopher! Come back here this second. Come now!"

I didn't hesitate this time. I ran straight to him and, when I got there, he was leaning over the body, pushing the hair back from the woman's face and reaching his other hand out to me across the room.

"Fabric!" he yelled, and I must admit that I did not understand him at first. "A tie, a shirt, a napkin. Give me something to stem the bleeding!"

I was wearing flannel pyjamas and, even if they hadn't been my favourite pair, they were too thick to tear, so I ran back to the room I'd just left and took a length of rope used for tying back the curtains and a piece of embroidery that was draped over one of the armchairs.

In a moment, I was with him once more.

"I don't know what is wrong with me, boy," Grandfather said as he applied pressure to the wound with one hand on her front and the other on her back. "I didn't even think to check whether she was alive. I'm at sevens and eights at the very least." He was evidently shocked by his own failings, but I hadn't done any better.

"What else can I do, Grandfather? Please tell me."

Frances was still lying on her side and had not opened her eyes, but Grandfather must have seen something that gave him hope. He took the thick fabric from me and pulled back one side of her blouse to hold it to the wound.

"Find Todd, or any other servants, but try not to wake the whole house. We'll need time to think before doing anything rash. Tell him we will have to drive the young lady to the nearest hospital. He'll know which is the best one for her. If you see any of our staff, they are to wake your mother and tell her that she will be in charge here until we return."

I was on the other side of the room already by the time he'd completed his instructions. I knew that Todd would be staying with the others in the gatehouse and called out to him as soon as I made it outside. I have a feeling that our most reliable employee sleeps with his boots on as he was up and out of the building before I'd crossed the courtyard.

"What is it Master Christopher?"

"Frances Horniman has been stabbed. You're to get the Rolls and bring it as close to the Saloon as you can. The French windows there should do the trick for getting her out of the house. I'll find Dorie to help us."

"Horsham would be the best hospital, sir. It's recently been rebuilt, and they have a machine that produces skiagrams. That's surely her best chance."

"Then that's where we'll go."

He said, *Very good, sir*, with a nod of the head, but I could see the emotion in him, just as plainly as I had with my grandfather. Todd had his head screwed on tightly, but he was only human.

Grandfather had told me not to wake everyone, but that was easier said than done in the densely populated servant's quarters. On finding our maid's bedroom and banging on the door, a ripple of noise travelled along the corridor as others in the building emerged to find out what was wrong. Of course, there was still nothing to rule out the staff as

196

potential killers, but I couldn't worry about that for the moment; we needed their help.

I returned to the house with Dorie and several footmen in tow, while more servants dispersed about the place to complete the tasks I'd given them. One went to call the hospital, and the police thereafter, to let them know an injured woman would be coming. Another went to wake the butler, and several more were yet again required to search the house to identify anything that could have been stolen.

"Has she lost a lot of blood?" I asked when I reached the injured woman, though I knew the answer and what I really meant was, *Is she going to die?*

"There's still hope," Grandfather told me as he tightened the cord that he had tied around her. "The knife didn't pierce her heart. I would guess that she ducked or flinched, and the killer missed his target."

"What about the damage it's done? She looked quite dead when we arrived."

"Yes, she'd passed out from the shock. It's amazing that she survived, but the most important thing is that she's breathing. While she's breathing, there is hope." I believe he repeated this expression to give us both strength.

Dorie had stood behind us this whole time, evidently unsure what her part would be. I can imagine it was her instinct to pick up poor Frances off the floor and toss the slim young lady over her brawny shoulder, but that could have made things far worse. Instead, we waited until two of the footmen had brought a long, low table from the library and, together, we gently moved the patient onto it.

"That's the ticket." Grandfather still lacked his usual determination, but at least he wasn't so drained of life as he had been. For a little while, it had been hard to choose the palest between Frances, the disheartened detective, and the white tiles on the floor beneath her. He watched as we carefully completed the manoeuvre, then clapped his hands together and led the way to the Saloon.

Todd was already waiting for us outside with the Silver Ghost. The door was just wide enough to put the makeshift stretcher through and slide Frances onto the back seat. With the table then removed, we followed her inside and were almost set to leave.

"Dorie," Grandfather remembered to say as Todd started the

engine, "tell my daughter what's happened. She'll know exactly what to do. The pair of you are to keep an eye on every last person here until we return. There's a monster in the house, but we will catch him."

The car was already moving away and so he slammed the door closed just as Delilah appeared from wherever she kept hiding. She ran down the drive after the car, clearly enjoying the chase, but Todd was too fast for her, and she eventually gave up. I watched her through the rear window as she stood staring after us until we'd disappeared from view.

Grandfather was kneeling on the floor, holding a clean towel to the wound, and I was squashed in at the end of the bench. Frances released an occasional moan but showed no other signs of consciousness. When we sped up, and I could no longer hear her breathing, I began to fret that we had lost her, but then the car slowed at a junction, and I caught a faint note again.

It was an eighteen-mile drive to Horsham, and I almost wished that we'd taken one of Grandfather's zippier vehicles, but Todd knew how to get the best from the Rolls and positively ate up the road beneath us. It was lucky that it was still so early, as there wasn't a car, cart or sheep on the country lanes along which we thundered. Should Grandfather one day wish to sell it, I doubt that the car had the same value as when we left Parham, but that was the least of our concerns.

There was a doctor and several nurses waiting for us at the door when we arrived, and the injured woman was soon transferred to a trolley. She disappeared into the bowels of the hospital, but I don't know exactly what happened to her after that. We were left in a waiting room while they did what they needed to save her and, at some point, Grandfather fell asleep. With his head on my shoulder, I soon did the same.

When I next woke, I was alone in the room, so I stretched out on the chairs and slept a little longer. The second time I came to, it was bright outside and Grandfather was back, pacing the room in his usual contemplative manner, and speaking to himself as he did so. Most of what he said was insensible mumbling, but I caught the odd expression.

"...wouldn't make sense... impossible to say...unlikely, improbable and fantastical..." he blathered, none of which sounded encouraging.

A doctor arrived to speak to us shortly after I'd woken.

"You're the family, I presume?" He was a serious young fellow with a pointed beard that was more suited to a German physician from the Victorian era than a modern-day Englishman.

"You could say that," Grandfather replied in a wavering tone before deciding to tell the truth, "but you'd be wrong. We brought the young lady here last night. My name is Lord Edgington, and I was investigating a pair of murders when Frances Horniman was attacked."

The doctor nodded, which was not the amazed reaction that many would have had. "Yes, I've read about you. You're one of those people who always find themselves in the paper. If murder has occurred, I take it you didn't save the previous victims?"

The implication that I took from this was that a doctor who could save people from their maladies was surely superior to a detective who investigated the deaths of those less fortunate.

Grandfather did not like his tone and made no attempt to hide the fact. "That is beside the point. The question is, have you saved your patient?" I was impressed that he could perfect such a superior tone whilst dressed in pyjamas and a velvet dressing gown.

"As it happens, I have." The doctor sniffed disdainfully. "But it's too early to say what the damage might be. The X-ray showed that she has no broken bones and that no part of the weapon that stabbed her remains inside the wound. She was lucky that the blade wasn't a large one, as it narrowly missed any vital areas."

I could tell that he had revealed what he'd come there to tell us, but I spoke before he could go. "Has she said anything? Is she awake?"

"Not yet, but you may wait in the room with her if you so wish."

He left just as brusquely as he'd appeared. He didn't tell us where to find Frances or guide us to one of his colleagues who could help. Perhaps he was an excellent doctor, but I've met dogs with a better bedside manner.

I would have left the room after him, but my grandfather held me back.

"It sounds as though Miss Horniman needs rest and is unlikely to talk to us soon. You must stay here and make sure that no one else sees her. I believe I can do more good back at Parham."

I believe what he really meant was that he didn't like to be seen out of the house in his nightclothes. I doubt he was too worried about me traipsing about the place in my pyjamas, though.

"Very well, Grandfather. But before you go…" I paused as I wasn't sure exactly what I wanted to know. "Can you tell me what you think is happening? Could the attack have been carried out by one of Uhland's accomplices?"

He straightened his back and looked about the room as if he hadn't taken the time to observe his simple surroundings until now. "It's possible. Yes, it's still conceivable that Uhland is to blame for the first two killings, as we know he forged and exchanged the Peake painting. What isn't clear is why anyone would have attacked Miss Horniman nor what she was doing awake at such an hour."

There were a hundred other concerns in my head, but the one that now emerged was, "Are you sure that we considered the right group of suspects from the beginning? Isn't it possible that one of the servants was working with the killer or has manipulated events to hide his guilt?"

He put his hand to the doorknob but didn't turn it just yet. "I'm no longer sure of anything, Christopher. But don't worry, my mind is not so foggy that I am unwilling to question all that we think we know. You can call me at Storrington 21 if there is any change in her condition." He remained for just a moment longer before opening the door and passing through it. "And don't let anyone see the patient until you hear from me – not even family or close friends."

When he'd left, I seemed to get stuck in space and – for all I knew – time. I just stood there with so many conflicting emotions and ideas circling my brain. It was quite unnerving, but I finally managed to break free and went to speak to the matron to ask after Frances.

Her room when I found it was small but bright and, as it was in a hospital, immaculately clean. The bed in which she slept appeared to have been made so tightly that she would not be able to get out of it even if she'd had the strength to do so. There was a square window that gave onto the elegant park behind the hospital, but most importantly, Frances herself looked perfectly serene there.

Her skin was still pale, but she had a slight smile on her lips as she slept and it was easy to imagine that she was a princess in a fairytale, awaiting better times. There was certainly nothing to suggest that she'd had a brush with death.

I sat down next to her, uncertain how long the chemicals in

her bloodstream would keep her unconscious. I sat listening to her breathing, which was much steadier than it had been in the car, and, in time, my thoughts turned to the case. For some reason, every time I tried to gauge Uhland's part in the proceedings and why anyone would have attacked poor Frances, my mind jumped back fifty years and the Anderson file was opened once more.

I'd read it enough times by now to know the salient facts, and I could even quote some of Grandfather's more expressive passages by heart. I can't say why this was necessary at that moment. Perhaps some previously unutilised part of my brain was keen on order and insisted that I solve cases chronologically, but I couldn't begin to think about Parham until I knew what had happened to Martin Anderson's infant son.

I flicked through the papers – though, in reality, they were back in my bedroom at Parham House – and key phrases stood out to me. There was the body in the road that made P.C. Robbyns think of sacks of grain, the grubby elderly couple who looked after the scene until he could return, the stuffed duck and clean nappies, the dead man's uninterested girlfriend and the priest-like gang leader. The answer was in there somewhere, and it's lucky that Frances slept all day, as it took me that long to work out what happened to baby Daniel.

Both my grandfather at the time and I in the present day had approached the problem from the wrong angle. The question we had asked was why someone would murder Anderson and take his son, but I could finally see that they were two separate concerns. It was telling that my mentor had given me a version of the case constructed after the fact. Some of the documents were from the time. There was a perfunctory police report and notes on the various interviews that had taken place, but Grandfather had reconstructed the facts for me, even going so far as to ask P.C. Robbyns to write an account of his initial discovery and the subsequent events as they unfolded.

This in itself should have told me all I needed to know. It proved that Grandfather had threaded the file with elements that would not have been included in a standard police file. I checked through my memories one last time and, in the end, it was a single word that gave the game away. "Childless"! He'd said that the old couple who lived right next to where the murder took place were childless, and that the man had white stains down his clothes when Robbyns knocked on the door.

If Anderson had been killed outside their cottage in the early morning, there's a good chance that they would have heard something. And yet there was never any mention of their admitting such. The only thing I knew about them was that they were childless, which is an entirely irrelevant piece of information to a police investigation. They were most likely also horseless, but no one talked of that. The white stains down the old man's clothes were similarly incongruous, and that was how I solved the problem. Why would someone have murdered a debtor like Anderson and taken his son? The answer was simple; they hadn't.

Anderson was killed with a hatchet on a sunny morning in March in a town called Wallington to the south of London. He was murdered because of the money he owed, but even a hardened criminal would be unlikely to kill the tiny, helpless boy who accompanied him. With so many other possible explanations eliminated, it made sense to me that the killer had left the child with his murdered father and that someone else had found him. I was sure that the old couple had taken him in, fed him milk and decided to keep him for themselves. And the reason I was so sure was not because of the facts of the case, but the facts as they were presented in the Anderson file. Grandfather had chosen exactly what to include, and as soon as I got the chance, I would open the sealed envelope with the solution and find out whether I was right.

Still, this wasn't the most important thing that occurred to me whilst sitting in that hospital room, waiting for the sleeping beauty to wake. What struck me, now that I'd fashioned a solution to the case from five decades earlier, was that we might still not be asking the right questions to explain the run of violence in Sussex that week. Grandfather had kept the Anderson case open for months after any normal officer would have given up on it. He questioned everything and re-examined every shed of evidence a hundred times until he finally discovered the truth.

Nothing at Parham House was clear or certain anymore, and so I went back to the beginning and started again.

CHAPTER THIRTY

It was lucky that I hadn't brought a book with me as I would have been distracted and not given the case its due consideration. I still hadn't read the most recent Dorothy Sayers novel, the tantalisingly titled 'Unnatural Death'. And I'd also packed George Eliot's 'The Mill on the Floss', but all I had in that room was a head full of thoughts. I'd solved one case, and perhaps the tedium of my stint in the featureless hospital could do the same trick for the attack on Frances Horniman.

She had begun to stir at midday, but fallen back asleep and, after I'd returned from consuming a ham sandwich in the canteen downstairs, she barely made a peep until evening fell. Different doctors came to see her a few times, and I had to conclude that the case was a curiosity for them. It can't be every day that a beautiful young woman is stabbed in the English countryside (unless my grandfather happens to be in the vicinity). I must say, though, I was impressed by the service they provided and hope that there will one day be such modern health facilities in every town in Great Britain.

I was there so long – with no word from my grandfather, I hasten to add – that the first doctor we'd seen that morning began a new shift. He was a different person after a good day's sleep, and I could only put his previous sullenness down to the demands of his arduous job.

"Ah, Mr Prentiss," he practically sang, "I'm glad to see that you're still here. How is our patient?" He was suddenly charming, though his beard was more devilish than wizardly.

"She's… Well, she's asleep." I don't know if I've mentioned it, but I'm adept at stating the obvious.

One thing of which I hadn't done a great deal that day was speaking. Not only did my voice come out terribly hoarse, the brief conversation roused Frances, and she immediately reached out to clutch her chest, causing the doctor to lunge forward.

"Be careful, Miss Horniman," he cautioned her. "You've had quite an ordeal, and you'd be wise not to move too much."

She opened her eyes and looked alarmed when she saw the doctor. Happily, she turned to me and began to relax a little. I'd rarely had that effect on someone, and it made me feel rather useful.

"You were attacked in the Great Hall, Miss Horniman," I told her as the doctor scribbled something down in his pocket notebook. "My grandfather and I found you. We thought you were dead at first, but we managed to bring you to a hospital before you could lose too much blood."

"You were clearly born under a lucky star," the doctor conjectured, which I thought a peculiar remark for a man of science to make. At least he wasn't grumpy any longer. "I'll leave the two of you to talk, but I won't be far away if you need anything."

He did as promised, and I poured Frances a glass of water. She shuffled higher in the bed, and I held it up for her to drink. It felt odd to be the one caring for someone a few years older than I was. I was so used to everyone babying me that I rather enjoyed this new sense of responsibility.

"Thank you," she said when she'd finished. "Thank you for everything." That memory of a smile was still on her lips, but it was mixed together with a hint of apprehension. "To be honest, I'm amazed that you stayed with me."

"I believe that, more than anything else, my grandfather left me here to guard you, just to be on the safe side. He can be a suspicious sort, and we're still not certain what's been happening at Parham."

She had finished her mouthful of water but had to swallow once more. "I've never owed someone my life before. I really don't know what to say."

She pushed her hand free of the bedclothes and held it out to me. I took it as gently as I could, and what I hadn't expected was that she would look at me, not as a boy who happened to have found her after the attack, but as the man who had saved her. It was a curious sensation, and I'm afraid that I pulled my hand away again rather rudely.

"May I ask what you were doing downstairs in the middle of the night?" I was wondering whether the killer had left her a note, just as he had for Mark Isaac.

"It was silly," she said, and turned away for a moment. "I'm silly."

"I don't believe that for one second. You and your sister both come across as highly accomplished young ladies."

She shook her head and tried to sit up, but the pain was too much, and she relented. "One can be accomplished and silly. I certainly manage both."

I had a sense of what she meant but asked her all the same. "Are you referring to the situation between yourself and Mr Lockhart?"

"I am." She pursed her lips together and breathed out angrily through her nose. "I was a fool, but when I met him, I was convinced that he was the man I would marry. When Vyvyan fell in love with him, too, I did something that only a true idiot would."

I couldn't help but smile at this. "Be careful. You've gone from being silly to an idiot in the space of a minute. If you don't slow down, you'll be a dunce in no time."

She apparently wasn't too upset by my thoughtless abandonment of her hand as she reached out to take mine once more. "I'm one of those, too. You see, I knew they loved one another, but Elton is so magnetically wonderful that I couldn't resist him. I should have left them to it and been happy for them, but I told him that he could have us both, and he and Vyvyan were too desperate to prove how bohemian they could be to reject the idea."

I didn't know what to say to that. I'd struggled to imagine how such a complicated arrangement had come to exist and, now that I knew, it was just as hard to comprehend.

"The worst part of it all is that I love my sister, and it almost tore us apart." She was evidently more upset by the situation with Elton Lockhart than the throbbing wound in her chest, as she hadn't even asked who'd attacked her. "We had always got on well, but we came close to strangling one another and never talking again."

I didn't feel that I'd had any experiences that were directly comparable, so I sought the nearest thing. "My brother once teased me in front of his handsome, charming friends that I eat too much cake. I don't think he meant it to be mean, but it made me feel awful."

"Did you forgive him?"

"Of course I did. It's hard to forget such moments, but our closest relatives have special dispensation when it comes to forgiveness. Vyvyan won't be worried about the past. I'm sure that she only has time for the future right now. And you will be there at her wedding to toast her happiness."

"I hope so. I genuinely hope so." Her expression became a touch more distressed, and I thought I'd said the wrong thing.

"Now, you mustn't worry about that. The most important task I have is to find out what happened to you in the Great Hall."

"I'm silly," she said yet again, and I was worried that we would have to repeat the whole conversation from the beginning. "I couldn't sleep for cursing my own bad behaviour. I drifted off a few times, then found myself so ashamed in my dreams that I would wake back up again. In the end, I'd had enough and decided to go for a walk to get some fresh air. I wandered downstairs and when I—"

As she was speaking, there was a knock on the door. It soon swung open, and Inspector Kirk entered with his usual cheery attitude apparent.

"I'm terribly sorry to interrupt, Miss Horniman," he said. "I was hoping you might be able to tell me a little of what happened last night."

His demeanour was so carefree and contented that it was quite at odds with the conversation we'd been having. It almost made me feel foolish for taking life so seriously.

"We were just about to discuss that," I explained, and we both turned to Frances. I crossed my fingers that she wouldn't say how silly she'd been for the sixth time – or was it the seventh?

She took a deep breath and began. "I couldn't sleep, so I left my room on the first floor and went for a walk around Parham House. Though I've been staying there for weeks, I had been so busy with my work that I hadn't taken the time to explore it on my own. Walking the halls by the light of a candle held a certain magic. I couldn't decide whether I was a character in a fantastical novel or a ghost story, and I was considering this very thing when I entered the Great Hall, and someone jumped out of the shadows to seize me. I should have known after everything that had happened that there was only one genre that would fit. I lay on the floor with my chest bleeding, finally aware that I was the victim in a detective story."

I frowned. Kirk smiled a touch guiltily, and Frances breathed in as a jolt of pain reminded her of the injury.

"Did you get a look at the man who attacked you?" the inspector tried. "Anything you can tell us might be of help."

"I'm afraid I didn't." She bit her lip, apparently taking some blame on herself because the monster who had tried to murder her had done so discreetly enough not to be seen. "He was behind me, and it all happened so fast that I didn't have time to look back at him."

"Was it definitely a man, at least?" I asked. "Was there anything in the way he moved, or perhaps his smell, that could tell you one way or the other?"

She took a moment to consider my questions before regretfully shaking her head. "I can't say for certain. He was strong enough to hold me as his arm reached around my body and plunged the knife through my chest. He had wide sleeves in a loose material and matching black gloves. That's all I can tell you with any certainty."

Kirk had become a little more cautious in his approach and coughed into his hand before asking a further question. "Is there any reason you can think of why someone might have wanted to hurt you?"

If anything, this only scared her more. She leaned forward a fraction and her big blue eyes caught the light. "You think someone was waiting for me there? Surely that isn't possible at four in the morning or whatever time it was. I must have disturbed the killer. That's the only thing that makes sense."

"It's just a question, miss," Kirk continued. "I didn't mean to upset you. It's just a question I have to ask."

I wished that my grandfather had been with me at that moment. I would love to have known what new ideas he had fathomed as to the killer's motives.

"I can't think of anyone who would have attacked me," Frances spoke more quickly now, a note of distress in her voice. "I would never have left my room if I'd thought there was any danger. I'm so sorry."

"There's no need for that, miss," the inspector reassured her. "We all believed that the killer was locked up in Pulborough police station. I took Eric Uhland there myself last night."

"Inspector, do you have an officer free who could wait here to make sure that Miss Horniman is safe? I feel I should ring my grandfather and find out whether he needs me back at the house."

"There are already two constables outside. One can drive you back to Parham if that's what you need."

"Thank you, Chrissy." Frances's hand shot out to me again, and I took it freely this time. "Thank you so much."

"I've really not done a great deal," I told her. "And to be honest, you saved me from a dubious lunch if our cook was in charge today. You never know what Henrietta will make, whereas the ham sandwich that I purchased here was delicious."

"I'm glad I could be of service." She squeezed my hand one last time and there was a mischievousness to her expression that made me question what she might say. "May I tell you one last thing before you go?"

I lingered beside her bed for a moment. "Of course."

"I do like your pyjamas. They're ever so fetching."

I looked down at the blue and white flannel and we both laughed. Once I'd said a proper farewell, I went out to the telephone at the front of the building. I felt bad for leaving her, though I knew I could do more to help in Parham. There was still a lot of thinking to do, but if Grandfather hadn't identified the killer by the time I got back, I was determined to do it myself.

"Operator," I said into the handset, and the line crackled for a moment, "please connect me to Storrington 21."

CHAPTER THIRTY-ONE

When my grandfather was perplexed by one of our cases, he liked nothing better than a good pace about the room. He could pace (and had paced) on the spot in everything from ballrooms to cupboards, and it often helped unlock some elusive understanding for him. I had tried to emulate him in a number of ways, but this was not one of the techniques that best served me. A day in a small white hospital room, however, had loosened the muscles in my brain and sent me off on a path that I greatly hoped would explain the mystery before us. As the constable drove me along the country lanes – at a much slower pace than dear Todd, of course – the sun set, and I began to conceive of a solution that I hoped would tie up every small, unlikely detail in a neat bow.

It was dark by the time I stepped out of the brown Bean 14 automobile and walked along the path to Parham House. I did not yet know who the killer was, but I knew that we'd spent much of the last day asking the wrong questions. Grandfather had felt certain that the culprit had designed a plan in order to distract from his criminal intentions. He'd continued to believe this when we identified Uhland as a counterfeiter and a thief, and yet I could no longer reconcile the two facts.

While it was true that the man still locked up in Pulborough police station was a criminal, he wouldn't have wanted to draw attention to the painting he was intending to steal. It seemed to me that Uhland would have been much better off swapping the real painting for the forgery without any prelude. Though he would have needed to do so without the nightwatchman finding him, with the help of his accomplice, it would have been easy to observe Mr Stanton's path around the house and make the exchange when he was far from the Great Parlour. I could only conclude that they had made the swap before the first attack and neither of the forgers was responsible for Mr Stanton's death.

I was more convinced with every passing moment that we'd got the wrong man and so, when I found Grandfather sitting in the library with Alicia and my mother, I was determined to tell him just that.

"Christopher, we've got the wrong man." I was barely in the room when he announced my own grand discovery back to me.

"I was about to say the very same thing!" I complained, but he wasn't listening.

"I should have realised that Uhland would not have complicated things to such an extent. If a forger is to be successful, he must direct attention away from himself. Our killer is a show-off. He wanted us to know that he planned to steal something."

"And he presumably wished to alarm Alicia," Mother pointed out.

Sitting just a few feet from her friend, our hostess's head dropped as she spoke. "He succeeded, but I still don't understand why anyone would go to such trouble." She exhaled deeply, and it was clear that her previous sorrow had returned. I could only imagine how she had suffered that week.

"What about the others?" I asked when the three of them fell silent. They were sitting in a set of armchairs arranged in equilateral formation before the fire, and so I walked closer to address them. "There are only three suspects left. Did any of them reveal anything significant when you spoke to them today?"

"No." Grandfather stared at the smoking fire in the immense grate, and I thought that was all he planned to tell me. "Each of them claimed to have been asleep at the time you chased the killer. I didn't tell them about Frances in the hope that one of them might give himself away. My plan didn't work." His words got caught in his throat for a moment, and I could sense his disappointment. "I confined them to their respective rooms for most of the morning but had to let them out for lunch."

"We were hoping you would come bearing good news," Mother said with a familiar optimistic expression on her face. "For the moment, we're all quite lost."

I went to stand by the fire as three pairs of eyes latched onto me. "Well, first things first; you've got far too much faith in me if you think I'll be the one to fix things."

"Please, Chrissy." Grandfather put one hand to his head as though to soothe the pain there. "This is no time for false modesty. I just want the facts."

"The facts are that Frances is awake and seems to be recovering, but she saw nothing. Except for a glimpse of black sleeves and the killer's gloves as he stabbed her, she had little to report."

"That sums up the day we've had." Grandfather looked as though he would clap his hands together, or perhaps even indulge in one last exasperated snap of the fingers, but he clenched his fists instead. "The servants found nothing missing in the house. No one heard or saw anything, and the suspects all act as if they're as innocent as newborn lambs."

"Yes, it really is a puz—"

"Don't say it!" He shot up from his chair to interrupt. "That word has become a thorn in my side. I should never have christened the problem before us. I feel I have cursed myself never to solve it."

I walked a step closer to put a hand on his shoulder. "Now who is being too hard on himself? We already caught Uhland in his scheme. You'll surely work out what else has been going on here and catch the real culprit."

"Were you not listening, boy?" He allowed the words a few moments' consideration before saying anything more. "I have discovered the limit of my abilities. I have finally found the case that shows me up for the lucky amateur that I have always been."

It was upsetting to see him so glum, and so I nipped it in the bud. "You sound like me a year ago, Grandfather. The only difference is that I've hardly solved any cases, and you have sent a whole legion of men to prison for their crimes. Just like the file you handed me before we left Cranley; the answer is in here somewhere."

"So you did it!" This, at least, made him smile. "You made short work of the Anderson file. It took me months, and you completed the challenge in the space of a few days."

"If the old couple had taken the child, then yes, I did." He did not contradict me, and so I knew that I'd got one thing right. "I'm sure I had it slightly easier than you did at the time, and if I can do that, then you can triumph here today."

Something in what I'd said had distracted him, but Mother rose from her chair to congratulate me, and I couldn't yet ask him what it was.

"That's wonderful, Christopher. He set me that same problem many years ago, and it was no cakewalk." I noticed that she decided not to tell me how long it had taken her. "As detectives, we are often too eager to link every element of a crime, and that case reminds us of the dangers of doing so."

"Perhaps I'm the killer," Alicia suddenly announced. She sat perfectly still in her chair and pushed a lock of hair into place on the top of her head. It was hard to know whether she was teasing us or putting forward a real possibility. The truth was that since she'd wound us up and set us to work, we'd had very little time to consider anyone but our six main suspects.

"Why would you—" Mother began before stopping herself short. "It wouldn't make sense if—"

"Alicia is right," I contradicted her. "I don't mean that she is to blame for anything that has occurred. I just mean that she feasibly could be the culprit and we haven't considered her guilt."

"Precisely, Christopher," she replied, with a proud expression on her face. "I might well have called you here for attention. Perhaps the stress of the refurbishments has taken its toll, and I've turned to murder and manipulation as a pastime."

I liked her even more than before. "I don't believe that for one second, but that's a very good point. We've made too many assumptions on this case, and now we must look at the evidence through fresh eyes, free from the preconceptions to which we've been clinging."

Grandfather seemed to come back to himself but gave no sign that he'd heard what we'd been saying. "What is the date?"

Alicia leaned forward to pick up an extremely well-ironed copy of The Times. "It's the twentieth of March. Why do you ask?"

He had to put his elbow on the mantlepiece to support himself, and I was more worried about him than I had been in months. "Of course it is. How could I have forgotten?"

"Oh, Daddy," Mother said in a sweetly sympathetic tone. "I'm so sorry. I hadn't thought."

"No, neither had I." The old man went to embrace his daughter, who put her head tenderly against his chest.

"What's the matter?" I asked, and Grandfather turned to face the fire as he explained.

"The twentieth of March. It was thirteen years ago today…" His words fell quieter, and I thought he would give up entirely, but then a torrent streamed out of him. "That's why I've been so out of sorts this whole time. I knew the anniversary was coming, but it quite slipped my mind after all that has occurred."

"I don't understand," I told him, though I really should have taken a moment to think.

"Your grandmother, boy. My Katherine was murdered on the twentieth of March 1915." He was speaking very quickly and had to slow down to explain his thinking. "You see, most years since then, I have locked myself up at home for the day. It seemed like the best solution at the time, and, for the first decade, no one noticed any difference. But when you came to live at Cranley Hall, Chrissy, it was suddenly more difficult for me to hide from the world. This is the first year that the date has almost passed me by entirely."

I wanted to comfort him, but his explanation stirred something in me. I'd only been a boy of six when my grandmother died and, as I stood watching him, the same dull ache I had felt as a child returned.

"I am so sorry, Lord Edgington," Alicia told him, and the empathy she felt was plain in her voice. "I would never have asked you here if I'd known."

"Thank you. Thank you, all." He stroked his daughter's hand appreciatively, then turned to address the room. "There is no need to apologise. But Christopher is right. The evidence we need in order to identity the murderer is here in this house, just as the solution to the disappearance of little Daniel Anderson was contained in the file I gave him. We've been looking at everything from the wrong perspective, but that's about to change."

CHAPTER THIRTY-TWO

The answer was before us, not that this meant I knew which of the clues we had gathered would be worth re-evaluating. I left the three of them talking in the library to return to the scene of the crime in the hope that something would come to me. If we set aside wild theories and tenuous connections, the one thing that felt stable was the house itself.

There had been three attacks, two of which resulted in murder. On our first night there, Mr Stanton had suffered a terrible reaction to chloroform and died. I considered it unlikely that this was the killer's intention, but if he'd gone there to steal something, he didn't have the time on that occasion. This made sense, as the nightwatchman's screaming would have made discovery more likely, but the same could not be said of the attack on Frances. She didn't cry out, and he would have had time after he stabbed her to take what he wanted.

Much like on the previous two nights, I was drawn back to the ancient centre of the building – the room where twenty generations had dined, entertained and celebrated. Two of the victims were found in the Great Hall, and I had to hope that the killer's secret would be uncovered there.

I stood in the centre of the immense space and took in every detail. There was the wall of weapons with one unoccupied space where, judging by its neighbours, a rather large sword had previously been. This told me very little, and so I looked about at the room's other treasures instead.

"Let me state things clearly," I said out loud, as I couldn't think of any other way to put things in order in my mind.

"If you so wish, sir," a voice from the doorway responded and there was Todd with Delilah at his side, just when I needed them. "Would you like an audience, or would you prefer to be left alone?"

Delilah ran over at a gallop, and I can't tell you what good it did to see them both. "No, come in, Todd. You'll have to put up with my rambling, but I'd very much like your thoughts on the matter."

"Of course, sir." He bowed and came closer as I motioned to a seat at the banqueting table in the centre of the room.

"I need to go through what's happened if I'm to understand any of it. Feel free to correct me if I make a mistake or you wish to offer some advice."

I must have fallen quiet then, as he gave me an encouraging nod and said, "Whenever you're ready, sir."

I took a deep breath and tried for the final time. "We came here because a friend of my mother's was worried about the goings on in her home. Historic artefacts were being moved about. A vase was broken, and two marble lions went missing entirely, only for them to turn up days later. On the very night that Lord Edgington arrived, Mr Stanton was murdered, and it seems that the first attempt to steal something from this room was made."

"It might also have been from one of the anterooms that lead off this chamber," Todd rightly pointed out, as Delilah sat down next to me.

"That is true. But if the motive is theft, I believe that we should concentrate on this part of the house. From the beginning, the culprit has gone out of his way to confuse what is before us. We fell into the trap of thinking that we had discovered a perfect motive when it seemed that Uhland had silenced his accomplice. What we should have questioned was whether Mark Isaac's death was just another distraction."

"Very good, sir!" he replied enthusiastically, though I was certain I'd only had this idea because my grandfather had made me study the Anderson file. "Yes, I believe you are on to something there."

I would have liked to walk over to the painting of the Prince of Wales at that moment, but Delilah looked comfortable standing next to me and so I stayed where I was. "If the purpose of the second killing was much the same as the disappearing lions' or the shifting portraits', the chances are that the attack on Frances Horniman served a similar function."

Todd could be as quick witted as my grandfather and immediately understood my reasoning. "Yes, if Miss Horniman was down here by chance so early in the morning, that would rule out the possibility that the killing had been planned."

I confess that I clicked my fingers at this moment as it actually felt as though we were getting somewhere. "So either that incredibly unfortunate thief was disturbed yet again before he could claim his prize, or he got up shortly before the first members of staff were set to rise and was waiting here for someone – anyone – to kill. But why would he do that?"

My smart young companion looked around the table as though there were other guests sitting with him. I don't know how this helped, but he managed to produce an answer. "It's difficult to imagine. Perhaps he just wanted us to know he had been in here."

I might well have issued a despairing cry as the endless variety of options overwhelmed me, but Todd spoke again. "There is the question of time to consider," he said, and I was glad he explained himself. "When Lord Edgington believed that Uhland had killed the nightwatchman, that would have made sense, as he and Isaac needed time to steal and replace the painting. If they weren't the killers, our chap could have had the same problem. He might have come here to complete a particular task rather than pocket a valuable. That would explain why nothing has been taken yet. Perhaps he wished to take something down from high up on the wall. Or maybe he's a forger like Isaac and he's been coming in here to copy the original before he gets around to swapping it."

I didn't like this latter option, if only because I felt that one talented counterfeiter in an investigation was plenty. I also seem logical that, after all that had happened, grandfather would have been on the lookout for another forgery.

Todd and I examined the upper part of the wall above the ornate wood panelling. There were plenty of paintings on display, not to mention the knives, plates and ornaments that were held to the wall with metal hooks.

"It was never going to be the cup," I said, having failed to notice anything. "Not only could he have taken it in five seconds without killing anyone, we would have instantly seen what was missing. He's trickier than that."

Still looking about the room, Todd rose to standing. "You're right, but that's how you'll catch him." He sounded ever so confident. I have no idea how I inspire such emotion in people. "He's done everything he can to distract you from his goal, but whatever he wants can't be invisible. We know it's in here somewhere and you're going to find it."

I sometimes wished that Todd had more time away from his duties to provide inspiration on a daily basis. His speech buoyed me nicely and, once Delilah had issued a few reproachful barks for leaving her, I was free to go on one last circuit of the room to compare it to my memory of the place when we'd first arrived.

"Todd…" I began before realising I only knew his Christian name and had never learnt his surname. Unless Todd *was* his surname. Perhaps his full name was Todd Todd. Anyway, as I was saying, "Todd, you're a genius. Come and look at this."

He strode over to see what I'd found, and I pointed to the rear of a large wooden chest that was a few inches from the wall at one end.

"It looks as though it has been moved and not put back as it was before. There's a clear mark on the floor where the leg would previously have stood."

For once *I* had made sense of something and *Todd* looked baffled. "What do you take that to mean, sir?"

"Well, it might just be that one of the servants cleaned it recently. But if we're lucky, we will look behind it and discover something extraordinary."

Without any prompting, he walked to the other end of the Tudor chest, which was decorated with half-moon patterns across the front. Together, we pulled it away from the wall, and I imagined what secrets we would find there. Perhaps there was a second priest hole, which the killer had been trying to access each time, or maybe there was an ancient inscription that foretold some mystical prophecy, or maybe there would be—

"Nothing," Todd said, and he looked just as disappointed as I felt. "I'm sorry, Master Christopher, it looks like your first idea was the more likely one. A maid probably pulled it out to dust behind it."

"It does look very clean," I conceded, before another idea entered my head and I took a few steps to the side.

I looked up at the line of blades that were still arranged in order of length, starting with the longest sword at the bottom of the wood panel and finishing with the shortest dagger high on the wall above. As we've established, I don't know much about weapons, but it looked as though there were examples from every era of history of the last thousand years. Some looked ceremonial rather than practical – there were rapiers with elaborate hand guards and intricate scrolling patterns on the blades – while others were little more than rusty old shards of metal with a few indecipherable words etched into them.

I looked at the space at head height where the killer had taken the weapon with which he'd attacked Frances. The neighbouring weapons were comparatively modern and had thick, wide blades. From the examples above and below, it looked to be a sword of some description, and yet the figure I'd chased up to the long gallery hadn't been holding anything.

"What have you discovered, Christopher?" my grandfather asked as he entered the room at just the right moment.

I didn't answer at first, as I couldn't quite believe my luck. I'd pieced together a possible solution, but I had to run through my logic a second time to be sure.

"Master Christopher?" Todd prompted me.

"I know what he was doing here," I said in a breathless voice. "No, in fact, it's more than that. I think I know who the killer is."

CHAPTER THIRTY-THREE

We left the Great Hall to look for our few remaining suspects. Mr Cridland was in the corridor and appeared to be counting the objects on a Welsh dresser for some reason. He was an odd chap, even for a butler, but he had a good knowledge of what went on in Parham House and directed us back through the Saloon and outside.

Dr Carbonell, Elton Lockhart and his sweetheart were at a table beside the house, drinking wine with the wide expanse of the estate stretching out before them. The remaining trio of historians consisted of a pair of former friends, and (overlapping, but separately) an engaged couple. I believed that only one of them had attacked Frances.

"Are you going to tell us what's been happening?" Dr Carbonell asked as soon as he saw my grandfather. But it wasn't the great Lord Edgington who could answer that question. I was as shocked as anyone that I was about to reveal a truly diabolical plot, with very little help from my peerless mentor. Of course, that didn't mean I knew where to start, but at least I had Todd and my grandfather there for support. Oh, and Delilah stayed at my side throughout.

Vyvyan stood up to address the detective in her usual soft, yet excited tone. "Please, Lord Edgington. Tell us what's happened. I haven't seen Frances all day and I'm worried."

"I'm sorry," Grandfather told them in as stern a voice as he could muster. "It's not my place to say. I'm going to keep my counsel and let my grandson explain what he has discovered."

There would be no good news for one member of our party, but then murder investigations don't tend to have happy endings. Vyvyan was clearly desperate to learn what I knew, but she sat in troubled silence, waiting for the truth.

I stood at the small metal table and, when it became clear that I would need some extra courage to get me through the discussion, Lockhart poured me a drink. He looked concerned as he served it, and this kindness was just what I needed to kick me into life. The gulp of strong red wine didn't hurt either.

"The mystery we have faced since we arrived at Parham House is quite different from the cases to which I have become accustomed.

Our group of suspects was not a tightly knit family or a pack of old friends but somewhat tangentially connected colleagues who had come together because of a shared interest in history. The twins didn't know Dr Carbonell well before this month. Elton Lockhart had apparently never met Eric Uhland, and none of you knew Mark Isaac."

"So we are not to blame then?" Whatever generosity the expert on ancient civilisations had just shown me was forgotten as he delivered his words in a bitter murmur.

My gaze locked onto his. "I didn't say that. I'm just trying to show you how hard it was to make sense of anything we've witnessed. First, there was a host of small, inexplicable events in the house for no apparent reason. Then the nightwatchman was killed without any apparent motive. Mark Isaac's murder, on the other hand, provided us with a stronger footing for our investigation; we identified his supervisor as the likely killer, as Uhland had stolen a painting from the Great Parlour and replaced it with a copy that Isaac had produced. When there was a further attack last night, it appeared to make our perfectly sensible theory null."

"Who was attacked?" Carbonell asked, but Vyvyan was ahead of him and rushed closer to demand the truth.

"Tell me it wasn't Frances! I couldn't live if anything happened to her."

Our time at Parham had been anything but a holiday and I was too tired to stay on my feet any longer, so I sat down in a free chair and took another sip of wine before continuing. "I'm afraid that she was stabbed early this morning. Grandfather and I found her in a pool of blood on the floor of the Great Hall."

The news crushed Vyvyan just as much as if I'd driven the Daimler straight over her. She opened her mouth to speak and held open one hand out in front of her, but it would do no good. Her sister was gone… to the hospital, not that she knew that. And, yes, I felt bad for keeping the truth from Vyvyan, but I had my reasons.

"Why would anyone want to kill her?" Carbonell asked, and I noticed that his old friend stayed silent.

I answered with a question of my own. "Why would anyone do anything that I've just described? The whole thing is a ruse wrapped up in a diversion, and it was only by accepting this fact that I could comprehend what was really happening."

Grandfather remained on his feet but looked proud of my success, even if he didn't yet know what I'd discovered. Todd stood ready as always and would no doubt launch into action if needed.

"As I implied before, this case would not be decided based on personal feelings or past grudges. The murder had nothing to do with Elton Lockhart stealing Dr Carbonell's fiancée, or the rivalry between Vyvyan and Frances – even if they nearly came to blows over their love for the same man. Any of us could have been victims, and it wouldn't have changed a thing."

"So you're saying that the killer is a madman?" Carbonell's eyebrows raised as he spoke. "You made the mistake of trying to predict the actions of a person whose psychology simply cannot be fathomed?"

I considered his point. "There is some truth in what you're saying. I believe that an element of insanity is required to kill another human in anything but self-defence. What I really meant, though, is that the evidence we found was designed for our benefit. My grandfather predicted that the killer's initial behaviour was a prelude to something more significant. He'd evidently had the chance to steal valuable items and not taken it, which suggested that he had a plan in mind. Stanton died when the killer was disrupted in his task. We found the chloroform that he'd used in Frances's bedroom, but this was another trick. He left it there for the police to discover, which is exactly what happened."

I don't normally have a taste for wine – except for the odd glass of sweet sherry, or perhaps a fruity rosé – but every time I stopped for a sip, I appreciated its strength more. It had a lit a fire in me and I wouldn't stop now.

"The first victims were killed for no reason other than to lead us to a finale. Any evidence we'd been able to uncover was planned by the killer and, last night after Frances was attacked, the treasures of the house still appeared to be in place."

I believe that Vyvyan would normally have been the one to ask questions, but she hadn't come back to herself, and stared off across the grounds as if she couldn't hear us. Instead, it fell to Dr Carbonell once more.

"So what was the point of any of it?" He was not the only one eyeing that rogue Elton Lockhart just then.

"To distract from a totally different crime, of course." I sounded more confident now. I knew what I had to say and what most of it meant, and I had no trouble choosing my words. "It was as my grandfather predicted from the beginning. We were called here because of a series of events that were staged to attract attention. In fact, the presence of Lord Edgington – far from scaring our killer as it did Uhland and his accomplice – only served to encourage him. He wanted us to notice the thefts and the valuables that were shifting around the house. He wanted us to find the chloroform and blame Frances, and when that didn't work, he wanted us to accuse Eric Uhland of Isaac's murder. The only problem was that Uhland was arrested before the real killer had time to enact the final part of the plan. When we were in bed last night, with the nightwatchman no longer an obstacle and everyone believing there was no threat to the house, he came down to steal the thing that he'd always planned to take."

"The monster in our midst is just a petty criminal." With tears finally coming to her eyes, Vyvyan inhaled in tortured astonishment. "Three people had to die… My sister had to die so that some blackguard could pinch a vase or a painting? Why didn't he just take it in the night and be done with it?"

Grandfather had promised to let me talk, but he couldn't resist explaining this himself. "Because every single thing in this house has been collated and catalogued by Clive and Alicia Pearson. It is almost impossible to take something without it being noticed and, if that item's true worth was still unknown, it's just possible that—" He caught my eye then and realised that he'd said too much. "My apologies, Christopher. Please go on."

"I appreciate your help, Grandfather," I told him with a smart bow of the head. "And you're quite right. Everything happened in this way because the killer wanted to do more than just steal a valuable. He wanted to conceal the fact that it had been taken. And what better way is there to hide a murder weapon than by staging a murder?"

There was a gasp then, not only from my mother and Alicia who, unbeknownst to me, were standing on the Saloon steps, listening to my tale. Grandfather was quite taken aback by the revelation, too, and I hurried to prove my point.

"None of us thought twice about the killer removing the weapon

224

he had used on Frances. The obvious conclusion was that it had his fingerprints on it, and he did not wish to be identified. But I came across the killer just after he stabbed her, and he was wearing gloves."

Carbonell looked quite confounded by the explanation and raised a valid point. "It still doesn't explain why he failed to take it on the night that Mr Stanton died. He could surely have pulled it down, even after the poor man had such an adverse reaction to the chloroform."

"He couldn't if it was high on the wall. He needed time both to reach the specific artefact he wished to take and rearrange the knives so that no one would notice which was missing."

"How do you know they were rearranged?" Grandfather rubbed the side of his cheek as he asked this, and I knew he was trying to follow the path of evidence that I had only just trodden.

"For one thing, I believe a chest had been moved so that he could reach the highest weapons. They were sorted by size, starting with the biggest at the bottom and reaching up the wall to the smallest at the top." I could see that he was about to interrupt me again, and so I talked over him. "The vacant space suggests it was a long sword which, if it's anything like the others beside it, had a thick blade. But the wound that Frances suffered was comparatively small, and it did not go all the way through her body, which suggests a thinner, shorter weapon was used."

"What were the weapons like at the top of the wall?" he could finally ask. "Why would anyone want to steal one?"

"Dr Carbonell will be able to tell me for certain, but, while some of them may have been very old, I don't think that any of the weapons on display had any great financial value when compared to the portraiture hanging throughout the house. This was another of the problems we faced as, surely, if the ultimate motive was theft, any expensive item that was stolen would be readily missed."

I paused to take in each person's reaction. Lockhart's normally arrogant gaze had dropped to the tabletop and would not shift for some time, but his fiancée stared straight at me. She was already distraught and now struggled to understand the implications of what I'd discovered. She was not alone; Carbonell sat beside her, puzzling over what any of it could mean.

"I examined each of the weapons before they were put on display."

He held his hat on his lap with one hand and scratched his bare head with the other. "You'll find my notes on them in my files, most of which I have already presented to Mrs Pearson. I can't think of any one of them that would be worth killing three people to obtain."

"Perhaps I can explain then. You see, on our cases, my grandfather is loath to accept the idea that any of the murders we investigate could have been carried out by a madman, but I believe that a certain kind of obsession was required in this instance. Did any of the weapons date back to Anglo-Saxon times?"

"Yes, there were three small daggers that were over a millennium old. They were discovered in the excavation of Chatterton Hall in the 1880s."

Her face pale, Vyvyan glanced at the man she loved. He looked more nervous than I'd seen him before – his usual brash manner dimmed – and I believe she'd sensed it too.

I spoke more quickly so as not to prolong the matter. "The killer was consumed by a period a thousand years past and the idea that the Anglo-Saxons had possessed pagan magic that had been lost to time. He saw the inscriptions in an ornate casket as a prophecy of how to achieve power beyond human reckoning."

Todd quietly sidled over towards Lockhart as I spoke.

"Even before he arrived here, the killer conspired to steal other items from a previous excavation and pieced together a formula to follow in the footsteps of an ancient hero who turned from a man into a god." There was the definite feeling in the air that something was about to happen, and if I didn't speak faster, I wouldn't get the rest of the story out. "On the casket here at Parham, the mythical character of Ægil is depicted holding his knife up to the sky on the night of the spring equinox, which falls around the twentieth of March. There are three dead bodies at his feet, and his people are bowing down before him as worshipers. It was not the exquisite cup in the Great Parlour which the killer identified as his prize but a simple knife that he believed had once belonged to—"

That was as much as I managed to say before Lockhart lunged away from Todd. To be quite frank, it was a farfetched tale, and I didn't blame him for interrupting, but the rage that surged out of him was truly frightening.

"Raymond, you utter swine!" he bellowed, and he would have caught his former friend on the chin if Carbonell's chair hadn't tipped backwards. "You're nothing but a murderer!"

CHAPTER THIRTY-FOUR

I should probably say at this point that I was just about to identify the real killer when Lockhart pipped me to it. I'm not so egotistical that I need constant praise, but I would like it noted that I picked the right man (for once). And now that is clear, I will continue with the story.

A mêlée was only just avoided as Elton Lockhart fell sprawling on his belly, and the expert on antique weaponry seized his pith helmet and rolled clear.

"I'll get you for what you've done, Raymond," Lockhart shouted again, but the killer was up on his feet by now, and there was no one close enough to seize him.

Todd, Grandfather and even our dog waited to see what Carbonell would do, but the table blocked their path and Carbonell turned on the spot to dash away from them. Somehow, I was the first to react and jumped from my seat to give chase. The land on that side of the house was flat and open, and there was nothing to slow him down. I really should have questioned why he was so attached to that hat, but I was too busy wondering what a younger version of myself would have thought to see me running towards danger rather than away from it.

I could suddenly remember what it felt like to be hunted around the schoolyard by my most consistent bullies, the Marshall brothers. The feeling in my stomach wasn't so dissimilar to seasickness, though I had no intention of hiding in a bush or taking cover in the school chapel. Instead of being afraid of what was about to happen, I ran all the faster. It certainly helped that I could hear Todd's quick footsteps not so very far behind me, and Elton Lockhart was still shouting insults farther back. Delilah was soon at my side, bounding along with her tongue hanging out, as I believe she had mistaken all this for a jolly game. Either way, she wouldn't have offered much in the way of help if it had come to a fight.

A thick bank of clouds rolled in from the east to cover the moon, but there was a faint light on the horizon that illuminated the field in front of me. It was as if someone had turned off one light and switched on another, and I could make out Carbonell quite clearly. He looked as though he'd never run so fast in his life, but I could see that his hands were full, and he was struggling with something. A moment later, his hat came sailing over his shoulder and almost hit me. I considered shouting in complaint, but after all he'd done that week, this was a minor offence.

Just as we reached the Parham House cricket pitch, he held his hand up to the sky. He kept running at first, but then the oddest thing happened. The faint light I'd noticed in the distance became brighter, much as if a motor headlight had been turned up to its zenith. It was like a beam sent to earth from… well, I almost dare not say it, but it looked very much like it was projecting down from heaven. It was far brighter than the Milky Way, but I could see the stars of distant galaxies most clearly within it. I was so shocked by this inexplicable phenomenon that I stumbled and went sliding down the pitch towards the killer.

Carbonell stopped at silly mid-off. He must have noticed the light too, as he turned back to me, and the dark blade in his hand glimmered like the sea in the moonlight. I looked up from a few feet away and there was a triumphant smile on his face. It was a terrible sight, and even Todd stopped beside me and wouldn't approach him.

"It's Dísablót. Tonight is the equinox!" the lunatic with the knife declared, and then he closed his eyes and started chanting something about Ægil and sacrifices and a few of the Anglo-Saxon gods.

I should have done more than just lie at his feet in fear, but it's not the sort of situation one finds oneself in very often. Before I could decide what to do next, Lockhart came thundering past to launch himself straight at his childhood friend.

Carbonell folded like a newspaper as the dashing figure crashed into him. There was a resounding "Oof!" and the blade he'd been holding shot into the air, spinning as it went. It plunged back down to earth in what, looking back, feels like half speed. At that moment, though, everything happened very quickly, and I only just had time to pull my leg away before the knife hit the ground in front of me.

"You grotesque, hypocritical swine!" Lockhart said as he pinned the culprit's arms and legs down with his own.

I'm fairly certain that things would have turned violent if Todd hadn't pulled the men apart. Vyvyan was there to embrace her brave fiancé, but my eyes were still on the defeated killer.

Carbonell was a wreck now and there was no risk of his escaping. He lay on his back, looking up at the celestial light, and tears sprang from his eyes as Todd stood over him.

"I was so close!" he whined. "I was so close, and you ruined it." He shook his head and felt sorry for himself.

"No, you weren't." I was only too happy to correct him as I got to my feet and brushed the grass from my clothes. "Frances is alive. We got her to the hospital just in time. You only killed two people."

"Oh, Chrissy. Do you really mean it?" Vyvyan's jaw fell open, and I had to hope this meant she wasn't angry with me for hiding the truth for so long.

"Yes, she's in Horsham Hospital, and you can visit her whenever you like."

The look of disgust on Carbonell's face was overwhelming, and he released an anguished wail up to the sky.

My grandfather arrived just in time to pass judgement. "Don't be a fool, man. You were never going to become a god. You're obsessed with a fairy tale, as so many men before you have been. There is no such thing as a knife that can turn humans into immortals."

"But the light," he replied, pointing to the horizon. Whatever it was, it had changed shape and intensified and was now more like a cone spearing down to us.

"The brightness you can see," Grandfather said as Todd pulled his prisoner up to standing, "is a common phenomenon at this time of year; it often coincides with the equinox. It's known as zodiacal light, and there's nothing magical about it."

Carbonell struggled under Todd's strong grip. "I know what really happened, you confounded sceptic. I was so close."

"You're a madman, Raymond," Lockhart exclaimed, and I doubt anyone there would have contradicted him. "I'm truly sorry for the part I played in driving you to this sad state. I'm sorry that I've been a liar and a cheat. But one thing I've never been is a murderer, and you chose to kill those people."

"It was the only way." Carbonell's eyes were wild; he looked at his friend as though he were a stranger. "They had to die so that I could fulfil the prophecy. The nightwatchman wasn't supposed to be my first victim. Unluckily for him, he changed his normal route and met his ill fate."

It was tempting to shout and yell or at least try to convince him he was wrong, but we did not take the bait. I picked up the knife, and Grandfather nodded to his factotum to deal with the wretched creature. I'd met enough murderers by this point in my life to know that there was no reasoning with a man like Raymond Carbonell.

Vyvyan had fallen silent again, but I imagine that it had finally sunk in that her sister really was alive – and that her fiancé really wasn't a killer – as she let out a cry and dropped to her knees.

"Oh, my darling," Lockhart turned away from Carbonell to lavish his attention on someone more deserving. "Oh, you poor thing, what must you have thought?" The pair embraced and, no doubt shattered but filled with relief, Vyvyan sobbed into his shoulder.

Grandfather put his hand on the flat of my back to guide me to the house. "You do know that you could have told her the truth from the beginning?" he pointed out, and I was quick to answer.

"But I didn't want Carbonell to know that his plan had failed." I admit this had seemed very important at the time, but it was hard to fathom what I'd been thinking now. "I didn't want him to kill again to fulfil the prophecy."

His expression instantly changed to one of quiet pride. "Then you did the right thing, Christopher. Everything worked out for the best. And what a beautiful night this is." Delilah was already sprinting off ahead of us, barking with excitement as the first constables ran from the house. "Of course, the 'false dawn' we have just witnessed is only visible when one is far from brightly lit cities and the moon is well hidden. Even the light of Venus can overwhelm it, but we were lucky tonight to enjoy a true spectacle."

I was dazed by just about every last thing that had happened. So to discover that the sky put on a show for us at night without anyone knowing was hard to comprehend.

"But what causes it? Can you be sure it had nothing to do with the killings and Anglo-Saxons and all that flummadiddle?"

"Scientists still can't agree, but it's most likely the light of the sun bouncing off tiny particles of rock in the atmosphere. It certainly has nothing to do with a mythical figure who may or may not have existed during the dark ages. Much like a rainbow, zodiacal light will make you neither rich nor lucky."

"Hmmm," I said, when I could think of nothing else. "I see."

His moustache wriggled, and I believe that he held back a smile. "Christopher?"

"Yes, Grandfather."

"I was very impressed by what you achieved this evening."

"Oh. Thank you." I should probably have been more appreciative, but there was something on my mind. "Grandfather?"

"Yes, Christopher."

"Do you think there's any chance I could have some dinner? I've only eaten a few ham sandwiches since I woke up this morning. To say that I'm famished would be an understatement."

"I'm sure that we could ask Henrietta to conjure us up one of her cheese flans."

"With apple cake for dessert?"

He really laughed then. "We'll see what she's got in the pantry."

"Very good," I replied, though inside I was shouting *Yes! Food! Hurrah!* "I would very much appreciate it."

CHAPTER THIRTY-FIVE

When the time came to leave the next morning, I felt quite perplexed. We'd solved the puzzle, so I wasn't worried about that anymore. In fact, the crime itself was one of my lesser concerns. After a hearty feast the night before, I'd given a report of my findings to Inspector Kirk, who, I believe it is fair to say, was an even more ardent admirer of that noted detective Christopher Prentiss than he had been when we'd first met.

The news from the hospital was positive too and, although Frances would need time to recuperate, her prospects were good. Her sister and future brother-in-law had been to see her, and she was apparently sitting up in bed full of the joys of spring – it being the twenty-first of March and all that.

No, what troubled me was the feeling that I was leaving a part of myself behind at Parham House. Alicia and her daughters came to see us off in the stable yard, and I had a chance to speak to my prospective assistant, Veronica. She had already turned me down for the position once, and I decided not to offer it again.

"Well done, Christopher," she told me, sounding particularly grown up. "It's almost as if you're a real detective and not just a boy playing at being one."

"You're absolutely right," I said without a hint of offence. "It's the darnedest thing, but I think that I did rather well this time. It took me a day or two – and I probably only managed it because my grandfather was distracted by the memory of one of the three greatest tragedies that have occurred in his life – but I'm still quite proud."

Little Dione let go of her mother's hand and rushed over. "Will you come back to play with us again soon, Chrissy?" she asked.

"Happily," I replied before realising that Grandfather was listening and trying to turn this into a grammatically complete sentence, "…is my answer to that question."

He grinned contentedly and went to talk to our hostess.

"You must have made a good impression on Dione," Lavinia told me. "She doesn't normally like anyone."

"Yes, I do," she replied in her contrary manner. "I like Chrissy."

She stepped forward to give me an unexpected hug, and I believe that I blushed as brightly as a spell of zodiacal light on a clear spring night.

The bride-and-groom-to-be were next, and they both shook my hand most enthusiastically.

"You know, Christopher," Lockhart began, "I'm going to be singing your praises for years to come. In fact, we may well name our first child after you."

"I don't know why you're being so complimentary," I responded. "You knew that Carbonell was to blame before I even said his name."

He tipped his head back reflectively. "That is quite true, but I had you at a disadvantage."

"Oh, yes?"

"That's right." He leaned closer to whisper his secret in my ear. "As soon as you sat down at the table on the patio, I felt sure that one of us had to be the killer. Well, I knew that it wasn't me. And I'd been with Vyvyan when Isaac was killed, so it had to be—"

"I think what you mean," his companion interrupted, "is that you never imagined for one second that the woman you love could be a murderer."

He hit his forehead with the heel of his palm. "That is it, my darling. You took the very words out of my mouth." He bent forward to kiss her cheek, and she rolled her eyes.

"We know each other so well." She gave him a loving stamp on the foot and then turned to talk to me. "I owe you a million thanks, Christopher. Without you and your grandfather, Frances would have died, and who's to say what Raymond would have done. You really are a marvel."

"And you really are too kind." This was another opportunity for me to turn red, but I tried to take the compliment as it was intended.

"Chrissy," Mother called as she emerged from the house. "I've just heard from Cranley that your brother and father have got into an argument over something to do with actuarial tables. They're both sulking in their rooms, and I'm afraid we must leave."

She bade farewell to Alicia, and when all the goodbyes had been said, I turned back to look at the house itself. Parham was still a building in progress, and perhaps it always would be. Generations of people had left their mark on the place, and Alicia and her husband were no different. While previous owners had tried to modernise or embellish the house, the Pearsons were driven by the desire to preserve it for posterity.

And if there was one thread that tied together the group of people I had met there, it was the importance they gave to the millennia of history that preceded the present day. Lockhart and his acolytes adored the ancient past. Carbonell had become obsessed with one specific period of it, and the Pearsons gave the weight of history the respect it deserved. It was hard to know whose approach was best – though it was easy to pick the worst.

"Do come along, Chrissy," Grandfather called from the Aston Martin. "We have a very short drive ahead of us." He laughed at his quip, and I got into the car beside him as Mother, Delilah and our staff boarded the other vehicles.

He tooted his horn and the friends I'd made that week (and a couple of people we'd accused of murder) waved us off. Veronica and her sisters ran after us through the gatehouse and up the winding path towards the deer park. Dione was the first to tire, then Lavinia, and Veronica made it some way before coming to a stop at the top of the hill to watch us disappear.

Thinking over my time there, I realised that things really had changed over the last few years. I wasn't a brat in short trousers anymore and, while some might therefore conclude I was a brat in long trousers, I decided to give myself the benefit of the doubt. I was still considering the progress I'd made and just how long it had been since my brother and I had squabbled over a teacake or apple turnover, when Grandfather made a confession.

"Christopher…" He had to clear his throat before he said anything else, and I could tell it was difficult for him. "My boy, there are things that I didn't quite… well, I must admit that there were some facts of the case that I perhaps haven't understood."

I put my hand to my mouth in disbelief. "Do you really mean it? Has the great Lord Edgington been outfoxed?"

"Not at all!" he snapped in reply. "As you know, I wasn't myself this week, and I may have become distracted from the minutiae of the—"

"It's fine, Grandfather." My tone had turned more serious, and I patted him on the back to show that I was only teasing. "I'll tell you whatever you wish to know."

"Jolly good." He took one hand off the wheel to bother his snowdrop-white beard. "In which case, I'd like you to tell me how you knew that Dr Raymond Carbonell was the killer as opposed to his former friend. When you described your perception of the case last night, I was certain that you were going to tell us that Lockhart was to blame. After all, he was the one who had been accused of stealing the Anglo-Saxon artefacts, and he was reluctant to discuss the issue whenever we talked to him."

"Yes, but the only reason that we knew about those accusations was because Carbonell was there at the same dig. I believe that he was the one who stole from the graves, and whatever he found there made him believe that it was Ægil's knife that held magical powers."

"That is just the sort of thing in which a desperate man would invest his energy."

"Exactly, and we knew that Carbonell had suffered a psychological fracture of some kind after Lockhart stole his fiancée. He told us that he'd poured himself into his work to recover and that it fulfilled him in a way nothing else could. I believe that the chaos he attempted to create at Parham was a sign of his unhinged mind. It was apparent early in the investigation that the killer was motivated by more than just money. As soon as I realised that it was the knife he was after, I remembered the picture of Ægil on the Anglo-Saxon casket in the workshop. He was holding a blade up to the sky with three dead bodies at his feet and his people bowing down in reverence. It seemed logical that the expert on old weapons would be the one to realise its importance."

"Some importance!" Grandfather gave a derisory hoot. "I examined the knife against Carbonell's files last night and he'd described it quite differently. He might well have hidden its true description if you hadn't caught him. Not that his conception of it was in any way accurate. The only thing that made it unique was the inscription which read, *Ægil ME ÞORTE*. I confess that I had to consult one of Clive Pearson's books to make sense of the phrase, but I believe it means Ægil made me."

"So it really did belong to a legendary hero?" I asked, somewhat impressed by his discovery.

"I suppose that is theoretically possible." He was evidently reluctant to accept even this much. "But Ægil was a common name at the time. It's just as likely as my buying a tall, nineteenth century hat that once belonged to a man named Abraham and assuming it was President Lincoln's."

I laughed at this, then wondered whether he was speaking from experience. To change the subject, he asked another question. "And what of the voice that Veronica heard and wrote down in her notepad? She said it was Eric Uhland who called to Mark Isaac before he died."

"Yes, that threw me for a short time, too. I really felt that Uhland must have killed the two victims and that one of his accomplices attacked Frances Horniman to undermine the idea. But then I considered the possibility that he hadn't killed anyone and, if that were true, someone could have imitated his voice." I adopted the forger's dour, flat tone. "It's really not so difficult to make oneself sound a little glum and boring."

"You're quite right, though I must also compliment you on a fine impression."

Silence fell between us, and I took the time to reflect on the case again. "The lengths that Carbonell went to are beyond tragic. Of course my sympathy must lie with his victims, but there's something terribly sad about a man who is so confident in his beliefs even after he's been shown that they are nonsense."

Grandfather slowed down to ease into a bend before replying. "I wouldn't be too upset. For one thing, he's still a murderer, and for another, we can't say for certain that his belief in ancient magic was entirely wrong. The picture of Ægil on the ornate casket showed that he had sacrificed three people before his apotheosis, whereas Dr Carbonell only succeeded in killing two and stabbing another. One of those may have been an accident, too, and so he hardly followed Ægil's example to the letter."

I pulled my neck in and considered whether he really believed this. "You don't mean—"

He interrupted me before I could say anything stupid. "No, of course I don't. The killer could have murdered three hundred people, and he still wouldn't have turned into a god. It's all stuff and nonsense." This was one of his favourite expressions, and he decided to repeat it.

"Stuff and nonsense!"

"Of course it is," I began, willing myself to believe him. "Only children worry themselves with such petty concerns."

To make me feel better, he found something to brighten the mood. "There is no such thing as magic, and we have no need for it when more wonders abound in human society than in every mythology in the world combined. Think of the planes in the sky and the submarines in our oceans. Those are the real wonders of the modern day."

"Yes, Grandfather. You're quite right." I had to stop myself from admitting that I still hoped there were mermaids and unicorns out there somewhere, even if I did enjoy modern technology as much as the next person. So maybe I wasn't quite as grown up as I believed. Maybe I was still in the middle between infancy and adulthood. To be quite honest, I was looking forward to staying that way for some time.

His eyebrows angled downwards in a disapproving grimace, and I could see that we had switched back to our usual roles. "We have plenty of excitement as it is." His frown became an upturned frown. "We can only imagine what our next case will entail."

The End (For Now...)

Get another

LORD EDGINGTON ADVENTURE

absolutely **free**…

Download your free novella at
www.benedictbrown.net

"LORD EDGINGTON INVESTIGATES..."

The fourteenth full-length mystery will be available in **Autumn 2024** at amazon.

Sign up on my website to the readers' club to know when it goes on sale.

ABOUT THIS BOOK

I've rarely felt that I knew a setting for one of my books as well as I do this one. At the same time, I've never before felt that there was just so much history to a house that I barely knew anything at all. And to make sense of that apparent paradox, give me a minute to explain.

I first heard about Parham House through an Irish colleague of mine who writes historical fiction (check out Suzanne Winterly's books. They're great!). She is an old friend of Lady Emma Barnard's, the great-grand daughter of Alicia and Clive Pearson who has lived at Parham since her great-aunt Veronica died in the 1990s. Suzanne put me in touch with Lady Emma and, the next time I was in Britain, she gave me a tour of the property whilst my children played in the gardens with their mother.

What I particularly liked about the idea of setting a book there was that I knew early on that the house was undergoing dramatic changes in the 1920s. As explained in this novel, the Pearsons only bought Parham in 1922 before spending decades restoring and reinstating the Elizabethan features it would have had when it was first built.

The fact that this was not a pristine stately home in the twenties, but a building in flux, instantly gave me ideas for who would make up my list of suspects and what the mystery would revolve around. As nice as it is to have a beautiful house on the cover of this book, this was what really inspired me to get in touch with Lady Emma, and I'm so thankful she gave me permission to set a story at her family home.

Another important development occurred after we included the cover for this book at the back of our last release. I was contacted by an existing reader called Jayne Kirk who happened to have spent three years writing a book all about Parham House and the renovations that were carried out, not only by the Pearsons, but by each family who had lived there over the centuries. "Parham: An Elizabethan House and its Restoration" is an incredibly useful book, and I consulted it every five minutes as I wrote – when I wasn't bothering poor Jayne with more questions via e-mail.

As if that hadn't provided me with enough information, I also had two books that Parham House had produced and (perhaps even more significantly for the story I ended up with) Lavinia Smiley (née Pearson)'s memoir of her childhood. "A Nice Clean Plate" is a lovely read, and it provides an account of the games the children played, their relationship with their family and friends, and their unique personalities. I've tried to do them justice in this book and a lot of the quirkiest details are references to what I read there. Some examples of this include their father's forgiveness of a servant who stole from the house, an entirely separate half-Italian footman whom they adored, the beloved, newspaper-ironing butler Mr Cridland, the rude poetry game that the children played, and the war between their nanny and the cook, who really did communicate through the dumb waiter lift and ancient pipes.

In order for the plot I'd planned to work, I needed a nightwatchman. I thought it a bit unlikely that such a person would have existed, but I was wrong. Lavinia's book confirmed that there was a Mr Scutt working there in the twenties who would walk about the place checking that no burglars had got into the house. Oh, and the owls that were making all that noise in the trees outside Chrissy's bedroom, which make him think that a grunting killer was coming to get him, were also real. Lavinia and her sisters were nervous children, and they were just as afraid of these ominous noises as our anxious hero.

To return to my feeling of knowing everything and nothing, I've never had the chance to read so much about a property before, so I spent a lot of time not only researching the book but checking my facts when I forgot where I'd read a particular story or had to look up extra information. One of the problems I found was that, with so many different generations of owners, who all left their mark on the estate, it was sometimes hard to know exactly what was there in the twenties. I have done my best to be accurate in this respect, but as I warned at the beginning, this is primarily a work of fiction, and a very silly one at that.

One thing that was true in the twenties is that the painting which was thought to depict Queen Elizabeth I was hanging in the Great Hall just as it does today. You can read about it in more detail on the Parham House website, but the picture now referred to as "A Lady of Rank" was certainly bought as an image of that great queen, who was the

246

godmother of the original owner. There is much debate as to who this lady is, but there's no doubt that the picture has been at Parham for many centuries. Whoever it is, with her crown, pearls and distinct similarity to the Virgin Queen, she is splendid. So there's still a mystery about her, and who doesn't love a mystery?

When I revisited Parham a few days after I'd finished the first draft, I had the strange sensation of my book coming to life. It was a real thrill, but I was also left with the feeling that I hadn't done the place justice, which brings me on to the most important thing I will say anywhere in this book, which is that I recommend visiting Parham House for yourself if you possibly can. You'll be able to see the richness of the building and its phenomenal art collection, learn about the restoration work the Pearsons carried out, and stroll about the sensational gardens. You can even visit Veronica, Lavinia and Dione's Wendy House, which was added to the walled garden by Victor Heal, the architect who worked on Parham for decades from the twenties onwards.

Though Lord Edgington and his family are not based on real people, someone who did visit Parham in 1928 was George V's wife, Queen Mary. The Pearson family would have been in a welcoming party for her at the main gate, but sadly her driver got lost and they ended up entering through a farmyard on the other side of the estate. She was not the first monarch to visit, as Queen Victoria (though a princess at the time) called by in 1821, and it has long been rumoured that Elizabeth I herself was there for a dinner, which no one can prove or deny (so we might as well believe it).

Clive Pearson does not feature in this book as he really would have been abroad working for the Pearson corporation – which would later become Pearson Publishing – on construction and oil projects in South America in 1928. He was an incredibly driven man and, though he had little knowledge of historical architecture or interior design when he decided to buy Parham, he would devote much of his life to the project and collaborated closely with his architect.

His mother, Viscountess Cowdray, was an equally impressive woman who was not only an influential suffragist, but a philanthropist who promoted the cause of nursing all over Britain and earned the nickname "the Fairy Godmother of Nursing", as she helped establish the Royal College of Nursing, and even a hospital in Mexico City. It's funny to read her granddaughter Lavinia's account of her, in which, after a long list of positive adjectives (including, hardworking, benevolent and ambitious) she admits that her grandmother absolutely terrified her.

But there's one person who, in all the accounts I read, was instrumental to the many things that the family achieved. The girls' mother, Alicia, was the person who kept the home fires burning when Clive was abroad working for his family's company. She was also just as knowledgeable on restoration as her husband, and she was very hands-on with the work at Parham. You can tell from her daughter's description in her memoir that she was very much loved as a mother, and that's one of the reasons I was cautious when setting a murder mystery around her family. In fact, her great-granddaughter told me that Alicia was "a scholar, book collector, historian and expert in heraldry – all self-taught." She was also a very good writer and had a great way with words, and all three of her daughters inherited these points to some extent. Lady Emma finished by describing her great-grandmother as "very modest and quiet, but whoever met Alicia always had the greatest respect for her and never forgot her."

Something I did to try to distance the real from the imaginary was to focus on a totally fictitious cache of artefacts that has been brought into the house. In truth, there are no Anglo-Saxon treasures at Parham. In a feat to rival an over-the-top Hollywood movie, I strung together a bunch of ideas to create my own mythology. And now that I've been hard on myself, I will say that all the things that my experts discuss are based on fact. The carved whalebone box and the cup are based on real items from the eighth century. I went to visit the Franks Casket in the British Museum, whereas the Tassilo Chalice, though possibly forged by English monks abroad, was immediately sent to Kremsmünster Abbey in Austria, where it remains approximately twelve hundred and fifty years later.

Paganism and Anglo-Saxon culture faded away in Britain as Christianity gained power. We know surprisingly little about them, as I discovered when I tried to write a fantastical children's book about British folklore and paganism (that I soon abandoned to write my first mystery novel).

Although the Anglo-Saxon runic alphabet was in use for five centuries, there are fewer than two hundred items in the world which bear such inscriptions. The Franks Casket is particularly interesting in that it mixes pagan and Christian imagery. It has both a scene of the Adoration of the Magi and one of Ægil and his brother – not to mention Achilles, and perhaps the founding of Britain centuries before. Though I made him out to be a demi-god in this story, the only information we have on the mythological figure of Ægil comes from two Norse sagas which depict him as either the son of a Finnish king who marries a swan or a William-Tell-esque archer who saves his brother from imprisonment, which matches the scene on the Franks Casket.

The casket was made in Britain, but found its way to a French monastery, from where it was probably looted and, by the nineteenth century, ending up with a family who used it as a sewing box. It might have been lost altogether if, after the silver fixings were sold, the remaining pieces hadn't been located in a Parisian antiques shop by Sir Augustus Wollaston Franks, an expert on medieval art who developed the British Museum's collection of national antiquities. It was not until decades later that the missing panel was discovered by the family who had owned the box. They sold it to a museum in Florence, where it is still on display – I'm going there this summer and… big announcement… Lord Edgington will be passing through that part of Italy next year.

Another element I lifted from history (thank goodness it isn't copyrighted) is Elton Lockhart's dig in the Yorkshire Wolds, which I based on the Walkington Wold burials. In reality, the site was not discovered until the 1960s, and it is believed to be the burial plot of thirteen decapitated criminals. The reason for their deaths has been theorised as being caused by a massacre, a head cult, or more likely, an execution. The heads were all found away from the bodies with the jaws missing, which suggests that they were displayed on poles and eventually fell off. And that may be the goriest thing I've ever mentioned in any of my books!

Last but not least, you can see a good example of Anglo-Saxon weaponry in the Abingdon Sword. It was found in a bog near Oxford in 1874 and, though much of the blade has rotted away, its finely etched gold guards and pommel are still beautiful. Although this one does not feature any writing, weapons from the period have been found with inscriptions such as "Eric made me" or "Eric owns me", and a lot of the examples are little more than rusty looking blades, so it's a good thing that knowledgeable people identified them and kept them for posterity.

As for the March equinox, it really was a time of celebration in both Viking and Anglo-Saxon culture, and it happened to fall on the day on which I finished writing this book. The worship of the goddess Ēostre – who is thought to have given us the German and English words for Easter, whereas most languages use a derivative of the word *Passover* – is only recorded in a single eighth-century text from the English monk and scholar, Bede. He goes into some detail about the month devoted to worshipping her in Anglo-Saxon culture and links the use of the older term to the modern celebration of Easter, which had already taken over by 673 when he was born. Ēostre is believed to have been the goddess of spring, and she may have been the English incarnation of a more widespread European goddess – the facts of which are still debated by scholars. In fact, people thought that Bede had made her up until the 1950s when a list of 150 inscriptions to various goddesses was discovered in Germany. Right, that's enough ancient history. I think you can see that I have casually stitched together a lot of references in order to create the legend that fitted my plot, though it is not quite as far-fetched as that may sound.

One thing that is far more substantial is the house which inspired all this. Not only is it a wonderful place to visit, it is run as a charity. When Veronica died, she transferred the ownership to a charitable trust to ensure that the house and gardens can remain open and visited by the public in perpetuity. It is still home to Lady Emma and her family but, from Easter Sunday each year until the middle of October, you can walk its halls and see its marvels. I feel very lucky that both Lord Edgington and I have done just that.

If you loved the story and have the time, please write a review at Amazon. Most books get one review per thousand readers so I would be infinitely appreciative if you could help me out.

THE MOST INTERESTING THINGS I DISCOVERED WHEN RESEARCHING THIS BOOK...

I very much doubt I've previously dipped into such a range of eras in my research as I did for this book. From the seventh century, I went right through the Elizabethan era and on to the 1920s, and these are some of the most incredible facts I stumbled across...

Where better is there to start than with narwhals? I often think that nature is even more incredible than fantasy, and this animal is a perfect example of that. As their name suggests, narwhals are a type of whale in the same order as dolphins and porpoises. They can grow up to five and a half metres and, of course, the most incredible thing about them is their tusk. Only males have one (or sometimes even two), and they can grow to an extra three metres in length. Its main function, be it for breaking ice, mating rituals, or fighting, is debated, but its size is known to signify social superiority between animals. It also works as a thermometer and is so sensitive it can tell the animal all sorts of information about its environment. There's a lot still to learn about narwhals, but some scientists believe that they even communicate between themselves by rubbing horns.

For a long time, it was believed that their tusks were actually unicorn horns, and there was a healthy trade in them – hence the four-hundred-year-old specimen which really is in the Great Hall at Parham. Vikings made weapons out of them, but by the Middle Ages they were apparently worth more than their weight in gold. Even Elizabeth I accepted that they had magical healing properties. She had one which was said to be worth £10,000, and the Danish coronation chair (or "unicorn throne") was made using them. Such legends could presumably live on for so long as narwhals keep to arctic waters and few people had actually seen them.

Sticking with natural history, Sir Joseph Banks, to whom there is a whole room dedicated at Parham House, was important for all the reasons that

Lord Edgington lists. He was a shipmate of Captain Cook's, president of the Royal Society for forty-one years, and he helped establish Kew Gardens by sending out botanists all over the world to collect specimens. He was also an important natural scientist in his own right and there are more than eighty species of plant named after him. He was the first European to document at least 1400 species, and he introduced the Old World to the acacia, the eucalyptus and the kangaroo.

From kangaroos to a crocodile… of sorts. René Lacoste had been the best tennis player in the world for two years by the time this story takes place. He helped end American dominance of the Davis Cup after six years of consecutive US victories, and when they played again in 1928, France built the Roland Garros stadium, which is still used for the French Open today, specifically for that much feted tournament. He was such a lethal player that he was known as "le crocodile" and that is why, when he founded the Lacoste clothes company in 1933, the logo was a little green reptile with a lot of teeth. He won seven grand slams and, in the 1960s, he revolutionised the tennis racquet with a new, hollow steel design that moved the game away from the previous wooden incarnations. It was kind of heavy and difficult to string, but it helped Jimmy Connors and Billie Jean King to emulate his title-winning ways.

Something quite unbelievable in a different way is zodiacal light, which definitely sounds as though I made it up, but is a real phenomenon which can still be observed at the right time of year if you have a clear view of the sky away from light pollution, and the moon and even other planets are obscured. In the twenties, the cause of it wasn't firmly established, but as we now know, it is caused by sunlight scattering in the sky as it meets minute interplanetary dust. Brian May, the guitarist from the rock band Queen, started his doctorate on the topic before the band became famous, and he went back to complete it thirty-six years later in 2007. It was only in the 1970s that the source of the light was confirmed by NASA missions and very little work had been done on the topic in the meantime, so May could pick up where he'd left off. I like to mix the seemingly supernatural with the real in my books, and I was very happy to stumble across this phenomenon, thanks to it often occurring around the spring equinox. I've tried to create believable conditions for it, so the end scene in the book is on a plain facing west, at the right time of the evening, far from light pollution and at the right time of year. And in case anyone is curious (I very much doubt it) the spring equinox occurred at 8:44 in the evening in 1928.

Moving on to another kind of electromagnetic radiation now, a significant innovation that came about in the time of Lord Edgington was the X-ray machine. X-rays themselves had been discovered in 1895 by a German scientist called Wilhelm Roentgen, who would become the first winner of the Nobel Prize for physics. He gave them the name X because he couldn't say what they were at first, and they are still known as Röntgen rays in many countries around the world. His discovery was so far ahead of its time that many people thought that they must be some form of paranormal power. However, it was soon realised that they could be used to see inside things, and by the (Meet Me in) St. Louis World's Fair in 1904, a fully working machine had been produced for medical purposes. The invention would become even more important during the Great War when Marie Curie helped to develop portable machines that could be driven between hospitals close to the frontline.

Although the dangers of X-rays were discovered almost at the same time as they were, in the 1920s, machines were developed to help people choose the right shoe size. Known as pedoscopes or shoe-fitting fluoroscopes, they used X-rays to show the amount of space in the shoes that shoppers were trying on. Which sounds pretty crazy, right? What's even crazier is that they weren't totally phased out until the 1970s in some places. X-rays, to me at least, still feel quite futuristic, so I would never have imagined that they had been discovered so long ago (or used for such a silly purpose).

Something else that can both help and kill is chloroform. I got the idea to use it as a weapon from a real-life case known as the Pimlico Poisoning Mystery. It concerned a woman called Adelaide Bartlett who almost definitely murdered her husband but got away with it. Her lover, a Wesleyan minister, bought chloroform at her request and, a short time later, her husband was found dead.

The pair were arrested, and Adelaide was put on trial. It's not clear how she got such a good barrister to defend her – a secretive father with connections to the monarchy, perhaps? – but he was very good and convinced the jury that, as the chloroform that had killed her husband showed no signs of burning his lips or throat as it went down, it was impossible to say for sure how the poison had been administered. Of course, the likely answer is that she gave it to him and told him it was medicine, so he swallowed it straight down, but the jury bought into the question of doubt and Adelaide was acquitted. What's particularly fascinating about the case is that, though it caused a media furore, the suspected killer soon disappeared from the public eye and was never heard from again.

That story, on the surface at least, doesn't seem to have much to do with this novel. However, it reminded me of the idea that chloroform really does not have the properties that most people think it has. I read an interesting book all about chloroform, so I know more about it than I can shove into a few paragraphs, but the good news is that I'll soon forget everything I learnt, as I'll be planning another murder in no time. What I can tell you is that the potential use of chloroform as an anaesthetic on humans was explored in the 1840s after a Scottish doctor called James Young Simpson had experimented with it on himself and his friends. Anaesthesia before this point consisted of either laughing gas, the even more dangerous ether, or (I assume) a whack on the head with a mallet.

Chloroform seemed like the perfect solution, especially as Simpson became very good at administering it in small enough doses to offer pain relief without burning or killing his patients. He was so successful, in fact, that even Queen Victoria used it during the birth of her eighth child. Her approval of the procedure was so often talked of that it became known as "childbirth à la reine". Years before that, to prove its effectiveness, Simpson attended a meeting at the Edinburgh Medico-Chirurgical Society. After his presentation, each of the worthy gentlemen there took a big huff of the stuff on a hanky and passed it on to the next person. Every one of them said they enjoyed the experience, and some asked for seconds as it felt like instant drunkenness. No one that day suffered hallucinations, heart attacks or death, but over the next seventy-five years, it is estimated that a hundred thousand people died unnecessarily from incorrect administration of the chemical.

That didn't stop chloroform from burnishing its reputation, though, and to this day, people – or at least lazy writers – believe that it is effective at knocking out unsuspecting victims without terrible side effects. That's despite the fact that *The Lancet* was already asking for definitive proof that it could be used as a knock-out drug in 1865. The risks and benefits of the drug were debated for decades, with fierce advocates on both sides of the argument, but by the 1920s its use as an anaesthetic was greatly in decline. To give Dr Simpson his dues, he also helped pioneer the use of forceps in childbirth and even developed a vacuum technique that was almost a century ahead of its time. He was motivated by a desire to reduce his patients' suffering, which, believe it or not, was a controversial issue at the time, as some believed that it was God's intention for women to suffer. That sounds so absurd that I'm going to have to give my source. If you don't believe me, check out the British Medical Journal's video "James Young Simpson: A New World is Born" on YouTube. Insanity.

Another important substance is… whatever gases make up the sun. Until 1859, we didn't know exactly what the sun was made of. Along with Dr Bunsen (that's the famous chemist who invented the Bunsen burner, not the Muppet) a German physicist called Gustav Kirchhoff created an instrument for analysing electromagnetic spectra, which he used to identify the elements within our nearest star. The two men achieved any number of impressive feats which still feed into our understanding of science today, but what I particularly like about Kirchhoff is his reaction to his banker, who heard of his client's landmark achievement and asked, "Of what use is gold in the Sun if it cannot be brought to Earth?" the Royal Society had just been given Kirchhoff a prize for his work, and so he handed over the gold sovereigns he'd won and said, "Here is gold from the Sun."

Moving on to another great discovery, I added the comment about Alexander Graham Bell because one of my early readers considered the telephone an American invention. I admit, it is a contentious issue to this day. The simple facts are that the appropriately named Bell was born in Scotland, initially remained a British citizen, and lived between Canada and the States when he patented his design for an "acoustic telegraph". However he also had a laboratory in Boston, and it was in the US that he received the patent, but I think it's fair to claim it as a British invention. I'm not going to get into the even more heated debate over whether it was Bell or his rival Elisha Gray who actually designed it first. It seems fair to say that, regardless of when patents were filed, Bell had the biggest impact on the wired telephonic device you can still find in most homes today.

More interesting than such arguments is Alexander Graham Bell himself, who had a simply incredible life. Far from considering his famous invention to be the pinnacle of his achievements, he felt it an intrusion on his real work and wouldn't even have one in his laboratory. Just imagine what he would have thought of smartphones! Various members of Bell's family worked with speech and elocution and, from an early age, he was interested in experimenting with sound and the human voice – though his first invention, aged just twelve, was a machine to dehusk wheat for his friend's family's flour mill. His main interest, though, was inspired by his mother's deafness, and his father, who was famous for inventing a system called visible speech which could be used to help deaf people learn to speak. Due to these influences, he tried to build a speaking automaton and it was such experiments that would lead to his understanding of the technical aspects of sound.

When he moved to first Canada and then the US, he taught his father's method at various schools for the deaf, before setting up one of his own in Boston, where he taught Helen Keller and his future wife, Mabel Hubbard. After his great invention and the establishment of the Bell Telephone company, he continued to be interested in many fields and was even the president of the National Geographic society for five years. He was an incredible man, whether we consider him British or American (nice try, Canada!) and would have lived a phenomenal life, even if he hadn't invented one of the most significant devices in human history.

Another very impressive family are the real-life Hornimans. I knew the name best through the museum in south London which is very close to the house where my parents lived when they were first married. It was established by Frederick Horniman, the heir to the Horniman tea fortune, (who was from Croydon, hurray!). Horniman's was the biggest tea company in the world at the turn of the twentieth century, which gave Frederick the opportunity to indulge in his passion for travelling and collecting natural specimens, historical and cultural items and musical instruments. He had a collection of over 30,000 artefacts by the time the museum was opened. It's a beautiful place, full of eccentric and extensive exhibits on just about every topic you can imagine. I really recommend a visit if you go to London.

On the topic of cultured fellows, I knew exactly what I wanted Raymond Carbonell to be an expert on: militaria! The only problem was that the word militaria didn't exist until 1964, and so I had to find an alternative term. I found the expression "war relics" in an American photo from 1918. It was a picture of a train which crossed America carrying captured German military equipment in a travelling museum to encourage people to buy "liberty bonds" after the war was over. In fact, allied servicemen in the Great War became hobbyist collectors and many searched the battlefields for memorabilia, with the classic German Pickelhaube – or pointy helmet – being particularly in demand. This made me rather happy as it fits with the story in the last Edgington book of the former soldier and his collection of scavenged wartime paraphernalia – which, I confess, I totally made up.

Dr Carbonell's name is borrowed from an incredibly interesting man called Eudald Carbonell, who is not only one of the world's foremost prehistoric archaeologists, he is my friend Nerea's uncle. Burgos, the city where I live, is famous for a number of things: its remarkably grand and beautiful cathedral; its blood sausage (which is a lot tastier than it might sound); its connection to the eleventh century hero, El Cid; and its UNESCO protected site at Atapuerca, where the world's largest collection of hominid fossils has been discovered. The real Dr Carbonell has been the co-director of the ongoing archaeological dig since the nineties. In that time they have uncovered not only the oldest examples of prehistoric man in Western Europe – from 800,000 years ago – but more hominid fossils than the rest of the world combined. And they haven't finished yet.

Atapuerca is a system of caves which have been used by many different ages of man for many different reasons – from simple shelters to functioning as a burial site. As a result, there are various layers to sift through, and the archaeologists remove no more than a centimetre of sediment from the caves each year, turning up new finds as they do so. You can visit the Museum of Human Evolution in Burgos and see reconstructed skeletons of humans and immense bones from lions, bears and extinct animals, who were either hunted or fell into the deepest caves and couldn't climb out. It's an incredible project that has reshaped our understanding of prehistoric man in this part of the world, and Eudald Carbonell is a real character. He is always pictured in a pith helmet (or explorer's hat) and my friend Nerea loves the fact that the Playmobil figure of an explorer looks just like her uncle. Why does my character have a Spanish name, you may ask? Well, I don't know, but there is a town in Shropshire called Ashford Carbonell, so I thought I could get away with it.

One thing that makes my job a lot easier is being able to look at newspapers from the very day that my books are set. I don't always reveal the exact date, but I knew that this one would be set around the March Equinox, and so I had a look at the newspapers on 20th March 1928 and was intrigued by the cover image on the Daily Mirror. It proclaims, "Woman's Fine Flight" and describes how a female aviator and her male co-pilot Captain William N. Lancaster flew from Croydon (hurray!) to Port Darwin in Australia. At the time, it was the longest air journey completed by a woman. They went 13,000 miles and, though it was only supposed to take six weeks, they had to stop because of bad weather halfway, so it ended up taking 159 days. What I found particularly interesting about this big front-page spread was the fact that she is only referred to as "Mrs Keith Miller, wife of a Melbourne journalist" and we don't even learn her Christian name.

Of course, this made me want to know more, and I soon discovered that the female pilot's name was Jessie "Chubbie" Miller, and she did not remain Mrs Keith Miller for long. Perhaps the two pilots' experiences flying halfway around the world pushed them together, as she left her journalist husband and moved to the States that same year with Captain Lancaster. She would go on to compete in The Women's Air Derby, an officially recognised women-only race from the West Coast to Ohio. She flew alongside Amelia Earhart and, in the course of the race, one of the pilots was killed in a crash, two appear to have been sabotaged – which caused a fire in one case and acid-destroyed wiring in the other – and both Earhart and Miller finished third in their respective weight-classes.

Just a couple of years after Miller's journey from England to Australia, the great Amy Johnson became the first solo woman to complete the challenge. Whilst writing this book, I was lucky enough to visit the still-standing terminal of Croydon airport, which is five minutes from my childhood home and was the most important airport in Britain until the end of the Second World War. It is featured in at least one Agatha Christie novel ("Death in the Clouds") and is also a simply fascinating place to visit, even if it is now hemmed in by a McDonalds, a KFC and a children's play centre.

Even more drama was to ensue for Jessie Miller as, when her boyfriend Lancaster was away in Mexico, she became enamoured with a writer called Haden Clarke, who convinced her to leave the captain and marry him instead. When Lancaster discovered this and returned to America, he shot Clarke dead and forged his suicide note. He also wrote one for Miller but did not go through with killing her. The strangest part of it all, though, is the fact that, when the case came to trial, Miller testified in the killer's favour, and Lancaster was found not guilty. It makes me wonder whether she promised this in exchange for her life or she really felt he deserved to be let off. Either way, Captain Lancaster did not get to enjoy his freedom for long. Short of money, he entered a high-speed race from London to South Africa and crash landed in the Sahara desert. From his log that he maintained for eight days after, it seems that he died exactly a year after he'd murdered Clarke, though his body would not be found until three decades later.

An even more despicable murder is mentioned in this book, and it wasn't the mystery that Chrissy has to solve, but the true story of the body that a gang of smugglers left in Parham Park. The Hawkhurst Gang were a notoriously violent bunch from mid-eighteenth-century Sussex. Though we might have a romanticised impression of smugglers and highwaymen, this lot were real savages. They were known for murdering rivals and witnesses to their crimes, but locals tolerated them as their smuggling brought jobs, money and presumably cut-price goods to the area.

The man who was murdered and left in Parham was suspected of stealing two bags of tea from the gang. He was interrogated, whipped and beaten to death before his body was sunk in the Parham House lake. The only person I know who would go to such lengths to make sure no one would take their tea is my mother, though I don't believe she would be quite so aggressive.

The Hawkhurst Gang would live to regret such actions... well, some of them would. After they'd enacted murderous revenge on an informer who had linked them to a daring raid on a customs house, local people were appalled by their extreme violence and raised a militia to bring them down. The Battle of Goudhurst led to the deaths of three of the criminals, while most of the rest would be arrested and hanged. Interestingly, one of the gang who was acquitted for his part in the raid was married to the illegitimate daughter of Sir Cecil Bishopp, who just happened to be the owner of Parham House at the time. Apparently, 75 members of the gang were hanged or sent to the colonies, and British people were so outraged by the case and the violent methods that the smugglers had used that it was something of a national sensation. Bloody stuff!

Which brings us on to Dracula – my goodness these segues are strong this time round! I've mentioned Bram Stoker before in these chapters, as he was the assistant to the actor Henry Irving who has cropped up many times. Irving gave a start to a young Irish actor called Hamilton Deane at the end of the nineteenth century, and twenty years later, when he had a company of his own, Deane approached Stoker's widow for the chance to adapt Dracula for the stage. The subsequent production was a huge success and, having played in London for several years, it went to America where a man called Bela Lugosi took up the role of the count. What's impressive about all this is the fact that much of the way we now picture Dracula comes from the Deane production – including the flowing cape, which is mentioned in this book. And when the first full-length Dracula film – ignoring the brilliant but unlicensed "Nosferatu" – was made in 1931, it closely followed Deane's adaptation and starred Lugosi as the antagonist.

There is not normally any garlic in game pies – okay, that wasn't so smooth a link – but they do sound delicious. They appear to have been around since Roman times and the recipe has developed with each new era. They were, at times, sweet, sometimes full of every bird going from herons to blackbirds, and they were even used for

260

entertainment – poor Charles I was once served one from which a dwarf popped out and, on another occasion, he cut his dinner open to discover a collection of live birds who flew forth, no doubt singing a song of sixpence as they went. There was a golden age of pie-making in the eighteenth century, when battalia pie, which Chrissy mentions, was popular. They were sometimes shaped like castles, and along with various types of meat, featured gravy, lemon and spices. For a while, it was also common to decorate a game pie with a dead bird on the top, and that's one tradition I'm glad we've lost.

From birds to Snakes (and Ladders)! The game, better known in the States as Chutes and Ladders, originated in India and was brought to Europe by families returning from the British colony. It was originally a very moral game with the ladders representing virtues and the snakes standing in for sins. To win, you had to live a virtuous life (or roll the dice enough times to get to 100 at least), and so it represented Indian spiritual concepts such as karma.

When I was checking its provenance for this book, I found a very funny article in the *Dundee Evening Telegraph* from 1929, in which a rather gloomy man describes "The Snakes and Ladder Demon". Ironically, for a game which was designed to impart a moral message, he complains that whenever he is forced to play it at "snake-and-ladder parties" it brings out the very worst in the players. He says that the game lasts for such an eternity, that people lose all sense and turn into monsters. I think there's an element of sarcasm in the text, but I believe him when he says, "I hate that game with a deep and enduring loathing". His attitude reminds me a little of the kind of opinion pieces we read today from people railing against modern trends. I think it's fair to say that, of all the problems we have in society, few were caused by Snakes and Ladders.

All that's left is for me to tell you about the songs in this book, and then I can have a rest… or more likely start writing another one. I was planning to use "The Laughing Policeman" as it has an interesting history, but that will have to wait until another time, as I ended up using songs that particularly fitted the Pearson girls. The poem they recite about their love for their dolly is included in Lavinia's memoir, and I cannot find any record of it online except as a traditional poem that parents would recite to their children. If anyone knows who wrote it or where it's from, please get in touch. The girls really did have to perform the song at dinners, and it doesn't sound as if they were particularly excited to do so. As for their presence at the dinners in the book, of course I'm aware that children at the time were rarely included in adult soirees, but in Lavinia's memoir she does talk about the odd occasion when they were. And if anyone has any problem with that, you can go back to the first page of this book, where I point out that this enjoyably silly mystery is fictional.

Their other performance piece, "If the World were Ruled by Girls" was written by C. W. Murphy and George Arthurs and made famous by the music hall comedian Whit Cunliffe. Cunliffe was far from being a feminist and sang "comical" songs about such topics as women's rights, tight skirts and force-feeding suffragettes in prison. Meanwhile, "(You're My Heart's Desire, I Love You) Nellie Dean", which Dorie the maid sings as they drive to Parham, was written as a ballad but went on to be a classic pub song – i.e. a song that is perfect for shouting out around a piano in a packed public house. It just has one of those rhythms which demands singing along, and a call and response element that is hard to resist (as Chrissy discovers). The song has no apparent connection, beyond a shared name, to the narrator of Wuthering Heights, though perhaps there is a subtle subtext that has so far been overlooked. There is a rather beautiful rendition of the song on YouTube from the 1930s sung by British soldiers around a campfire at the foot of the pyramids in Giza.

I will leave you with that pretty image. Thank you for letting me share all the things that so amazed me. I hope you enjoyed them too!

ACKNOWLEDGEMENTS

For once, I'm going to start with the people I normally leave until last. If you don't know what an ARC team is (I didn't until shortly before I formed my own) it is a group of ever so kind people who give up their time to offer feedback before a book is released. I haven't gone out of my way to find such helpful people, but through my e-mail correspondence with my readers, they have all come to me in ones and twos.

With the Marius books, the idea was that I would rely on the traditional editing method of a developmental, copy and proof editor but, as good as those people are, I found that it couldn't replicate the feedback I got from my big group of around fifty people. Crowdsourcing the editing process in this way doesn't just help catch typos, but enables me to identify issues that aren't working in the plot and change them where necessary. The team has been particularly important this time as I was feeling pretty drained after my insanely busy 2023 (one baby boy received, eight books written). I've had such a great deal of support from a brilliant group of people, many of whom I have exchanged getting on for hundreds of e-mails over the last three and a half years.

So I have to say a massive thank you to Rebecca Brooks, Ferne Miller, Melinda Kimlinger, Emma James, Mindy Denkin, Namoi Lamont, Katharine Reibig, Linsey Neale, Terri Roller, Margaret Liddle, Lori Willis, Anja Peerdeman, Marion Davis, Sarah Turner, Sandra Hoff, Vanessa Rivington, Helena George, Anne Kavcic, Nancy Roberts, Pat Hathaway, Peggy Craddock, Cathleen Brickhouse, Susan Reddington, Sonya Elizabeth Richards, John Presler, Mary Harmon, Beth Weldon, Karen Quinn, Karen Alexander, Mindy Wygonik, Jacquie Erwin, Janet Rutherford, M.P. Smith, Ila Patlogan, Lisa Bjornstad, Randy Hartselle, Carol Vani, June Techtow and Keryn De Maria. Thank you, too, to my extra-early readers – Emily Gowers, the Hoggs, and the Martins. And to my fellow writers who are always there for me, especially Catherine, Suzanne and Lucy.

As we're in reverse order, I'll finish by thanking all the kind and knowledgeable people who helped make this book a reality. It would never have come into being without the permission of Lady Emma Barnard. It would not have made as much sense or captured Parham's unique charm and history without Dr Jayne Kirk. And the cover would not have looked so good without the assistance of Geodime Ltd., the company that was hired to take aerial photographs of the house when the roof needed surveying. Thanks to all of them and all my readers too.

"THE PUZZLE OF PARHAM HOUSE" COCKTAIL

I didn't know the word shandygaff before writing this book, though I drink this drink in bars more often than any other. Shandygaff originally referred to beer mixed with ginger beer, but it is now more generally beer mixed with any soft drink. In Spain, beer and lemonade is called clara (meaning clear), but the German word Radler (meaning cyclist!) is also used here, and occasionally you'll find the now more typical English word shandy on cans and bottles.

There are references to shandygaff way back to 1853 and it was already being shortened by 1888. What's great about a shandy is that it is almost infinitely customisable. In Britain, it is common to ask for a lager or bitter shandy, and you can also specify how much you want of each to make it more or less alcoholic. My mother tends to send hers back for more lemonade, as anything more than a spoonful of beer goes straight to her head. In France, the name for a mix of beer and lemonade is panaché, but there is also a version called a Monaco, which adds a dash of Grenadine syrup to the recipe.

I don't work for the shandy promotion board, but I do think it's a brilliant summer drink, which is refreshing, but not too sweet, and doesn't get you drunk. It is the ideal option for sitting on a terrace in the sunshine in front of a Spanish bar (which is a national pastime here).

Having made it any number of times on family holidays, these are my instructions for the perfect shandy...

- **Fifty per cent lager** – in Spain I'd use Alhambra Reserva 1925 if I was being fancy. You can also use ale or bitter (a type of pale ale) for a different, fuller flavour.
- **Fifty per cent carbonated lemonade** – the best option for me is Fanta Limon or a cloudy lemonade with sweet and bitter flavours mixed in. I don't think clear lemonades like Sprite or 7-Up work as well.

Both ingredients should be chilled in advance. In the summer, you should also put your glass in the freezer for a few hours before serving to keep it perfectly cool as you enjoy your tasty drink.

READ MORE LORD EDGINGTON MYSTERIES TODAY

- **Murder at the Spring Ball**
- **Death From High Places** (free e-novella available exclusively at benedictbrown.net. Paperback and audiobook are available at Amazon)
- **A Body at a Boarding School**
- **Death on a Summer's Day**
- **The Mystery of Mistletoe Hall**
- **The Tangled Treasure Trail**
- **The Curious Case of the Templeton-Swifts**
- **The Crimes of Clearwell Castle**
- **The Snows of Weston Moor**
- **What the Vicar Saw**
- **Blood on the Banister**
- **A Killer in the Wings**
- **The Christmas Bell Mystery**
- **The Puzzle of Parham House**
- **Death at Silent Pool** (Autumn 2024)

Check out the complete Lord Edgington Collection at Amazon

The first ten Lord Edgington audiobooks, narrated by the actor George Blagden, are available now on all major audiobook platforms. There will be more coming soon.

WORDS AND REFERENCES YOU MIGHT NOT KNOW

Barmy in the crumpet – an old-fashioned expression for *somewhat eccentric*.

Mulligatawny soup and kedgeree – two Indian dishes that were brought to Britain. When I was a child, my mother once made me eat kedgeree (fish curry) and it may have turned me off fish for the next twenty years. Whether that version had fish heads in it, or I've embellished the memory, I cannot say.

Odd man – a person in a grand house who did odd jobs. There really was one in Parham in the 20s.

Pastry coffin – this was a common name for the pastry exterior of a pie.

Cyanosis – a change in skin tone because of a lack of oxygen, and a symptom of exposure to chloroform.

Cornery – literally something with a lot of corners, but when said of people it can mean awkward or a prickly personality.

Working away here like a dray horse – self-explanatory, but what I liked about this is that the simile was so ubiquitous that there is even a verb "to dray-horse", meaning to work very hard.

Dísablót – the Norse word for a sacrificial celebration in honour of female gods and spirits.

"What would you have me do? Strut about like I'm the master of Parham Park? Play hide and seek in the Long Gallery? Swim naked in the pleasure grounds just to show everyone what a rake I am?" – this response from Elton Lockhart is a reference to a late-nineteenth-century mistress of Parham House who, though only recently married, had a wild and very public affair with a young poet. They did all of the above and far worse… including sinking a boat on the lake, firing pistols on horseback, and trying on

267

the ancient suits of armour. She would throw the poet over for his cousin, but not before making her lovers stage a medieval battle for her enjoyment. It sounds like she would make a good character in one of my books.

Babblative – talkative, chatty – like Benedict, Amelie and Laraine Brown, for example.

Tut-Ankh-Amen – this is the spelling I found in newspapers of the day.

Scaramouch – a rascal. I originally knew this word thanks to "Bohemian Rhapsody", and it comes from a stock character in Italian *commedia dell'arte*.

The Zivoniev Letter – a fake letter published in the Daily Mail just a few days before the 1924 election. It appeared to be written by an important Russian communist and suggested that there was co-ordination between the Soviets and the British Labour party. As Chrissy points out, it was still being discussed in parliament four years later and, in fact, some people in the Labour party are still sore about it today as, at least partly because of this illegal intervention, they lost the election.

Baby farmer – people who would take in unwanted babies in exchange for money. There are some truly gruesome stories about them, should you enjoy reading such terrible things.

Poultry-flutters – a fit of emotion.

Blue boring stodger – a blue bore is a boring person and so is a stodger, so this sums up Eric Uhland nicely.

A pig's whisper / in an eyewink – I couldn't decide which to use so I included both. They mean a very short time, similar to *in the blink of an eye*.

Muntins – the word for the pieces of wood, metal or plastic that divide a window.

Pikelets – something that my mother often made us when we were kids, they are small pancakes, originally from Wales. They are very similar to drop scones or Scotch pancakes, and I like them best with raisins.

Mossbacked – I'd only heard this in "It's a Wonderful Life" but it seems to have been used in the UK by the 1920s. It means reactionary and old fashioned.

Promnesia – the term déjà vu wasn't very common at the time, and this is the more formal word for it. Would Chrissy have known it? Probably not, but we all pick up strange vocabulary, and he does read a lot.

Skiagrams – another term for X-rays.

Wizardly – I was surprised that this was a word, but it really is.

A motor headlight had been turned up to its zenith – I must confess that I didn't write this pretty phrase. I found it in a newspaper article on zodiacal light from the Bath Chronicle and Weekly Gazette on 9th March 1929.

Silly mid-off – a fielding position on a cricket pitch. It's called silly as it is very close to the batter and you are likely to get whacked by the ball, and it is the off-leg side of midwicket. No… I don't really understand it either.

Flummadiddle – nonsense.

Apotheosis – transformation into a god.

THE IZZY PALMER MYSTERIES

If you're looking for a modern murder mystery series with just as many off-the-wall characters, try **"The Izzy Palmer Mysteries"** for your next whodunit fix.

Check out the complete Izzy Palmer Collection in ebook, paperback and Kindle Unlimited at Amazon.

ABOUT ME

Writing has always been my passion. It was my favourite half-an-hour a week at primary school, and I started on my first, truly abysmal book as a teenager. So it wasn't a difficult decision to study literature at university which led to a master's in Creative Writing.

I'm a Welsh-Irish-Englishman originally from **South London** but now living with my French/Spanish wife and presumably quite confused infant daughter in **Burgos**, a beautiful mediaeval city in the north of Spain. I write overlooking the Castilian countryside, trying not to be distracted by the vultures, hawks and red kites that fly past my window each day.

When Covid-19 hit in 2020, the language school where I worked as an English teacher closed down and I became a full-time writer. I have two murder mystery series. There are already six books written in **"The Izzy Palmer Mysteries"** which is a more modern, zany take on the genre. I will continue to alternate releases between Izzy and Lord Edgington. I hope to release at least ten books in each series.

I previously spent years focussing on kids' books and wrote everything from fairy tales to environmental dystopian fantasies, right through to issue-based teen fiction. My book **"The Princess and The Peach"** was long-listed for the Chicken House prize in The Times and an American producer even talked about adapting it into a film. I'll be slowly publishing those books whenever we find the time.

"The Puzzle of Parham House" is the thirteenth novel in the "Lord Edgington Investigates…" series. The next book will be out in Autumn 2024 and there's a novella available free if you sign up to my **readers' club**. Should you wish to tell me what you think about Chrissy and his grandfather, my writing or the world at large, I'd love to hear from you, so feel free to get in touch via...

www.benedictbrown.net

CHARACTER LIST

Parham House

Alicia Pearson – the owner of Parham House. She and her businessman husband bought it six years before the start of the novel and have been restoring it since.

Veronica (12), Lavinia (10) and Dione (8) – the three daughters of Clive and Alicia Pearson.

Elton Lockhart – a dashing and adventurous antiquarian with a love of ancient cultures and a penchant for travel.

Dr Raymond Carbonell – an expert on military equipment and war relics. He grew up with Lockhart.

Vyvyan and Frances Horniman – twin sisters and acolytes of the great Elton Lockhart.

Eric Uhland – a very uninspiring expert on portraiture.

Mark Isaac – his young assistant. A student and artist.

Inspector Kirk – a local police officer based at Pulborough police station.

Mr Cridland – the Parham House butler.

Graham Perugino – the half-Italian footman whose main job is polishing.

Cranley Hall

Lord Edgington – my friend and yours, former Scotland Yard superintendent turned hobbyist detective.

Christopher Prentiss – his grandson and sleuthing assistant.

Violet Prentiss – Christopher's mother, Lord Edgington's daughter, and a regular helper to the detective duo.

Todd – everyone's favourite chauffeur turned semi-psychic man of all trades in the Cranley Hall household. He is Lord Edgington's head of household and factotum.

Halfpenny – the aged Cranley Hall head footman.

Cook / Henrietta – the Cranley Hall cook.

Dorie – the Cranley Hall mega-maid.

Delilah – the Cranley Hall golden retriever and an all-round good doggy.

Made in the USA
Middletown, DE
14 May 2024

54332655R00163